A Necessary Killing

Hilary Lloyd

UKA PRESS, LONDON

Published by UKA Press
UKA Press, 55 Elmsdale Road, Walthamstow, London, E17 6PN, UK
UKA Press Europe, Olympiaweg 102-hs, 1076 XG, Amsterdam, Holland
UKAPress, Anderson St, 108, 2-5-22 Shida, 426-0071, Japan
2 4 6 8 10 9 7 5 3 1

First published in Great Britain in 2006 by UKA Press
A CIP catalogue record for this book is available from the British Library

ISBN 1 905796 00 5
ISBN 978 1 905796 00 7

Cover photograph: 'Morning Frost' by Gracey Stinson, Ontario
Cover design by Don Masters (St. A)
Edited by Don Masters (St. A), Editor-in-Chief, UKA Press

UKA Press would like to express warm appreciation to the the cover adviser and formatter, Cait Myers

Printed and bound in Great Britain by Biddles Ltd., King's Lynn

A Necessary Killing

based on a true story

CHAPTER ONE

This room is filled with black stick men and women who rustle with whispers. They don't tell me what I do now. They don't talk. Most find it hard to look at me. They turn away, mouths quivering, though perhaps that's for the best because I don't recognise half of them, and the ones I know have changed.

Even Fiona tells me nothing. Though it's too hot she's in a thick black coat that devours her tears.

'Oh, Julie,' is all she says.

'I must check the sheep,' I say, longing to escape this mess, this whirligig of people with their heads down into a wind that isn't blowing, huddled up inside themselves as though they haven't noticed the sun's shining outside.

Heads spin round, as if I said I'm off to the moon.

'I'll go,' Jamie whispers.

What does he know about sheep?

'No, let me,' says Mike, already halfway to the door.

'They're my sheep,' I growl, fleeing outside.

Without looking back, I know they're all around the door and the window, watching.

The sun sits warm on my face as I stride across the yard.

Down on the road cars spin past in a kaleidoscope of muted colour, but their sound is different. I stop to listen to their muffled progress, and think of galloping horses with their hooves wrapped in sacking.

Why is everyone so quiet? They're like that in the house, creeping around, placing cups on saucers as though they're precious china and not plain old earthenware.

Someone comes up behind, breathing so hard it shifts the hairs on the back of my head. Spinning round, I see Phil. His mouth opens and a voice reverberates in my ears but I can't make out the words. Then he hugs me, something he's never done before, and when he pulls away I see tears plunge from his chin, too.

I turn and run for the shed, where the sheep are the same as they always were. Maybe they'll tell me what to do.

Death is love's first cousin.

Ben's death has turned my insides into the same grinding pit I had when I dared hope he'd want the rusty old battleaxe of me. I have the same difficulty breathing now as I had when he first brought me onto his farm, and the same void that apes hunger but has my stomach heaving at the sight of food.

But it's peaceful in the shed, in the crowded warmth of my pregnant flock. The ewes murmur, like everyone in the house, but at least I know what they're saying. The one nearest talks to her lamb, nudges to make it stand and feed. In the next pen, one ewe rumbles deep in her throat as she looks down at her sleeping offspring. Those ewes who are not in pens whicker to me, tell me they feel safe with me near.

I want to feel safe again. I want all those people to go home and leave me to tend my sheep. Until they go, I'll make a nest of clean straw and hold my aching stomach and try and work out what I'm going to do without Ben.

'Julie?' Fiona pushes the door open and the sheep run for the far end. Those in pens stop dreaming and crooning. Their guards are up, their heads down ready to attack anyone who threatens their lambs. Fiona's eyes fill with apology for frightening them.

I walk away from her down to the far end to grab a ewe, any ewe, and manhandle it into an empty pen, give it fresh hay and a bucket of water. Fiona is fooled. She doesn't come to watch. She knows that when I pen a sheep it means that sheep is starting labour and doesn't want strangers peering.

'I'll go,' she says, creeping out. I feel a wisp of regret for rejecting her, though there isn't enough left of me for anyone else.

But she stays on the farm.

Later, peering between the slats of the shed, I see her in the yard thanking everyone for coming. Guilt stirs, and I manage to stagger outside and fumble through a few words.

Carol and Jim each take one of my hands. 'You've only got to phone,' Carol says. Jim points at their farm on the other side of the road and mutters something, and I know he's trying to tell me their thoughts are as close as their home.

I must make an effort. I must tell them how much I appreciate their concern, but I'm afraid that if I let go of my pain even for a moment, Ben will leave me completely. I open my mouth, but can say nothing. Carol manages a smile before they link arms and walk away, heads down. Their closeness is a new pain.

Sarah next. She touches my hand and nods before she takes Jack's arm. Don't they know their affection for each other is a kick in my guts? Instantly, I'm contrite. Ben's death is a shock too, to these neighbours who saw him grow up, take over, and care for his mother through the long years of her decline.

'Sorry,' I mouth after them.

Mike next. He shifts his balance from one foot to the other, but when he speaks the words march out. 'I'll be along in the morning to give you a hand.' With that, he walks through the gate and across the lane into his own yard, and I watch him out of sight.

But when they've all gone – Jamie with a bewildered and frightened glance at me, Fiona with a promise to come back once she's seen to the children – I walk into my kitchen and stare at the just-washed cups and saucers and wiped surfaces, the chairs pushed back under the table, the fire stoked and guarded. That there isn't a speck of ash on the hearth or a crumb of sandwich or cake anywhere shows how sterile my home is without Ben.

What do I do now?

I go back outside and see daylight being wiped from the valley by the busy fingers of night, but it's later in the small hours, between two of my checks on the ewes, when I at last acknowledge my neighbours' kindness. This unleashes tears of remorse and grief and anguish that begin to fill the aching void Ben has left behind.

CHAPTER TWO

Another of those glittering dawns. Sitting on my bed, watching the sun heave itself above the hill opposite in a ridiculous blaze of orange, I hate its energy, the way it sets the frosty fields alight, the way the bloody thing just keeps on rising day after day.

A bout of shivering forces me into clothes – jeans and sweater over the T-shirt I've worn day and night for God knows how long, but it's too cold to strip off or brave a freezing bathroom, and anyway, what's the point of clean clothes or a clean body when an hour with the sheep will have me stinking again? I pull on thick woollen socks and turn to stare at the bed, at the hump down the centre that should be Ben but is only a line of pillows, a poor imitation I can't sleep without.

I've clung to my bed every morning for weeks, and though staying there is like prodding a bruise to see how much it hurts, I can't stop, can't let go of my obsession with pain.

Come on, Julie, move. Get out there – they need you.

I turn away from my pit of misery, and tramp downstairs.

Outside, the February sun is making diamonds of the frost on the yard and its dazzling light pierces my darkest corners.

There's animal warmth in the shed, and the welcome of a hundred ewes looking up when I enter thaws my bones. Some put themselves between me and their lambs, others nudge forward with rumbling bleats, and though it's cupboard love, I'm needed. I move through them, checking for signs of labour, and find one pawing the ground in the far corner.

'This way, sunshine.' I steer her into an empty pen.

Head down, mutinous, she stamps a foreleg in her demand to deliver her lambs in a remote corner of a field, not herded flank by muzzle with the rest of the flock.

Two orphan lambs gaze at her from the next pen, ears at half-mast, barely a week old and still shaky but filling out nicely. I remember Fiona's promise to collect them this morning, and a flash of pleasure displaces the hard grief of dawn.

But I always feel better working outside, so why do I ruin everything by going to bed? Surely all I need do is work myself silly all day and catnap in my fireside chair all night. But at four every morning an aching longing forces me up to bed to hug a line of cold pillows and complete a daily cycle I can't seem to break.

Fiona tells me not to try. Just let it all happen, she says, and hang on. Though I trust her wisdom, how does she know what it's like? She still has her husband. She didn't search for his broken remains after a tractor bent on suicide took him along for the ride. And she's had years with Jamie. I had only one with Ben.

I march out of the shed, load a bale of hay and sacks of feed into the trailer, kick-start the quad bike into life with something like anger, then cross my front field to fill the troughs and watch the ewes fight to get a nose in first. Their lambs dance round them in hooligan gangs, and I'm smiling.

Looking over the hundred and fifty ewes turned out from the lambing shed since the middle of January, I congratulate myself for the way I've taken over. Work's kept me going, kept me alive, and I know that by the time my younger ewes are back from wintering on Jack and Sarah's land at the end of the month, I'll have learned enough to lamb them with ease. All I need is energy. This clod of a body refuses to do what it used to.

The throaty cough of a leaking exhaust system drowns the sound of the bike as I chug home.

Squinting left, I see Fiona's red car cruising up the lane. I wave and press the throttle to race back to the yard, eager to see her although it's only a week since her last visit. I arrive first, and escort her battered Marina to a standstill.

'Hello, you lot.' I peer into the car.

Fiona climbs out, followed by her two young children.

'And why aren't you at school?'

The elder child bridles. 'It's half term, silly.'

Fiona frowns. 'Ellie, that's rude.'

'Sorry, Mum.'

I smile at Ellie. 'I am silly, sometimes – like when I forget to buy chocolate biscuits.'

Danny clutches Fiona's skirt. 'I like chocolate biscuits.'

I reach down, he laughs, and I lift him up and spin him around.

'Don't worry. The tin's full – waiting for you.'

I put him down, then carefully hug the willowy Fiona before leading them all over to the shed. I know they can't wait to see their new charges.

Half an hour later, Ellie's bursting with importance, the proud owner of two cade lambs and desperate to take them home. I put her in the pen to let her find out just how strong and greedy bottle-fed orphans can be. Fiona and I stand back to watch the lambs pump the bottles so furiously they lose hold and suck Ellie's knees in blind hunger. Danny watches through the bars of the pen, but I don't doubt he'll join in, the minute they get the lambs home.

I don't want them to go.

I need time with Fiona, need to see her reassuringly on the other side of my hearth, the curtains of her hair framing her face and her grey eyes fixed on mine, listening to my every word though saying little.

Back at the house, I take the children up to the bedroom where Ben's mother stored his toys and books for forty years in case they came in useful. Ellie and Dan love the old-fashioned illustrations, chipped tractor and trailer, plastic sheep, and faded plywood farm.

When they're settled, I run downstairs. There's so much to say, and I'm greedy as a lamb for Fiona's company. I wouldn't have got through the last weeks without it. She's absorbed all my wild thoughts and desperate feelings, then in a few words she's put them in order, arranged a lifeline for me to cling to.

She gives me her Mona Lisa smile as I sink into my chair.

'So how's everything at home?' I ask, for a moment my needs suddenly and inexplicably gone.

'Fine. The barn's ready for the lambs.'

'Started on the veg garden?' Just talking feels wonderful. 'And what about the wood – all that *coppicing?*'

She smiles warmly again. 'Jamie's finished the winter work. We've got tons of thinnings to saw up for firewood, and he's building an open-sided shed to store it all in.'

'And school?'

'Just the same – I've got some good kids. They're working on this year's play with stars in their eyes!' She leans forward. 'Your eyes look tired, Julie.'

I shrug, studying my soil-ingrained hands. 'I was up until four, with a problem ewe.'

I look at her then, and begin to talk about my loneliness, pain, anger and bewilderment, how my emotions leap from one extreme to the other for no reason and without warning.

'And I *hate* going to bed,' I lurch on, 'so I sleep down here between checks on the sheep, then…' I fight to keep my voice steady. 'Something makes me go to bed and I can't bear it there but nor can I bear to leave it.' My outpouring turns into a tidal wave. I tell her of my seesaw moods, and how, 'Work saves me, but I ruin everything by going to bed. It seems to undo all the progress I make during the day.'

'But you're *still going*,' she says, 'and keeping the farm alive.'

Alive. Why isn't Ben alive? Why can't he be here to help me lamb, to laugh at my thrown-together meals? And why can't I lie down at the end of the day, safe and needed in his arms? A sour image of Fiona, in Jamie's arms, creeps into my mind.

I wonder if she knows what I'm thinking. She mustn't. 'I like working with the sheep,' I stutter, 'but…I want the old me back, the one who coped with everything life chucked at me, the one before I met Ben.'

Her face is impassive. I must ease up on work, she say,s and get out more, drive over to see them, eat with them, inspect Jamie's wood, give them the pleasure of my company if only for an hour between checks on the ewes.

The pleasure of my company? What do they want with second-hand misery?

'You're such good company,' she says, as if reading my thoughts. 'The children think you're smashing – the way you know everything about animals, and all those stories you tell them about when you worked for a vet.' She pauses. 'Lambing isn't enough for you, Julie, especially at the moment. You need other people. Come over for lunch with us. Please?'

Doesn't she know how hard it is to go out, even to the village shop for milk and biscuits?

Simply being alive takes all my energy, and…I catch a distinct whiff of sheep and realise it's me, stinking, unwashed. Fiona hasn't recoiled yet, but…

'Okay – Friday, then.' And suddenly I'm planning out the rest of the week – light the boiler to heat the water for a bath, find clean clothes, bung the rest in the washer, change the bed. Yes. Change the bed. And I need a few days to sort my mind, too.

'Your lambs will be settled by Friday, and Ellie will know what she's doing.'

As they leave, I lean against the gate to watch the car crawl down the lane and turn left for the village. I lose them now, but their warmth will stay with me. *Thanks, Fiona*, I telegraph to the red beetle of her car as it emerges from the village to crawl up the hill opposite. Thanks for pointing me in the right direction.

At a suggestion of movement to my right I turn. Mike Corley is pushing four sheep and six new lambs out of his yard into his front field. The ewes tread carefully, heads on swivels as their lambs leap into a new green world.

I wave. Hundreds of yards away, Mike waves back.

Farmers drive tractors, round up hundreds of sheep or bury their attention in a drainage ditch, and they still notice everything going on in the valley. I wonder if I'll learn to do the same, now I'm a proper farmer managing eighty acres alone.

Alone. The familiar ache sneaks back, but I put it aside and head for the shed reciting my formula for survival, the one that works when I'm not in bed – *food, sleep, and company*.

'Phil? It's Julie. I've got a problem – triplets, I think. She's too bad to bring in.'

'Right. About an hour do?'

'Fine. How's things?'

'Busy – see you.'

I go back to the shed. Not that there's anything I can do for the ewe, but it's better to add more straw to the deep litter, fill the water buckets in the pens – anything but watch her writhing with a bellyful of knotted lambs.

I hate it when I can't help them, when I can't make use of my thirty years as a veterinary nurse and perform a caesarean, or just put the poor thing out of its misery.

At last I hear the car, and rush out to see my former boss unfold his lean frame.

His old rubber waterproofs squeak as he walks round to the back of the car.

'I shouldn't tell you what to do,' I say, 'but I've set everything up for you to do a caesar.'

He yanks a yellow plastic crate out of the boot.

'I wish all my clients set me up. I just spent the last hour chasing ponies round a paddock because the owner couldn't be bothered to get the lame one in.'

Rumbling like a distant jet, he follows me into the shed.

'Ever thought of coming back to the practice? We could set the animal world to rights, with you keeping all the stupid owners in order. Shouldn't say that, but I'm tired – knackered through and through.' He parks the crate by the pen and stares at the bale I put there. 'God, Julie, I miss you.'

'Come off it, Phil – you've got a smashing team of nurses.' I drop easily into the old banter. 'I should know, I trained them.'

'They can't read my mind, like you.'

He grumbles on while soaping his hands in a bucket, but I ignore his way of coping with the tension of a busy day, and hoist the ewe onto the straw bale that will be its operating table.

The ewe and one lamb survive. We leave them to recover and head for the house, where I plug in the kettle.

'Thanks for coming so quickly.' I pick the cleanest mugs from the stack in the sink, rinse them, and make tea. 'Three sugars, for after-shock?'

'That sounds good. Shouldn't stop, I know,' he says from the fireside. 'It's been one of those days, and everyone's in a panic.'

'Why?'

'Don't tell me you haven't heard – are you so wrapped up in this farming lark that you haven't time for a bit of telly?'

I pass him a mug of tea, and sit down with mine. 'What's the point? It's all doom and gloom. Anyway, lambing takes most of my time, and I'm still learning. Then when I'm not in the shed, I'm napping.'

Or stumbling through despair, aching for Ben, desperate for something in life to feel normal.

Phil cradles his mug, and I know he sees the pain around my eyes and mouth.

I avoid mirrors, scared by what I saw in one recently, my sturdy body somehow crumpled, face gaunt, eyes out of focus, hair spiked up as if in horror.

'Bloody not fair,' he says. 'You deserve better, especially after all those years working for a miserable old basket like me.'

The years I worked for him struggle to come into focus, but my mind won't let them – I zoom instead to the summer before last when Ben had walked into Phil's practice with an ancient dog in his rusty arms. The dog died, but we lived. We grew from its pain and distress.

'I'm okay, Phil.'

'It's a bloody shame.'

I have to get him off the subject. 'So what's this news, then?'

'You're bloody brilliant.'

'That's on television?'

'I meant you're bloody brilliant for keeping the farm going.' He scowls. 'Lambing all those sheep…'

'Ah, but I've had so much help. You've no idea how supportive they are around here. Being a good neighbour is a farmer's first commandment. I think it's etched upon their tablets of stone.'

He sighs.

'You're going to need that. Foot and mouth disease is back and spreading fast. If it's anything like the sixties' epidemic, all hell's about to break loose.'

CHAPTER THREE

I don't remember much of the sixties' foot and mouth epidemic. In my early teens, I'd had far more important things to think about – my dog, for one.

But Phil had just left veterinary school, stuffed to the eyebrows with ideals about protecting the health of the animal kingdom, and armed with comprehensive lists of drugs and procedures to do so. Taken on by a rural practice, he soon discovered how useless his ideals and drugs were for stopping the spread of foot and mouth, and the decimation of thousands of sheep, cattle and pigs. Talking about it now, sadness and futility deepen in his eyes.

His phone bleeps. Heaving himself up to head back to the surgery, he gives me a wry warning about listening to old sods who should have been put out to grass years ago.

I begin to watch news bulletins, and install a radio in the shed for updates, but I switch the thing off after two days, tired of twitterers. To a man, they assert that the disease is contained.

Strengthened by Fiona's and Phil's visits, I get through to Friday lunchtime, and glance in on the sheep before heading for the Land Rover.

Climbing in, I allow a second of smugness. I haven't phoned Fiona with an excuse, and I've eased off work all week.

The nights haven't changed. I can't sleep, and can't break the pattern of dreading going to bed, and hating to leave it.

Determined, I start the engine. It's cold and stubborn, because it's hardly used. Short trips to the shop don't get the engine warm.

I heave the bonnet up to give the engine a what for, managing to cover my scrubbed self in oil, and pollute the air with a filthy cloud of diesel fumes.

But then I'm off down the lane, on my first proper outing for weeks. I turn into the main road and speed toward the village.

I'm out. Done it.

Days of preparation have cleaned me up and steadied my mind. I'm visiting people who seem to like me, despite my emotional state. What more can anyone ask?

Fiona and Jamie take me straight to their barn, where Ellie straightens and beams like an amiable bishop, and Danny skips around the lambs who stand side by side and stare.

'Look at mine,' shrieks Danny. 'It's the biggest!'

'Greediest,' Ellie shoots back. 'It'll get as fat as a pig.'

'They both look good,' I say. 'You're feeding them well.'

'We're all at it, actually,' Jamie mutters. 'Guess who gets up in the small hours to feed the blighters?'

Fiona glances back from the pen. 'Me mostly, you old grump.'

He laughs.

'Ah,' I say, 'and who'll be feeding them every four hours next week when the children and Fiona go back to school?'

Jamie groans, but his dark eyes wink like beacons.

'Dad, don't be *difficult.*' Ellie wrenches her gaze from her new charges. 'These lambs will teach you a great deal.'

'Like what?'

Her mouth forms a prim line. 'How to be *nicer*, for one.'

He pulls her into a hug. 'I'm already nice, sometimes.'

'When you're not going on about what a wonderful thing nature has created in a tree.'

'This kid's too clever.' Jamie turns. 'Let's go in for a beer.'

I shake my head, knowing that even half a pint in my state of sleep deprivation will have me unconscious inside an hour.

We go in to eat, instead, and I manage some pasta.

The children suck on spaghetti strings until Jamie delivers a lecture about noisy slurping – and I realise I've missed the children's antics.

Does this mean I'm mending?

I watch the familiar procedure. Ticking off the children, quietening them down, the beginnings of the next round. The laughter and ping-pong conversation shine into my murky corners.

Finished, the children tog up and rush outside. Jamie gets up to make coffee, then plumps the cushions in the old chair next to the Rayburn. He always parks me here, opening the lower oven door, so I can prop up my feet in their size ten boots.

He hands me a coffee. 'Comfy?'

I nod, warmed that he hasn't forgotten, grateful for these scraps of familiarity.

'So just what does this foot and mouth scare really mean?'

I have to scramble some words together. 'Oh, nothing. According to the *radio*, it's been contained.'

'Thought you had more intelligence than to believe the radio.'

'Cynic.'

'Rightly so. All those in-depth discussions are just gloss, and as for the experts – most wouldn't know a grass root if it was served up on toast.' He notices my grin, and scowls. 'You're as bad as the kids, nudging me onto my soapbox. Now tell me, really, about foot and mouth – you're the expert, not the media.'

It's hard to organise my thoughts and relay what knowledge I've acquired – most remembered from Phil earlier in the week, the rest official stuff I used to read up on at the practice. But I manage to explain most of what I've gleaned, surprising myself.

An hour later when I leave for home, Jamie gives me an awkward hug at the gate.

'You're amazing, Julie,' he says. 'Keeping all those acres going while I find three acres a problem. Come and see us more often – some of your expertise might rub off.'

Expertise? I feel embarrassed, but Ellie saves me.

'We need you to come to *inspect the lambs*,' she says, 'because only you know if we're doing it correctly.'

'You'll know, Ellie,' I tell her. 'If they eat well, and play a lot in between, they're thriving.'

I drive away, thinking the same applies to people.

Stopping at the village shop for bread and milk on the way home, I find a knot of people outside.

My neighbour Sarah greets me, the grey coils of her perm trembling as she speaks. 'Doesn't look good – Jack's worried.'

'Mum remembers the last one,' says Carol. 'It started like the war. Nothing happened for ages, then bang, everyone was in it.'

I'm concerned by this anxiety. 'Is there more news?'

An elderly man shifts the angle of his cap. 'A farm in Cumbria's got it, from stock bought at a market up there, the other end of the country from where they first found it. The Ministry banned animal movements today to stop it spreading, but I'm betting it's too late.'

'Today? When?'

'Just been on the wireless, but we've expected it all week.'

'Sarah, what about my young ewes on your top fields? I was going to bring them home next week.'

The old man adjusts his cap again. 'Well, you can't now.'

Sarah attempts a smile, but her voice is soft and tentative. 'Don't you worry, Julie – the Ministry says it'll be over soon.'

'I can still go up and check them, though?'

'Shouldn't if I were you,' says the old man. 'Best not to walk on other people's land now – never know what bugs you're fetching on your boots.'

Sarah frowns at him, then turns back to me. 'You carry on. Our cows won't be outside until May anyway, so there's no risk.'

I drive out of the village, resentful that the glow I found at Fiona's has faded, and disturbed by my neighbours' limp responses. Their voices had been hushed. Even roundly pregnant Carol was as gaunt and stringy as I am.

In the lane, I find Mike pouring evil-looking liquid over a vast mat of straw across his entrance to his gate.

I stop and open the passenger window. 'Has it come to that?'

His shoulders lift a fraction. 'Don't know if it does any good, but what else can we do?'

'Should I do the same?'

'Up to you – got any disinfectant?'

Mike is almost off-hand, no longer his usual self – my easy-going, kindly neighbour who, with so many other farmers, has helped since Ben died.

Whenever I've needed to unload a feed delivery or move sheep to a fresh field, all I had to do was phone, and there they were in my yard, standing ready, as though they had all the time in the world for a stricken woman.

With hardly a word, they were all there for me – Mike, Sarah and Jack, Carol and Jim. Even Mike's son Davy, working his father-in-law's farm ten miles away, came over to lend a hand.

With their support, my farm has been kept going.

Now Sarah and Carol have fear in their eyes.

And Mike is distant.

'Better make sure it's on the approved list.' Mike trudges away, and disappears round the corner of an old barn.

I'm out of the Land Rover, fumbling with the gate catch, charging across the stinking straw with more energy than I've had for weeks. He's leaning on a half-door, staring inside.

He says, not looking at me, 'I bought sheep from market last week, and they're tracking everyone who bought and sold there.'

'How do you know?'

'Davy rang this morning – seems our market had sheep from Cumbria. He phoned the auctioneers and they said the Ministry's tracing every buyer.' He turns, face as grizzled as his hair. 'Best if you don't come inside my gate for a bit. Foot and mouth's the last thing you need now you're managing things again. I don't want to spread it, so I'm not going anywhere, nor will I let anyone in.'

I leave, carefully securing the gate on my way out, and drive on the few yards to my entrance with an urge to lose myself in the lambing shed, anything to stop joining the ranks of the afraid.

The sheep don't help. Something's changed.

As though through a fog I look at them, aware of a growing lump of fear inside.

In all those years as a veterinary nurse and one of farming, I've never been through an epidemic. I know about dealing with them in theory, all the procedures needed to stop the spread of infection, but not what it means to my living, my flock.

But the sheep need nothing, so I walk to the house – with the things Phil explained, and Mike's mood, sitting inside me like ice.

Mike rings two days later.

'The Ministry just phoned,' he says in an even voice. 'The sheep I bought might be carriers so I'm now a dangerous contact. They'll be here in a day or two, for the cull.'

I must ask. 'Just the sheep you bought?'

There's a long pause. 'My whole flock.'

'Oh God, Mike, I'm so sorry.'

'Best really. I don't want to spread it. I couldn't live with myself if I gave it to anyone else.'

I search for words. 'Can I do anything?'

'Just keep your sheep away from my boundary – move them up to your top fields. The sheep I bought aren't near yours but it's best to be on the safe side. And don't come calling, for a bit.'

I go outside to look at my ewes and lambs in the front field, divided only from Mike's land by the narrow lane we both use. The thought of moving them makes me so tired I put it off. I've already wallowed for two days in a deep and aching inertia and now I don't even have the energy to do the one thing Mike wants.

For the rest of the day, I try to work out how else I can help him, a lone farmer now totally marooned because he doesn't want to spread the disease. The phone seems the only contact. He's often used it since January, said he'd be along in an hour, or that he expected Davy for the afternoon, so did I "need another pair of hands for anything?" Because he's been through grief too, when his wife died five years back, he must know that keeping up with routine work helps build a pattern to the days.

I call him that evening, squashing the feeling I'm being a nuisance. 'Any more news?'

'I rang the Ministry today – someone'll be out tomorrow to plan what's needed for the pyre.'

The ice inside me splits into shards.

Since Friday, I've been mesmerised by televised images from the mouth of hell, blazing infernos grotesque with the upended corpses of Cumbrian cattle and sheep. 'Mike, what will…?' I can't ask. 'Need any shopping done? I'll go into town tomorrow, to the supermarket…'

'Not eating much. Only drink tea, and I've got that.'

'Let me know if there's anything.'

He doesn't phone back, so I set off next morning – not to the supermarket, because I'm not hungry, either – but to the village shop, for milk. Quarantined and drinking tea, he'll be short, and leaving a bottle at his gate will help me feel less useless.

My night was full of fear. In the shed at two am, I even wondered why I'd bothered to get up to check on the sheep.

Why put myself through this sleep deprivation when the Ministry might make a bonfire of them?

But Mike's needs won, and it feels good to be thinking of someone other than myself.

On the way to the main road, I meet one of his lambs in the lane. It looks at me in panic then squeezes under the fence and bolts bleating back to Mum. Has it been under my fence, too? Has it danced its way through my ewes that I still haven't got round to moving? All I can see is the virus, lurking on the tarmac where the lamb stood, waiting to leap onto my tyres, eager to be taken to the village and back, into my yard…and shed.

I slam into reverse, push the screaming Land Rover all the way home, and run into the house to grab up the phone.

'Jamie? Fiona there?'

'Half term's finished – she's back at school. Can I help?'

I can't speak.

'Julie, are you okay – shall I come over?'

'No!' I didn't mean to scream. 'No,' I repeat more calmly. 'I'm all right – just wanted to hear a friendly voice.'

'Won't mine do?'

I relax. 'Of course, Jamie – sorry. Touch of panic, that's all.'

He's quiet, and I know he's remembering just such calls when I was in despair, almost suicidal and desperate for normality, even for second-hand glimpses from other people's lives.

'I'm paranoid, that's all. All I can see is the virus.'

'Not surprising after what we're seeing on the news, and I heard about Mike. When are they…?'

'Soon.'

'Don't be alone when it happens, Julie.'

I force myself to think calmly. 'I have to be – got to stop it spreading. You mustn't come up.'

'Then I'll phone often. Fiona will ring, when she gets home.'

'Please.'

Angry for being weak, I search for and find a train of rational thought during the rest of the day, force myself to work, and eat a little between spells in the shed. Not able to face anything but lambing, I bed down in the chair by the fire between shed checks and listen to audio books Fiona lent me, and UB40, Mozart, Dire Straits, anything but the news. Fiona's call helps, a one-sided conversation about how her drama students are doing, or how the lambs are entertaining the family. Her even voice soothes my panic and reassures me I'm not falling back into the pit again.

By the time the sun crawls over the hill the next morning, I've turned my fear into energy. I make a mug of tea, phone Mike.

'No word from the Ministry,' he says, 'so I'm lambing.'

How he can keep bringing lambs into a world that slaps a death warrant on their first breaths?

'About that shopping,' he says, 'I'm out of milk – drunk too much tea. I wouldn't mind another pint, if you're going.'

At last – something I can do for him.

'Put it by the gate – I'm a dangerous contact, with my sheep.'

I tear down the lane towards the village shop, driving straight over where the lamb had stood, and buy milk, tea, bread, and chocolate, a bag for each of us, then speed back to Mike's gate.

His head appears round the corner of the shed after I sound the horn. I get out and hold up a bag.

'Just leave it there.'

'No, Mike, come and chat.'

'Best not.'

He looks exhausted, grey all over, but a new strength courses through me.

'I'm not leaving until you do.'

Shoulders slumped, he walks up and stops three paces away.

As we stare at each other, I thrash around for even a wisp of my old bossy self, the one Phil said kept animal owners in order, the one that forces recalcitrant Land Rovers to start, the one Ben claimed to be as energising as a fried breakfast. I've lost it though, just when I need to show Mike that he's my neighbour.

Instead of scrambling for words, I reach into a bag, break off two wedges of chocolate, and hold one out. After a moment, he steps forward and takes it.

'Shouldn't be doing this,' he says, his gaze distant.

'We're neighbours, Mike. You taught me what that means.'

'That's different.'

I munch on the chocolate, though it tastes like axle grease. I tell him about the shop's new deli counter of alien pâtés and cheeses, and about Jamie's tree surgery business, and his plans for greenwood furniture-making and charcoal-burning, when his coppicing is established. I talk about anything except livestock and foot and mouth.

By the time I resurrect last year's village panto, when director Fiona turned my bossy character into a Wicked Queen, Mike has relaxed and is leaning on the gate in much the way he used to. Better still, the grey is leaving his face.

'We missed you in the panto this January,' he says. 'You were good last year – looked about ten feet tall in that black cloak. I liked your spell scene best.'

'Hubble, bubble, boil, brew.' I make claws of my hands.

He smiles. 'Kid behind me burst into tears. Scared me a bit, too. Reminded me of a teacher back in junior school.'

I laugh softly.

'Didn't know you had it in you, Julie.'

'What, evil? Don't tell me you haven't heard me kick buckets round the yard – I'm the devil's own, when roused.'

He smiles.

'People said afterwards we could do with a Wicked Queen to help stand up to the Ministry and the bank manager.'

I laugh properly, one of my old sort.

This booms round his yard, disturbs the sheep in the shed.

A ewe bleats, its lamb responds. Mike hears it too, and I see by his face that he's done enough contaminating for one day.

As he steps back from the gate, the outside bell of his phone clangs, and his eyes dilate in fear.

I wait, in case it's the Ministry, but he emerges minutes later to shout that it was just Davy.

I go home to collapse, drained by the effort of it all. But I've done it, made contact, forced myself out of the shell of grief. And I've given something back.

Is this what happens? Do all those who mourn emerge one day to find other people's needs greater than their own, and do they find it as exhausting?

I haven't the energy to work it out, so go back into automatic pilot where work-eat-sleep keeps me alive.

Some of the pain has gone though, and I notice that the brilliant sunrises now get me out of bed, instead of making me want to burrow down and hide.

I plod on for another seven days, a week of looking over to Mike's fields to see him carrying on as usual.

Every morning he brings more sheep and new lambs out from the sheds, takes sacks of feed to their troughs, and fills the racks with hay, and I know I'm waiting for the morning when he's had the call from the Ministry and is too frozen in shock to come out.

Through each day, my gaze constantly drifts towards his front field to see if his sheep are still there. I look before I enter the shed, when I leave it, and before I go inside the house. I wake from naps to rush to the window, and abandon mugs of tea or a sandwich when I hear the sound of a powerful engine, in case it's the arrival of the Ministry and its machines.

Determined to witness it all, share it with Mike even from a distance, I play the waiting game and wonder how the poor man is coping with his wait. I phone him every day, sometimes twice.

I also phone Fiona and Jamie to say I've isolated myself to protect my sheep and will make only essential journeys. Though true, I need to be at home, as most farmers are, hiding behind barricades of disinfected straw and hoping against hope that the virus doesn't spot us.

Phil phones on the fifth day for a chat, and says he's just diagnosed a case six miles from us, to a farmer who's flatly refusing to acknowledge that his life's work and that of generations before him will go up in smoke.

'And how are you?' He sounds exhausted.

'Afraid – terrified – but still lambing.'

'Best to be busy.'

There doesn't seem anything else to say.

On the seventh day, I see the first pyre.

Just before dusk, a cloud rumbles into view. Miles away at the far end of the valley, a ferment of black smoke is rolling into the cold air, the top flattening out into a mushroom like one I've seen in Jamie's wood – thin-stalked, wide-capped and poisonous.

I stare, unable to move yet dreading seeing the fire beneath it when the day fades completely. It's only when I hear the bawl of a ewe in labour that I flee to the shed.

CHAPTER FOUR

Mike rings at first light next morning. I've spent most of the night mesmerised by the distant fire, and now I'm limp.

'Definitely tomorrow,' he says, his voice flat. 'The heavy stuff's on its way now to build the pyre.'

The grind of machines starts before I put the phone down. Going outside, I see a lorry crawling up the lane from the main road with a vast red caterpillar digger on its back. Loaders and JCBs follow, their dandelion paint glowing eerily through the freezing dawn mist. Rumbling trucks come after, then cars and white vans. The heavy plant disappears through Mike's gate to grind to a noisy halt in the field behind his buildings. Men in fluorescent yellow jackets and white paper boiler suits stud the grass like an early crop of buttercups and daisies.

Clanking begins soon afterwards, the diggers silhouetted on the skyline, their arms and buckets dipping and scooping out a vast pit in a macabre dance that goes on all day and into the night under powerful lights. I stare at it all – determined not to avoid whatever meets my eyes or assails my ears – and dread what the following day will bring.

Mike phones after the machines have stopped for the night. He sounds different, clipped and businesslike, when he tells me the pyre is finished, with hundreds of sleepers in place over the pit, then all his hay and straw, and sixty tons of coal on top.

'And how are you, yourself?'

'Not so bad,' he says, 'just relieved it's started.'

'I'll be thinking of you tomorrow.'

'The smoke will head in your direction,' he says. 'Better close your windows.'

They start at nine the next morning.

Mike and three men in white suits walk into his front field. His sheep look up and begin to walk towards him, hungry to the last, but they falter at the strangers, call their lambs and trot away.

Slowly, the men circle them and push them up the slope towards the farm.

The sheep go quietly, until the last moment when four lambs break away from the flock and rush leaping into play. Mike lumbers in their trail, tries to get beyond them – but the game is too good, and he leaves to help drive the rest into his yard.

The silence that follows holds me by the throat, and glues my legs rigid. I know what will happen next.

He shouldn't be alone today, I rant to nobody.

No son to prop him up, no grandchildren to make him laugh, no neighbour to remind him of good times, nothing to keep him busy, only an invasion of his life and land by men and machinery and guns.

Anger roars through me. I want to tear down to his yard, screaming, arms waving, to fight off his intruders and scatter his sheep.

'Oh, Mike,' I whisper into the thudding silence, 'you poor bugger.'

And then he appears again, riding his quad bike at full speed – standing in the stirrups, like a jockey pushing his horse to the finish line.

The bike screams after the escaped lambs who flee to the hedge at the bottom, then turn and run back towards the farm.

They aren't playing now.

The phone rings halfway through the afternoon and forces me away from the sight of loaders ferrying corpses to the pyre site.

'It's Mike,' he says quickly. 'The Ministry vet's checked them all and he doesn't think they've got foot and mouth. He's done blood tests too, so I'll know properly in a few days. I'm just glad it's over, all that waiting and thinking I was spreading it to everyone else. Davy helped me buy those sheep from market and his farm hasn't got it, so maybe I didn't pass it on, and…Julie?'

'I'm here.'

'Your sheep should be all right now, and that's good.'

'It is, Mike.' I try to inject relief into my voice.

Does he care so much for his neighbours that the killing of his stock comes second?

I mutter platitudes, say I hope he'll sleep easier tonight, anything but scream my rage about the Ministry's policy to kill first, and test later.

So much pointless death.

They light the pyre at dusk. I watch men torch its base, see the flames hesitate before a hundred-metre wall of fire roars skywards into towers of angry black smoke. Only then do I turn away to seek refuge in the warm life of my lambing shed and try to hide from the images of infernal carnage.

But I can't escape the obscene light. It flashes between the boards of the shed, floodlights my yard then chases me into the house where it fills each room with angry snakes. The smoke's already there, oily pungent filth that lines my nose and stings my eyes. And the sound – a crackling spitting din so persistent I can't drown it out with either loud music or the radio turned up high.

I belt upstairs to my bedroom, pull the heavy curtains across, and then dive beneath the duvet – fully-clothed and cold to the bone. 'Ben,' I whisper into the pillow. 'I can't stand this.'

The phone by the bed shrills, and I lift my head. Seams of orange light are framing the curtains.

'Yes,' I mutter into the receiver.

'It's Fiona – we can see it from here.'

Tears come – raging tears of fear and horror, of tension from the interminable wait, the futility I feel about Mike, all the anger and isolation mixed up with surges of resurrected grief for Ben.

'I *can't bear…*' I'm finally able to say.

'I'm with you, Julie. I'm not going anywhere.'

'I'm in bed,' I say, daring to sit up, 'but I can't escape it.'

'How long before you have to check your sheep?'

'Not for an hour or two – all's quiet in there.'

'Fancy a cup of tea?'

I manage, 'Yes.'

'Go downstairs,' Fiona says, her voice firm. 'Put the kettle on, and pick up your kitchen phone. I'll still be on the other end.'

I fly downstairs, ram the kettle plug in, and grab the phone.

'I'm here,' she soothes, 'and I'm staying, all night if necessary. Now, make a pot, then get yourself comfy in that wonderful chair you make me sit in when I come to call.'

'The mucky job by the fire?'

'That's the one.'

'But it faces the window.'

'I know, Julie, but we can't hide from it. It won't go away. We'll talk instead, or sit silent. I just want to be with you, and this is the only way.'

Listening to her calm, gently undulating voice, I feel my distress subsiding, just as it has so often since January when I've needed company or was in a panic of grief. Fiona never seems ruffled, and she uses words in the same way I use my arms to give hugs and comfort. And she listens to anything from wild ramblings to storms of anger. No wonder the volatile Jamie adores her. No wonder their children are growing so strong and true.

She stays with me until it's time for the next lambing check when she makes me promise to ring back if I need company.

I go out armed into the fiery night.

The killers have gone but the machines haven't. I trudge exhausted into the next day doing everything possible to ignore them and the still raging pyre. My eyes can't take any more.

The sounds intrude though – the screech of white vans arriving, men's laughter carrying on the wind, the grind of diggers pushing in the edges of the fire and a cacophony of bangs and crashes from Mike's yard. It all assaults my ears.

I phone Mike mid-morning. His voice has slumped again but he says the clean-up has started and his yard's brimming with men and machines emptying the sheds. 'They've got to get everything out then power-wash and disinfect the whole lot, even the rafters.'

'But you didn't have foot and mouth.'

'Still got to do it – it's the rules.'

He sounds to be on autopilot and my heart goes out to him.

'And what are you doing?'

'Nothing. Don't want to see them…'

'Come over, Mike, and get away from it for a bit.'

'Can't – the rules.'

Bugger the rules. He needs to get out. 'So break them, when it's dark, when they've gone home. Come over for a drink.'

Silence.

'Mike?'

'Maybe – I'll see.'

At lunchtime, Sarah phones. 'Are you all right, Julie?'

I collapse into the fireside chair and put my feet up. 'I think so, just exhausted. Yesterday was so awful.'

'We're tired too,' she murmurs, 'but I think that's what fear does to you, and being up half the night. We couldn't stop looking at the fire, and thinking of Mike. Poor man, coping with all that on his own – I hope he's all right. I phoned him earlier and he sounded so flat.'

She pauses. 'These are dark days, Julie. Take care of yourself.'

Mid-afternoon, Carol phones. 'If you want a visitor,' she says cheerfully, deliberately avoiding what we all witnessed yesterday, 'we could go to the bottom of our lanes and yell across the road to each other. I haven't been out much, and I feel like a prisoner.'

For her sake, I try. 'Me, too. See you in five minutes?'

'Make it ten – don't seem to have much energy today.'

I stump down my field, not the lane past Mike's, and the ewes think it's feeding time. I let them bombard me, grateful for the noisy bleating of their cupboard love. It drowns out the sounds from Mike's yard.

As I reach the hedge by the main road, Carol is starting down her lane. Though I can't make out her expression, I guess she's preparing a grin of welcome. Carol's like that. But when she reaches the crossroads, a truck thunders between us, its turbulence lifting her hair, and her face contorts in an ugly scowl.

'Monster,' she yells after it then shouts across to me. 'Maybe this wasn't such a good idea.'

'It is, Carol. I'm starved of company.'

'How are you, love?' Three cars and a white van streak between us. 'Can't you see a conversation?' she bawls after them.

I laugh, my tension unfolding like creased washing pegged out in a breeze. It's absurd to yell across a busy road. Something in me wants to stride across, give her a hug and sod the virus, and the powers-that-be for their warnings to farmers not to mix. Isn't farming solitary enough without an occasional visit from a neighbour, and what are we supposed to do for a bit of cheer? This

God-awful plague's bad enough, without depriving us of support.

But she'll back away if I go anywhere near her.

'I'm okay,' I call back, over the noise of more traffic. 'What about you and the family?'

She pats her pregnant belly. 'This one's fine, better off for not knowing anything about this crazy world, but Mum's not good…It's brought back all her memories of the last epidemic. I've set her making a cake for the kids.'

'Are they all right?'

'No – they're afraid,' she shouts across. 'Off their food, don't want to go to school, all the signs that something's wrong. I couldn't settle them last night.' She looks beyond me to the site of Mike's fire with such sadness that I know she's thinking the same as everyone else. He shouldn't have to cope with that alone.

Above the grind of machinery in Mike's yard comes a wave of men's laughter. Carol scowls again.

'And I know what I'd like to do with that lot,' she calls, rage flashing in her eyes. 'They have the sensitivity of boiled carrots!'

We talk about Mike until we're interrupted by the approach of the school bus. Three sets of feet appear beneath it until it lumbers away and I see Carol talking to her children. They turn as one to wave at me, but there's none of their usual exuberance. They look tired out, listless. The youngest, Amy, holds up a painting she's done. Even at this distance I see it's a maelstrom of red, orange and black daubs, and I recall the times they came over to see me with Carol, how they sat quietly at the kitchen table with coloured pens and paper. The pictures Amy drew then were of houses framed by lollipop trees and rainbow flowers.

'Bye,' they call, before they turn for home.

'It's done me good, Julie,' Carols shouts. 'I hate being deprived of my friends. We'll do it again soon. Take care now.'

I watch them go, then plod home to phone Mike. He doesn't answer. Perhaps he's outside with the men.

He doesn't come over in the evening.

I try phoning at eight next morning, and at nine and ten, but get the engaged tone. Something's wrong.

Throwing caution over my shoulder, I fly through my gate to find the lane a sea of earth and grass sods from the digger-ravaged verges. Cars and vans are parked all over the place. Nipping between two white Transits, I reach Mike's gate and stare at the devastation in his yard, the piles of broken concrete and bricks, heaps of straw litter and ruts of earth. The din is astounding.

The kitchen window has its curtains drawn across. A light glimmers through the thin fabric.

I wave wildly at the driver of a digger reversing out of one of the sheds. He stares back, then opens his door to shout at someone. A short youngish man in wellies and a white disposable suit marches round the corner towards me.

'You can't come in,' he orders, raising a clipboard between us.

Despite my exhausted state, something about him shoves energy through the roots of my hackles. 'I don't want to come in but I want to check that Mr Corley is all right. Please go and see.'

'He's fine. Saw him a minute ago.'

'Where?'

'Where d'you think – down the pub? He's not allowed off the farm until we've disinfected.'

My bristles sharpen to icy points and I stretch to my full five feet ten.

'Don't take that tone with me, sunshine. Who do you think you are?'

His eyes narrow. 'I know who I am, the supervisor of this clean-up, but who are you?'

'A neighbour.' I turn to point at my buildings. 'Mr Corley isn't answering the phone, and I'm worried about him. He's been through…'

The man softens slightly. 'He's just staying indoors – don't blame him really. Bit of a mess out here.'

Forcing my voice to come out evenly, I glare.

'Would you please let me know if he needs anything.'

His expression says he has far more important things to do than carry messages between neighbours, but after a second's thought he nods politely, makes his excuses, and walks away.

I stare on at the house for a while, then go home seething.

CHAPTER FIVE

My phone has never been so busy. Fiona rings daily to send everyone's love and thoughts and to say she can't wait to come and visit – the moment Mike's tests are confirmed negative. Sue from the shop phones, to say she passed the end of the lane and saw it blocked with vehicles, so if Mike or I need supplies, she could meet me at my lower boundary by the road.

They're all still out there, still caring, concerned and wanting to help in any way they can, yet I can't do a thing for Mike, not with that pillock guarding his gate.

I lurch on, trying Mike's number occasionally but still getting the engaged tone, and it's not until two days later that I decide to storm his defences. I have to do something to stop pacing and prowling or I'll go right round the bend, pushed there by a clipboard-brandishing bureaucrat. I won't stand by and let Mike rot in isolation, not after what he's been through, not after what he's done for me.

When the pillock and his crew go home at dusk, I march down to the filthy lane, ignoring the accusing voice inside me that says the owner of sheep and an ex-veterinary nurse is acting irresponsibly. By the time I'm picking my way across the Somme of Mike's yard, the voice shuts up. It feels good to be back in control, and with someone else to think about.

The side of the house reflects the glow of the pyre embers and my hand casts a monstrous shadow as I hammer on his back door.

It opens a crack, enough to show at least three days' stubble on Mike's chin and his eyes dull, despite the light from the pyre.

'Hi there, neighbour,' I say briskly. 'I think your phone's out of order.'

'Go away, Julie. You have to go away – it's not safe.'

'Bollocks! Excuse my French but you said the vet gave you the all-clear. I used to work for a vet, in case you've forgotten, and they don't make many mistakes. You need company, Mike, and so do I.' I heave a rucksack from my shoulders.

He doesn't move.

'Going to leave me out in the cold, then?'

He shakes his head, opens the door, and stands back.

The single bulb in the kitchen ceiling illuminates every detail of his 'shutdown.' The table overflows with paper, reams of official stuff, and the floor is a sea of discarded boots, coats, and crumpled blankets. Balled paper fills the hearth, the coal bucket stands empty, and no fire burns in the grate. It's cold in the room, the sort of chill that crawls through flesh.

The sink isn't piled with dishes, as mine is when I've better things to do, and there's no evidence that he's eaten much recently. A bread wrapper and an empty milk bottle stand bleakly on the draining board.

'I'm a bossy old sod when I want to be,' I say, 'so here's your orders. We're going to pile up all this paper and put it away.'

He stares at me.

'Come on, Mike, I need your help, otherwise we'll never get a drink down us.'

He bends to lift one sheet, then another.

I clear the tabletop, pile everything into a corner, then pick up the coal bucket. 'Now, where's your coal shed? I'm freezing.'

Within minutes, I have the fire going, all the cooker burners alight and the temperature up by ten degrees. I park Mike in a chair by the fire with a blanket over his knees and a coat round his shoulders, then take a box of eggs and a loaf from the rucksack.

'Don't worry,' I say to his vacant eyes, 'there's whisky and beer, but we'd better eat first.'

He doesn't respond, so I get on with scrambling eggs and making toast. I give him a portion, and sit down on the other side of the fire. By staring, I force him to eat. He takes tiny pieces, hardly more than crumbs, but they go down and stay down.

Finally he leans back in the chair, and closes his eyes. 'I couldn't stand the phone clanging, not with that noise outside – all those machines, and the men laughing. I want to kill them.'

Bastards. Cold, caculating, cruel bastards.

'It's quiet now, Mike.'

'Too quiet.' Tears squeeze from his closed eyes and zigzag down through the stubble.

‘Tell me,’ I say softly.

His eyes snap open, but he doesn’t look at me. ‘Can’t – too bloody awful. You must have seen.’

‘I did. I watched.’

‘It’s like they’ve taken me as well.’ He lifts a hand and stares at it. ‘My body’s still here, but I’m not.’

I wait quietly, wanting to bawl and yell and scream.

‘Sorry you couldn’t get through,’ he says eventually. ‘Davy must be trying as well – he’ll be worried.’

‘Phone him when you’ve warmed up.’

His gaze swings towards me. ‘In a bit.’

I get up and pour two small measures of whisky into a pair of mugs. Diluting them well from the tap, I hand one to him. ‘Here – to warm the old cockles and help you sleep.’

He sips, and shudders.

‘Not good?’

His mouth relaxes into a sort of smile. ‘It’s good.’ He takes another sip and this time doesn’t shudder. ‘Thanks, Julie.’

‘I don’t want thanks, Mike. I’m only doing what you’d do for me, what everyone’s done for me since January. All I want is you to look after yourself a bit.’ I grin at him. ‘Food and stuff. And if you don’t, I’m sending the Wicked Queen round to sort you out.’

He gives a half-smile at my weak joke. I’m winning.

CHAPTER SIX

Mike's tests come back negative in mid-March, but mixed feelings run through the valley. Some are shaking their heads at the apparently pointless killing and destruction of Mike's living, but most farmers are sighing with relief that the valley feels virus-free, even though foot and mouth rages to the west and smoke from numerous pyres fills the horizon.

The wind has backed to the south and sent the smoke packing.

It's also coaxing the ground out of hibernation, and celandine sprawls along the verges, daffodil spears are breaking through the soil, and gardeners have reached for their spades.

The news isn't good, with five hundred cases of foot and mouth nationwide, and ministerial talk of a fire-break cull on farms around infected premises, but Mike's results have given us all a respite. We continue to douse our straw mats and sluice our vehicles with evil-smelling disinfectant, yet now nurse a germ of hope that the virus has passed us by.

Despite advice from the Ministry that farmers shouldn't socialise until the epidemic is under control, I've been visiting Mike every evening after his clean-up crew go home. If his animals weren't infected, then there's no virus to take home, so bugger the Ministry. Surely Mike's health is more important than advice from so-called experts? And he's so much better – still drawn and exhausted, but his face has lost much of the grey.

Propping him up helps me, too. We sit in easy silence by his fire, or talk about Davy, or exchange stories and snippets of the history of our farms. Though exhausted myself, I find purpose in his company, something apart from the need to lamb the sheep successfully, and keep the farm going. But it's when we talk about how the epidemic is being handled that I know I'm emerging from the trough of lethargy I've wallowed in since Ben died.

'The Ministry must know what it's doing,' Mike comments one evening, after I've criticised the rate at which the disease is spreading.

‘Why? Just because they pay us subsidies doesn’t mean they know it all. They’re not God, Mike, only pen pushers and agents for the nation’s taxpayers – just remember that. Most don’t know the difference between a sheep and a goat.’

He shakes his head, so I grin and hand him another beer. We’ve graduated from drips of whisky to generous mugs of ale, and from teaspoons of scrambled egg to sausages and chips. His living might be decimated, and the silence on his farm wrings out my insides every evening when I cross his yard, but he’s climbing out of the hell I found him in on my first visit.

With a responding grin, he changes the subject. ‘How’s your lambing going?’

‘Tail end now – only a few to go of the older ewes, then it’s the younger ones, when I’m allowed to bring them home from Sarah’s land.’

‘Many casualties?’

I wonder how he can ask such a question after what he’s been through, but he looks genuinely interested. Will I ever get used to this overriding concern he has for his neighbours?

‘Just a few,’ I say.

‘Happens on the best of farms.’ His head droops, but he lifts it almost immediately. ‘Can I come up to your place tomorrow night? A change of scene might do me good.’

Yes, yes, yes, I want to yell, but I keep my voice even. ‘You don’t need to ask – you’re always welcome.’

‘Don’t think I’m supposed to go off the farm without some licence or other, but… sod the Ministry, eh?’

And he chuckles.

He’s learning.

Mike’s need to venture out prompts mine. I phone Fiona, stress I’m ‘clean’ and invite myself over. Turning up their lane out of the village and driving past their neighbour’s farm with almost a tune in my heart, I see Frank Holmes in his yard and wave. Pushing on up the hill, I look forward to a riotous welcome back into Fiona’s fold.

I approach their gate hand on horn, and Fiona emerges from the house. In the vegetable plot, Jamie parks his spade and walks over, then Ellie and Dan race from the barn followed by two leaping lambs.

'I've got *two hours*,' I yell, climbing out.

Fiona grapples with the gate catch, then beams. 'It's so good to see you, Julie, and you look well.'

'It's bloody wonderful to see you lot,' I say, wrapping her in a spine-cracking hug. Dan runs up for his usual twirl round my head but Ellie waltzes round us, showing off the lambs which have filled out remarkably in the three weeks since I last visited.

Bucking and skipping, they prance the steps of the innocent.

'Goodness,' I say. 'You feeding them on Horlicks?'

Ellie is severe. 'We went to town to get proper lamb milk powder from the farmers' shop. Our car had to be disinfected before we went in, then we had to wash our wellies in a stinky bucket. *Daddy's wellies leak!*'

'So his feet can't catch foot and mouth,' Danny adds.

I grin stupidly at them all, with the feeling that I've just been rescued from a desert island.

Jamie heads for the back door and yanks off his earth-laden boots. 'Coffee?'

'Please, and a biscuit, then I want a guided tour out here. I haven't seen what you're all up to for ages.'

In their cluttered and cosy kitchen, the children gulp down fruit juice, tell me about the lambs, then rush back outside. Jamie says they have to be forced indoors these days. He refills my mug and studies me. 'You're looking better.'

'I am now – I've missed you all. But you'll be pleased to hear I haven't been totally isolated.' I tell them about seeing Mike.

'Poor bugger,' Jamie mutters. 'He must have been through hell. Bet he's wondering now why he had to lose his stock.'

'His biggest concern was infecting his neighbours, so he's much more relaxed since the tests came back negative.'

Jamie shakes his head. 'Farmers seem to take everything that's thrown at them – bad weather, ruined harvests, low prices, interference from government, and now even total wipe-out.'

I have to agree. 'Ben was like that. Must be in the blood.'

Fiona stirs from a reflective silence. 'But it doesn't mean they don't feel anything. How could that carnage and the awful fire not affect anyone?' She traces the rim of her mug. 'Maybe people like us – from town – maybe we let our feelings show more.'

I think of Mike, as he was when I first forced my way through his defences. His feelings were blatantly obvious. When I tell James and Fiona how shell-shocked Mike had looked, Jamie starts to pace the kitchen, heading for the soapbox.

'Poor sod,' he growls, 'and I bet *not a scrap of official support* is offered. Just a pay-off, compensation or whatever you call it.'

'But he needs that – to restock,' Fiona puts in.

'Of course,' Jamie snaps back, 'but he should have emotional support, as well. The man's spent his life rearing sheep for the nation's food, but when things go wrong he's put through hell in total isolation, handed a cheque, and ignored. And all he can do now is sit round on his bloody farm waiting for six months until he's allowed to restock.'

He stops pacing and stares at me. 'And all those poor bastards on contiguous farms in Devon and Cumbria – thousands of healthy animals slaughtered to stop something that's already spread beyond them. It doesn't look to me as if the epidemic is under control, as they keep claiming.'

A streak of fear grips me, that the virus has not passed us by, and Fiona sees it in my face. She looks up at Jamie and shakes her head almost imperceptibly, but I notice.

'Don't stop him, Fiona,' I say. 'I need to talk about it all. The worst thing is being holed up with only the media for company.'

'We've heard such harrowing reports,' she muses. 'It makes me want to rush onto the farms to be with those poor people, or protest at their gates, even try and reason with those Ministry men about the way they're trampling over people as well as their land.'

'I've wanted to do that,' I admit, and tell them about the officious clean-up supervisor and the noise his men make.

Jamie's been quiet long enough. 'I know what I'd feel if a team of men marched in here,' he mutters, his eyes dark with rage. 'I'd beat them round the ears with a tree trunk.'

Fiona stands up. 'Let's show Julie what we've been up to, outside.'

'Don't worry about me, Fiona,' I reassure her. 'I wanted to beat that supervisor round the ears with his clipboard.'

'You're bloody wonderful,' Jamie says, as he heads for the door. 'Not many would do what you've done for Mike.'

'Yes they would, and if you've got that tree trunk handy, chuck it in the back of the Land Rover and I'll see to Mr Clipboard on the way home.'

He laughs, heaves on his boots, and stomps outside.

'I do admire your courage, though,' Fiona says. 'You must have been worried for your sheep, going to see Mike before the test results were back.'

I shrug. 'Much as I love my ladies, and I wouldn't inflict anything on them if I could help it, somehow Mike's needs came first. And, joking apart, maybe I should have demanded more consideration for Mike from that supervisor.'

Fiona puts her hand on my arm. 'Don't take the world on before you've put your own back together.'

'But I *am* putting it back together. These last weeks have prised me out of that awful nothingness, and I want to help people the way they've helped me.'

'Yes, I'm sure you do, but please take it steady. I don't want you to…'

I grin. 'Nah...I promise not to use a tree trunk. Now, show me what you're all up to, outside.'

She frowns, but leads me out to inspect the vegetable plot, then the pasture already occupied by scratching hens and a pair of geese, soon to be joined by two sturdy lambs.

'I want this mess out here cleaned up,' I say to Mike's Mr Clipboard on my way home. I point up the lane, at verges ploughed out by turning diggers, earth mixed with straw from the yard and driven and scattered halfway to the main road by the team's cars and vans. 'Get it done before you leave tonight.'

He hugs his clipboard, and takes a step closer. 'What for?'

I straighten to my full height and glare down. If tiny Fiona wants to stand up to burly men from the Ministry, I can deal with this pipsqueak.

'Because I use this lane, and I have sheep. You've all driven on and off Mr Corley's farm bringing out all this muck and I don't want to take it home on my wheels.'

He shrugs. 'It wouldn't matter – his tests were negative.'

'It does *bloody matter*,' I roar. 'Who knows what you bring in every day off the main road and grind into this mess? I haven't seen much wheel-arch cleaning or disinfection going on when you arrive each morning.' I lean closer, and lower my voice. 'And I can see everything from my yard.'

He squints up at my buildings. 'Not without binoculars.'

I grin at him. 'Which I have. And you'd be surprised at how much I see – like how early you all clock off, and how late you arrive in the morning. Funny hours you civil servants keep.'

A shadow crosses his face.

'Nothing better to do than spy on us, eh?'

'I've nothing better to do than protect my sheep,' I shoot back, 'and I will not put up with shoddy biosecurity, especially from Ministry officials who should know better!'

He backs off then, and I beam in triumph. True, I've been keeping an eye on them, out of concern for Mike rather than a desire to timekeep, but challenging these men strengthens me, boosts my resolve that if strangers have to invade Mike's farm then at least they should work as hard as he always has.

'I heard about all that this morning,' Mike says with a grin when he arrives freshly shaved at my kitchen door. 'I've never seen the lane so clean – the tarmac's almost polished!'

I lead him to a chair by the fire, pour him a beer, and sit down opposite. I've always assumed that he's in his sixties, but now I'm not sure – he could pass for late seventies. But at least the harrowed depths have gone from his eyes.

'I cleaned my kitchen a bit, too,' I say with a grin. 'Thought I'd better practise what I preached to the pillock.'

He surveys the room, but doesn't seem to focus on the results of my puny attempt to clean up months of clutter and dust.

'Had another pillock round this afternoon – two of my wooden barns have got to come down. Too old to clean properly, or something.'

I gape, astounded at a Ministry intent on wrecking the fabric of his farm as well as his living.

'I told him where to get off,' he says.

'Good!'

'I'm not demolishing everything just so he can spray disinfectant more easily. The farm's for Davy, if he or his kids want it, and I'm going to leave it to him in a workable state. I know the Ministry would put up concrete sheds instead, but there's nothing wrong with my old ones.'

'How long have they been there?'

'Hundred years or so, maybe two.'

I shake my head in disbelief, knowing that his ancient oak-framed buildings would be standing long after modern farm buildings crumbled. Speechless, I get up to put the greens on, and drain the potatoes. While I work Mike talks on, slowly at first as though picking his way over a mountain of words, but by the time I've finished the gravy and hauled one of my better toad-in-the-holes out of the oven, his talk is seamless.

I'm keeping him plied with beer, knowing it'll help him to get things out of his system, and by the time we've eaten and returned to the fireside, he's told me every detail of the pyre building, the cull and the clean-up.

I didn't expect him to talk about the cull. My stomach turns at some of the details, and I wonder at his courage in insisting he stood by and witnessed the killing.

'They were my animals,' he says, 'so it was my duty to see they did it properly.'

I hardly dare ask. 'And did they?'

'Mostly – the older slaughtermen were better at it. Some of the younger lads seemed a bit…' He pauses. 'A bit excited, like. I heard the vet having words with them.'

He sags, and I see the full extent of his trauma.

'Tell me about that clipboard man,' I say to divert him.

He shrugs. 'He's far too young to manage that lot under him. They're leading him a dance, all right. You should hear what they say about him behind his back, especially today when he told them to clean up the lane.'

I can imagine. Serves the pillock right.

'But then those men are better at skiving than work,' he goes on. 'They pinch stuff, too. I thought it odd how they all have diesel cars, but I've seen them filling up from the tank brought in for the diggers and loaders. One of the perks, I suppose, but it doesn't seem quite right.'

'And it's taxpayers' money.'

He frowns.

'It's making themselves at home that I don't like. They go into my workshop for tools they've forgotten to bring, then don't put them back. I mentioned it to the supervisor, but he couldn't even find my hammer. I suppose it's ended up in someone's pocket and gone for good.'

'Stolen.'

'Don't like to quite say that – it's easy to lose a hammer or a wrench.'

I glare at the fire.

You trusting sod, Mike. I know what I'd do if an uninvited guest accidentally stole anything of mine. The urge to give them a taste of their own medicine settles in a corner of my mind, and I promise myself the future pleasure of working out the details.

Mike's grinning when I look up.

'Don't worry, Julie, I've got everything in the front room now – can't get in there for tools and gear, even my generator!' He heaves himself off the chair and sways. 'I'd better go. I'll not be able to walk home if I go on drinking like this.'

'A bit of a drink helps you to sleep.'

He gives me a knowing glance, and reaches for his jacket.

After a long session in the lambing shed the next morning I walk up the fields behind the house, then through my three-acre wood to inspect my younger ewes that are still on Sarah and Jack's top land because I can't get a licence to move them. I clamber over the fence and cross the lane to find them lining the hedges eating early hawthorn shoots, and nosing through the gaps for any blade of grass they've missed.

In the three weeks since they should have come home, they've eaten the field down to the roots, and it will be a month before the grass starts its strong spring growth.

I've been bringing bales of hay and feed up the lane in the Land Rover to try and keep them in reasonable shape for lambing in April and May, but it's not enough. They need grass.

After looking them over, I walk slowly back down the bramble-ridden path. I like the wood, especially in winter, the way the trees arch over me in a vaulted nave. It's peaceful as a church.

Feeling slightly more positive by the time I reach the gate to my back field, I lean on my favourite oak and inspect the valley.

Made up of small farms, most of which have been worked by the same family for generations, the land is a kaleidoscope of small fields ringed by hedgerows and clumps or stripes of ancient woodland.

Some fields are ploughed ready for barley, some are emerald with winter wheat, some a bleached khaki – a sure sign of over-grazing. Movement restrictions are already leaving their mark.

Sweeping my gaze along the opposite hillside beneath the swathe of conifers stretching along the summit, I focus on the crescent of Jamie's broadleaved wood round their house. In the clear air, I can even see the two white specks of their geese moving across their tiny field.

Another white shape catches my eye. I wonder if Ellie's dancing with her lambs again. Next moment I'm running down the hill, fear propelling my legs. That speck is far too big for a lamb. It's a man in a white disposable suit, and he's at Jamie and Fiona's gate.

CHAPTER SEVEN

I know the system. I know why there's only one white suit. I race into the house, grab the phone and dial Fiona's number.

Jamie answers, his voice shaking. 'The vet's been at Frank Holmes' for hours. I saw him examining their cows in the yard, and he's just been up to our gate to say he's blocked the bottom of the lane, and we're quarantined and can't go out. Does it mean Frank's got foot and mouth?'

I can hazard a guess. 'I don't know, Jamie. Just stay inside, and don't let the lambs out.'

'So the Holmes have got it. But we're contiguous – they won't take our lambs, will they?'

'No – that's only in badly affected counties, but keep them in all the same.'

He gives a sort of sob. 'Come and get the children, Julie. We're so near the Holmes, and I don't want them to see this.'

I think quickly, knowing I can no more cross the vet's barricade than swim the Channel, but it won't be long before hell lets loose – maybe this evening, possibly tomorrow – it depends on how soon a slaughter team can be brought on site.

'If the vet said you can't go out,' I say quietly, wanting to scream, 'then no one can move on or off. I'm so sorry, Jamie. If there was anything I could do, I'd do it.'

He groans. 'I know. And you've got your sheep to think of, so you mustn't come anywhere near. But I've learned enough about this bloody epidemic to...' He pauses, but I have no words to fill the silence. 'Julie, will we hear it?'

How can I tell him they use rifles for cattle? How can I repeat what Mike told me about the bloodbath in his yard?

'Stay inside,' I say.

I go back to window-watching, dreading what I'll see and hear but somehow powerless to stop looking. Crashing through the afternoon, railing against my inability to storm the vet's barricade and whisk Jamie and his family away, I give the sheep what they need with my mind elsewhere, and a compulsion driving me to constantly scan the valley.

Sarah phones, fearful for her own herd – with their land divided from the Holmes only by the B-road.

After seeing the vet's car arrive, she walked to the end of her driveway to stand on her disinfected straw and watch the cows brought out into the yard for inspection.

Then the vet took the Holmes back inside the house, and she had a long wait for nothing else to happen, keeping vigil for her neighbours.

'Our cows have been inside all winter,' she says, 'so I know there's been no contact, but I can't rest. And God help Frank and Maisie – they'll be in the house, waiting …' I hear her breathing. 'What about your friends up there, the Caseys? They must be worried sick.'

'They're quarantined. Jamie wants to get the children away, but I can't do anything for them.'

'It must be like being in prison,' she muses. 'You and I can go out – not that we do, for fear of bringing the virus back, so heaven knows what they're going through.'

I ask after Jack.

'He just sits at the kitchen table, head in hands. He's scared, hardly daring to go and milk for what he might find, and he's dubious about the milk tanker coming on – thinks they're the ones spreading the disease. He may be right, of course. Tankers go on and off farms twice a day, every day, but we've got to sell our milk. Money's been tight enough the last few years.'

We talk on, trying to reassure each other though preoccupied with our own fears, but it's better to be with someone, even over the phone.

Nothing's happened. It's dark now and I can see lights on in the Holmes' house and sheds. It's almost as though life's ticking over as normal. But animals, like children, need constant tending so the Holmes will be carrying on with their milking routine. I wonder where they've found the strength.

After my last ewe check of the evening, I phone Fiona and Jamie again.

'I'm still here.' I say evenly. 'I haven't abandoned you.'

Fiona thanks me. 'And we've calmed down a bit, and the children are asleep. Nothing will happen tonight now, will it?'

I pray that it won't, banking on the fact that even in a crisis, overworked vets, slaughterers and digger drivers need sleep.

'We're all right, Julie,' she says, not waiting for an answer. 'The children picked up our panic earlier, but they're okay now, and maybe they're not old enough to work out what's going on.'

Maybe not Danny, I think, but Ellie's a bright nine year-old. 'I wish I could bring you all over here.'

'No, Julie, you can't. Remember what I said the night of Mike's fire? We can't hide from it, and if this is part of living in the country then we'll put up with it. If we can't go out then we'll concentrate on the garden, and I can get to grips with next term's teaching plans. Those students of mine won't know what's hit them when I get back to school! I could even start writing next year's village pantomime – what do you think to Sleeping Beauty? It'd have to be spiced up a bit, of course, but you'd make a great Wicked Fairy!'

It's not like Fiona to prattle. She's a listener, eyes fixed on the speaker's face absorbing every nuance, every expression.

Now she's putting all her energy into protecting the children, and reassuring Jamie and me that they can cope with this. I know that even Fiona will find it hard.

My vigil stretches into two days.

I emerge from a long session in the shed to see a cluster of cars and vans in the Holmes' lane.

Why didn't I see them arrive – how long have they been there?

Why didn't I leave that ewe to fend for herself, and has Fiona tried to ring and now feels abandoned?

I belt into the house, and grab the phone.

'It's Julie,' I say to Jamie, fighting to keep my voice steady.

The sound of shots come loud and clear down the line, then a child screams.

'Daddy!'

The phone goes dead.

I run outside to hear muffled bellows and shots reverberating through the air.

Every shot batters my chest but I stand silent, frozen, unable to go in.

It goes on for two hours.

An unholy stillness blankets the valley for days afterwards and normal routine lumbers on. Though every farmer within three kilometres of the Holmes' farm has received a restrictive D notice from the Ministry, life goes on – milk tankers and the school bus crawl along the main road twice a day, people go to work in town and children, apart from Ellie and Dan, go reluctantly to school.

Farmers, restricted or not, stay at home as much as possible and speak in hushed tones to their neighbours over the phone.

Though everyone for miles heard the sounds from the Holmes' yard – the shots and frenzied bellows, men shouting, the clanging of metal hurdles – no one wants to discuss it, no one wants to resurrect the horror we all felt.

We wait instead, for the disposal team.

It still hasn't arrived by the weekend. I hear on the radio that the Ministry hasn't enough disposal teams to go round and that infected farms now have to wait days, sometimes weeks, for carcases to be buried or burned. I can hardly bear to think about the Holmes' yard, of Frank having to disinfect his dead stock daily, and what the mild weather is doing to the carcases.

And I bleed for Fiona and Jamie. Feeling totally useless, apart from phoning them at least twice daily, I seek Mike's company and read in his face that he's mourning too, not only for his own living but for the Holmes' as well.

'It's not good enough,' he says one evening over a bowl of tinned soup and hunks of bread and cheese, 'and you were right, the Ministry isn't God. He wouldn't allow that torture. Poor Frank and Maisie – no one should have to go through that. It makes me want to run down there and start digging holes to bury their cows.'

'But you haven't got a digger.'

'Got a spade, haven't I?'

I stare at him. 'For two hundred cows?'

'Better than nothing,' he mutters into his soup.

It is, Mike, I want to shout. A burst of resolve shoots through me but, as usual, it's short-lived, running out of steam within seconds of its coming. What can I do, anyway? The Holmes' farm is sealed off, out of bounds to everyone, and so is their lane. Searching for the smallest crumb of comfort, I can only be grateful that at least Fiona and Jamie are upwind of two hundred decomposing carcases.

'I want to do something, Mike, anything. For the Holmes and the Caseys. Any ideas?'

He puts his spoon down into an almost full bowl of soup and shakes his head. 'That's what gets to me – being useless.' Leaning forward on the table, he gazes at me. 'Hope you don't mind me saying this but back in January when you were a bit down…'

'You mean after Ben died? If I can say it out loud, Mike, then you can. I miss him dreadfully, but I'm learning to live with it.'

He looks embarrassed. 'You're a brave lady.'

'No. I had a lot of help, especially from you.'

He shakes his head. 'But I could do things, help keep the farm ticking over, give you a hand when you couldn't do everything. This foot and mouth's different – no one can help anyone else. We're not even allowed to drop by to cheer each other up, and I can't start digging holes for Frank's stock any more than I can bring my own sheep back to life.' He shivers, and seems to shrivel. 'But it comes to something when a man can't do anything for a mate. I've no stock to get the disease, yet I can't even go and meet Frank for a pint.'

My mind whirls. I've broken rules by visiting Mike at home, so why not break more and storm the barricade?

Then I shiver, too. With a real case of foot and mouth, I'd be risking my sheep and everyone's stock by setting even a boot on the Holmes' lane. Live bugs are out there, and until the disposal and clean-up teams have done their work, there's absolutely nothing anyone can do.

But I *have* to do something.

Pacing inside and worrying about Jamie and Fiona isn't doing any good. Anguish about Ben has returned in force too, stopping me getting enough sleep to build myself up for the next day. And I'm losing weight, in all the fear, dread and sympathy for my friends. In under a week of finding food dry as hay, I'm tightening my belt a notch and wondering why my skin no longer fits.

And I alternate between being glad Ben can't see his valley, and wondering how I can be pleased he's not here.

Didn't he make my *life* sing? Didn't he transform the blunt instrument of me into a malleable lump with his teasing, adoring eyes, and strong hands?

Ever since the Holmes got the virus, I've lurched between surges of wild energy, and feeling as limp as a sopping dishcloth.

I've charged outside to hammer in a single fence post, then crawled back to the nest of my fireside chair to recover. I've driven hay up to the thaives, only to collapse in the Land Rover afterwards until rested enough to drive the half mile home. Mike's company is the only thing that gives me any comfort, even if we do nothing but discuss foot and mouth or sit in silence by the fire.

But I have to do something. I have to prise myself out of this inertia, if only for my own peace of mind.

It's a week since the Holmes' cull and the diggers still haven't arrived, so I plant an image of Mike with a spade burying a mountain of corpses firmly in my mind and phone the Ministry's Midlands Office.

'I want to speak to someone responsible for this area.'

After a few transfers and a long wait, I get through to a clerk and give him the exact location of the Holmes' farm. 'It's seven days since the cull and there's still no sign of the disposal team.'

'There's nothing we can do about it.' He seems to be stifling a yawn. 'We're a bit busy.'

'Doing what – sharpening pencils? Can't you see what torture the Holmes are going through, surrounded by rotting carcases and forbidden to leave the farm?'

He sighs. 'What can I do?'

'Get your finger out and organise something!'

'No need to be rude. If you're finished, I've got things to do.'

I know shouting won't help, nor being rude.

'*Look*,' I say when I've got a grip on my anger, 'it's not just the Holmes. There's a young family up the hill who are marooned because the lane stops at their house. Until those carcases go, they can't go to work or shop for food, never mind see anyone. Being so near, they must have heard the slaughter last week and the children will be traumatised – the youngest is five. They're not farmers, not even country people, so…'

Another sigh. 'So what are they doing in the back of beyond? They shouldn't live in the country if they can't take the strain.'

'I want to speak to your superior,' I say icily, fighting the urge to call him every bloody name under the sun, 'and I'm not getting off the line until I do.'

He makes a muffled aside to someone in the office that he's got a trouble-maker on the line, then there's silence. I wait.

'The office manager's had to go out,' he says five minutes later. 'You'll have to phone tomorrow.'

'I am not hanging up until I get someone prepared to listen.'

'Have you any idea how busy we are? We're in the middle of an epidemic, in case you haven't noticed.'

I can't hold back any more. 'You haven't the slightest fucking idea what it's like to be in the middle of an epidemic! Have your children been through hell? Are you cut off from the world surrounded by stinking carcases?'

The phone goes dead.

Next morning brings a small miracle, the familiar convoy of red and yellow machines rumbling towards the village. When they turn up the Holmes' lane, I send up a prayer of thanks to my own god, knowing that the arrival of the disposal team has nothing to do with my tirade to some lowly bureaucrat.

Then Jamie phones to say an official has been to their gate, and they're quarantined until the Holmes' farm has been through a preliminary disinfection. He sounds brittle, and there's none of the normal background noise, no children laughing, no sounds of life.

When he's gone, I curl up by the fire and weep.

Then I'm charged with another surge of energy, and ransacking the shelves for the Ordnance Survey map of the valley.

Pouring over it, I see I can get to their house by driving up the parallel lane to theirs, the one past Carol and Jim's farm.

If I park by the forestry land at the top and walk through it along the ridge, I can drop down through Jamie's wood to their house. Didn't my friends storm my defences when I shut myself away after Ben died? Didn't they force their company on me, knowing that hauling me out of the pit even for half an hour would stop me sinking further? I rescued Mike from his pit, so why can't I do the same for Fiona and Jamie?

I spend an hour, and sort it all out. I'll wear a clean pair of overalls and Ben's old wellies once I leave the Land Rover to walk through the forest, carrying a bucket of disinfectant and a stiff brush to scrub myself down afterwards. The overalls and wellies can be sealed in a plastic feed sack and...

But it's no use. Mad even to think about it. Would I ever forgive myself if I spread the disease or brought it back? Far better to buckle down, concentrate on the sheep, batter in fence posts, do what I can for others by getting on the phone to prop them up – not risking their animals with manic schemes. After all, I'm no more God than the Ministry.

Smoke from the Holmes' pyre fills my house and sheds. It sneaks into cupboards and drawers to taint the clothes. Recoiling from clean shirts and underwear stinking of burnt diesel and barbecued rotten meat, I fling everything into the wash and get on with lambing the last of the older ewes, though the lambs come infrequently. I fill time fixing fences and half-heartedly servicing the Land Rover and quad bike, but still have empty hours.

The state of my thaives plagues me, too. I'm taking hay up and hauling it into their field, but it does little good. They're not only hungry, they're drowning in mud.

The mild dry weather has gone. It's rained relentlessly for days, a steady vertical downpour that soaks the earth and surges through ditches in torrents.

Devoid of grass, the thaives' field has quickly turned to a quagmire, especially where they stand to strip the hedges of every new shoot as soon as it bursts from dormancy.

Though I choose a different place each day to dump the hay bales, their fight for food has turned most of the field into a sticky boot-sucking bog. I can hardly bear to inspect them each day. I've applied and re-applied for a licence to move them, but haven't received a thing. Part of me wants to open their gate and simply walk them home down the lane.

Anxiety keeps me tossing into the small hours, waking with a start as soon as I've dropped off. During the day, I traipse through work, resenting not only my lack of energy but the way my hard-won plans for the future seem to have gone up in the smoke of foot and mouth.

Maudlin now, I worry about my neighbours constantly, their isolation, their financial straits.

Most farmers have overdrafts accumulated over years of plummeting farm incomes, and this is the time of year to sell stock and knock a slice off their debts or help pay another feed bill. I can't imagine how they're coping, especially people like Sarah and Jack whose son Alan also works on the farm.

If the income tumbles further, how can it keep him and his wife and baby as well as his parents?

And what about Carol and Jim with three school-age children and an elderly mother? Restrictions make it impossible to sell a single animal until well after the epidemic is over.

My widow's pension pays for the basics, but their overdrafts must be soaring.

God help them, for I can't.

CHAPTER EIGHT

I spend the two weeks of Fiona and Jamie's quarantine in a quagmire, so deep I can't climb out.

Then, in the middle of April, Jamie phones. His voice is even and cold. 'We're allowed out. We've survived.'

I search for comforting words, find only platitudes. 'It's over now, then.'

'It certainly is for Frank Holmes.'

'How are you all?'

'Disinfected.' His voice cracks. 'And scarred. I'll never forgive the bastards, and I may have been imprisoned against my will but I haven't been idle.'

'I'm sure you haven't, but…'

'Do you mind if we come over – now?' His tone has altered, the edges are frayed with desperation. 'I know we're contiguous to an infected farm, but we need a change of scene and… We'd leave the car at your gate and change our shoes, and we won't go on your fields or anywhere near your sheep.'

'I'll put the kettle on.'

I go to meet them at the gate, but they stand by the car with blank expressions, so I make my usual lunge for Dan and whirl him round. Ellie stares up, hugging Fiona's side.

'Come on, folks,' I say, leading them up the yard, 'or the kettle will be boiled dry.' I turn to Dan. 'Biscuit tin's full – want to go and get it out?'

He takes a small step, then breaks into a run.

'Straight inside, mind,' Jamie yells after him. 'Ellie, go with him, but please stay in the house.'

Jamie puts his arm round Fiona's waist. 'We're not beaten,' he says, his eyes full of flames. 'I've joined an action group. I'm going to do what I can to fight these bureaucrats. Will you help?'

Fiona slumps against him. 'I won't forgive them for that cull,' she murmurs. 'It was barbaric, then afterwards…all those corpses. The children…'

'Come on,' I coax. 'Inside. We'll talk more later.'

I lead them up to the house, then light a fire. Despite the mild weather, they look as though they need a bit of warmth.

I don't say anything as I make coffee and pour juice for the children, but my mind races. Jamie asked for my help. At last someone's given me something to get involved in, yet I'm reluctant. I can't leave the sheep for long so how can I join demonstrations and wave placards or hurl abuse at politicians?

And anyway, it's my friends and neighbours I want to help, people who stood by me when I needed them. If I joined one of Jamie's crusades, and I know he's been a valiant protester over all sorts of global issues in the past, I'd neglect the rest of the valley.

I hand out the mugs, and Fiona smiles up. 'Don't worry.'

Jamie sits back. 'Sorry, Julie. I'm a right activist when I get wound up. I want to sort the world out, right here and now, just sharpen my sword and barge in. I can't sit round helpless, especially when my family's threatened. I have to do something.'

'Me, too.' I explain the aborted plan to sneak along the far hill to see them.

'We wondered if you'd try something,' he says with a grin, 'but I'm glad you didn't. You've got to think of your sheep.'

Fiona leans forward. 'But you wanted to come and that's the important thing. We knew you were with us in spirit.'

I have to fight back tears, three weeks of tension looking for a sluice gate. 'It's feeling so *bloody impotent* that I hate.'

Dan giggles. ''Bloody's naughty!'

'It's only naughty for children,' Ellie tells him. 'Daddy says it all the time.' She turns. 'I don't want to go home. Can we stay?'

I laugh, for the first time in ages. 'Best idea I've heard for weeks! Now, tell me about the lambs.'

'Gynormous,' Dan stretches his arms wide.

'And greedy,' Ellie adds. 'It's a good job they don't have many bottles now, because they nearly pull my arms off!'

'They're eating lamb pellets,' Dan says proudly. 'We bought them before the men locked us up.'

They fall silent.

Jamie explains more about his crusade later, after the children have gone up to the back bedroom to empty the cupboard of toys.

'I've found out from this website just what's going on,' he begins. 'It's also a support group, with a chat-line, and they've been so understanding over our situation. It's made up of all sorts of people, everyone who's concerned about what's happening, and there are lots of experts on hand for advice, and different localities have set up groups to organise ways of giving practical help – food at people's gates or being prepared to stay on the phone all night with someone who can't cope, and even getting children off farms before the slaughter.'

His jaw clenches. 'I found out that Ellie and Dan could have been taken off the farm before the cull – that vet was wrong when he said no one could leave. I tried to insist, but he wouldn't listen.'

'I should have come and fetched them,' I say, in knots.

'You didn't know.'

'*I should have tried.*'

'No, Julie, I won't have you blaming yourself. The fault lies in the lack of information available, even to vets on the ground. He was only young and probably not briefed properly. His orders were to examine animals then start the awful killing machine. People didn't come into it.' He touches my arm. 'No one could do anything – don't feel bad.'

Oh, I do feel bad. What have I done but wallow in self-pity? I can't haul my young ewes out of the mire, never mind my friends.

'And it could have been worse,' Fiona muses. 'Culling on contiguous farms is now in force round here. A week earlier and the lambs could have gone too. I can't imagine ...it was bad enough helping the children through the Holmes' cull.'

I get up to pace the kitchen then grab the mugs and bang them down in the sink. Then I shove chairs back under the table so violently they squeal on the quarry-tiled floor.

Jamie laughs, a strangled version of his old humour. 'We could do with a tigress clawing for us,' he says.

I spin round. 'I haven't got the claws of a kitten.'

'But you'll find them again, Julie. Join this group we've set up and you'll find any number of claw-sharpeners. Now sit down.'

They both grin.

'You've no idea how wonderful it is to see you again,' Fiona says, '*especially* all fired up like this. You're just what we need.

But can you calm down enough for us to explain?'

'You want me to calm down just when I've found a bit of energy?' But I do sit, and tell them I've never felt so powerless or lacking will to fight. 'I don't even know who the enemy is – this foot and mouth is bloody dire but it hasn't got a face I can punch.'

'Punches aren't needed,' she says, serious. 'Hundreds of people all over the county need someone to phone, someone to give them accurate information, someone to lean on when they've been culled out, and a voice to speak for them when they're too shell-shocked to do anything.'

'So we've formed a local group for everyone affected round here,' Jamie says, 'not only farmers and their families but local businesses, people in tourism, outdoor pursuit centres – there's even a hot air balloon enterprise going bananas because trade's slumped to nothing since the Ministry closed the countryside and those awful televised pictures of pyres deterred visitors.'

'We've been running for a week now,' Fiona says, 'and without something concrete to do, we'd have gone bananas too.'

'But you couldn't get out,' I say, 'so what could you do?'

They tell me they phoned everyone they knew within a thirty mile radius, all the staff at Fiona's school in town, and every one of Jamie's customers and contacts, to ask if they'd like to help.

The ones who joined then phoned their friends. In a week, countless people throughout the county were ready to do what they could – just listen and sympathise on the phone, organise visits to gates with food boxes, track down legal or official information, start fundraising – anything.

Then Jamie persuaded an official at the Holmes' gate to post a bundle of leaflets he'd printed about the group to local farmers and rural businesses, and his phone had started ringing.

'Why didn't you ask me?'

'Saving the best till last,' Fiona says with a smile. 'I knew you'd be a driving force but I didn't want you rushing off on your usual charger.'

Would I do that? The old Julie maybe, but the lump I am now?

'I haven't got a computer so I can't help there,' I say, 'but I'll do anything else, apart from donate hay. I'm running a bit short.' I won't mention the thaives.

‘Our phone hasn’t stopped for a week,’ Fiona goes on, ‘and even the children pick it up now. Ellie’s getting her own scheme going, too, a sort of child line where they talk about anything worrying them.’ She stops. I see her suck her lip. ‘Only yesterday she was talking to someone who’s obviously going through what she has. I heard her say that it wasn’t for ever, even if it felt like it, and the best thing to do was draw lots of pictures or write stories because that helped to stop hurting.’

Little Ellie, counselling children. I gulp at the image. ‘You’ll have done that with Ellie and Dan.’

She nods. ‘They can’t put their horror into words like we can – painting and writing serve the same purpose.’

‘Anything’s better than doing nothing,’ Jamie says after a moment, ‘and I’ve started my own private war and that’s what I need your help in.’

His eyes flash with their old crusading light.

‘It’s giving me great pleasure to bombard the Ministry with protests about delayed disposals, or requests for up-to-date information about the epidemic, or just point out that people are deeply affected seeing their life’s work go up in smoke – I’ve found some sort of pleasure in telling them about the Holmes’ botched cull in lurid detail, and I’ve written reams to the regional manager about what it did to the children. I’m also plaguing the local Trading Standards office with demands for licences to move sheep marooned by movement restrictions. They haven’t enough staff to cope with the demand, but that’s no excuse for letting lambs drown in mud. In normal times, the RSPCA would be down like a ton of bricks on any farmer who let his sheep suffer like that, so why should it be okay now, just because the government didn’t have a contingency plan and local councils haven’t put aside any money for emergency staff? It makes me wild.’

Me too, I think, picturing my thaives up to their knee joints in mud, and me with no licence to move them.

‘You’ve already stood up to Mike’s supervisor,’ Jamie goes on, ‘so how about a bit more official-bashing? I’ve got a list as long as your arm to deal with.’

‘Got it with you?’ I’m spoiling for a fight, and a way of climbing out of the bog of my mind.

He pulls a folded sheaf of pages from his pocket and passes it over. I scan each sheet, horror growing with every mention of isolation, distress, frustration and trauma.

'This is all going on round us? Why don't we hear about it?'

'Can't you guess?'

I can, and in that moment I haul out the old battleaxe, dust her off and recall Phil's words about how he misses me when it comes to awkward clients. Just let me at 'em.

'Starting tomorrow,' Jamie says, interrupting my thoughts, 'I'm also visiting some of the farmers who've lost their animals. I thought they might like a sympathetic ex-townie at their gate as a change from Ministry officials, and maybe by chatting to them I'll find out if they need any practical help. I bet their pride gets in the way of asking directly.'

He notices my eager expression. 'Better not come with me, Julie. Even though I'm only visiting ones who've had at least their preliminary disinfection, it's still a risk. You've got to think of your sheep.'

'But you're a sheep owner too,' I point out, 'and I've been hiding behind my flock for long enough. If we wear a separate set of clothes and thoroughly disinfect ourselves and the car, where's the risk?'

'No, Julie,' he insists. 'I'll put your number on the helpline list but I really want you to take on the Ministry and wake up the media to what's going on.'

I sit up straight and glare at him.

He pulls a face. 'You look just like in the panto last year!'

I make a swipe, and he ducks. 'Don't you see,' he laughs. 'One word from a wicked queen over the phone, and we'll have every official running to do as they're told!'

I have fire in my boots now, almost leaping out of bed to drive up and feed the thaives. Then I tend the sheep and lambs in the front field. There are no more ewes to lamb in the shed and I'm clearing it out for when the thaives are allowed home. Come home they will, and soon, even if it means hours on the phone bullying clerks in the local Trading Standards Office about my licence, and the tens of others desperately needed by farmers on Jamie's list.

The rest of each morning is for Jamie. After I've finished the chores, I give him a quick call for an update, then in a fury of determination I phone officials about issues on his list. They're all out of the office for the day, of course, and though I'm promised a return call, none comes. By Monday, it's hard to hold on to my repertoire of foul language, and though I try to be mindful that it's the office juniors' ears I'm bending, I rush outside after every other call, to vent my frustration on a bit of shed-cleaning or a pile of straw litter. On Monday morning, I phone Trading Standards for what seems the hundredth time. I've just come down from feeding the thaives, and cannot dispel their pathetic condition.

'Not you again,' says a young female.

'Yep, and this time I want action. Whether or not I get a licence today, I'm moving my sheep home tomorrow morning.'

'You can't do that.'

I think for a second. 'Have you got a dog or a cat?'

'What business is that of yours?'

I let my breath out in a steady stream before replying. 'Come on, sunshine, humour me. Let's have a bit of light relief in all this mess. Have you got a pet?'

'Well, yes,' she admits. 'A terrier.'

'And you love it to bits.'

'Of course.'

'I bet you spoil it – ball games and walks, lots of nice nibbles.'

Silence. 'I know where this is going,' she says after a moment. 'You're going to tell me your sheep are pets.'

'Even I'm not stupid enough to try playing ball with hundreds of ewes. No, I'm going to tell you that I used to work for a vet and I've tended dogs that have been neglected, starved, given birth outside in the middle of winter then got mastitis after the puppies died in the wet and cold.'

'Don't,' she says.

'Why? It's the only way I can get through to you. I'm responsible for the health of my sheep and not only are they starving, they're lambing in a field of mud. Some ewes lies down and can't get up again. Lambs are being born into mud and they're dying like flies from hypothermia. Shall I stop now?'

I hear a choking sob as the line goes dead.

Rage shoots through my legs. I try to kick the stuffing out of the old chair by the fire before sinking into it, sobbing for my sheep and a week of discovering how many others are at the mercy of unresponsive people in remote offices.

When the phone rings, I glare at it then remember my number's on the helpline list. Taking a deep breath, I pick it up.

'Mrs Sumner? Alan Smith here, Chief Inspector, Trading Standards. I will not have you terrorising my staff like this.'

I leap up. 'Someone phoned back!'

'I phoned to ask you to stop upsetting my staff.'

'I've spent a week trying to speak to someone higher than a clerk and now I get the boss,' I yell. 'Hang on a tick while I put the flags out.'

'Mrs Sumner, please don't be facetious. We are working our way through a crisis as best we can and it doesn't help to frighten my staff. They're doing their best in difficult times.' His patronising voice turns the flags red.

'And I'm doing my best to save my sheep,' I bellow, 'which is a lot more important than filing paper.'

'If you'll listen a minute…'

'No, you listen to me while I'll repeat what I said to your clerk. If you don't give me a licence to move the sheep by tomorrow, I'll do it without your permission. Then I'll go and help everyone else round here to do the same.'

After slamming down the phone down I charge outside to kick buckets around the yard.

CHAPTER NINE

At dawn next day, I walk up to inspect the thaives in torrential rain. The sheep don't rush towards me expecting food – they can't. Even I find it hard to walk across the field in working boots with a decent tread on them. The sheep have no chance. Sinking in at least six inches, every step is a trial.

I cross to the far side where ewes line the hedge. They aren't eating shoots now.

Every scrap of energy is reserved for staying alive, and the ones who've lambed aren't going anywhere, not even for food, not when their lambs can't wade through the mud after them.

I bend to pick up a lamb, obviously born since my last visit yesterday evening. It hangs over my hand, slimy with mud and lifeless. Its ewe noses about, searching the spot where it had lain. Caked in mud from thrashing in labour, her fleece hangs in stiff rags. She whickers, so I put the lamb down at her feet. Moving along the hedge, I find three more dead lambs and one dead ewe with twin lambs perched on her side, the only dry ground available.

I've been up three or four times each day since they started lambing; in the night too, with a torch. I've helped ewes through labour problems then found their lambs dead in the morning. I've tended the sick animals and watched them rally, only to die next day. I've given them penicillin, injected vitamins and minerals, applied antiseptic sprays to sodden feet and infected umbilical cords, all the time knowing that remedies for drowning in mud don't come in bottles. I can't help these sheep any longer, even if I were to spend every minute of every day here, or administer a whole pharmacy of medicines.

After one last look round the field, I go home to fill the Land Rover with bales of straw, bucket of disinfectant, stack of hurdles, and all the tools I need, then drive back to rescue my sheep.

It's not hard to flout the rules, especially after brick wall treatment from Trading Standards, but I know it would be difficult for the thaives to walk the half mile home down the lane even without the extra weight of their sodden fleeces.

With caked and probably infected hooves, some will find walking on tarmac a problem, others won't leave their lambs. But rescue them I will. No more nonsense.

Overnight, in the icy calm that followed my rage of yesterday, I worked out the best way to move them – directly over the lane and into my wood. There they can take their time. I'll encourage the healthier ones gently down the path through the trees to the field behind the house then return to help the lame ones. I can even take the really sick ones home in the back of the Land Rover, four at a time. It might take me hours, even the rest of the day, but rescue each one of them I will.

Traffic isn't a problem. The lane winds on along the contour line of the hill to a crumbling cottage of Sarah and Jack's, one they've planned to turn into a holiday cottage but can't afford to restore until farm incomes improve. No one will come up while I'm getting the flock across the road, no one will stand on their horn and no one will see me. The last thing I want is interference either from friendly neighbours or law-abiding passers-by. I'll do this alone, and take the consequences alone.

First, I cut and peel back some of the fencing along the top of the wood then use a sickle to clear the path of knots of brambles. Within an hour, I'm down to the gate to my back field. Trudging back up, I spread straw right across the lane and empty a bucket of disinfectant over it for propriety's sake. Hurdles come next, two lines of them straddling the road on each side of the straw mat.

Opening the thaives' gate, I walk slowly round the perimeter of the field pushing the healthier ones into a bunch then on over the road into the wood. It's easier than I thought. Leaving them there to find their own way home, I rig another hurdle across the gap to stop them returning then go back for the rest.

I spend most of the day coaxing the weaker ewes with lambs across the field by walking backwards holding their offspring a foot from their noses. My lower back burns with the strain of bending double but I'm winning, even if the pace is agonizingly slow. Once they're all in the wood, I try to move the sick and the lame across the field with a combination of gentle shoving and lifting. Some collapse with the exertion but I haul them upright each time and urge them on, determined to get them all out even if I have to work into the dark and use the lights of the Land Rover to guide me.

I haven't finished by nightfall. Apart from the casualties of the last two weeks, eight barely-alive ewes still lie under the far hedge and one's started to lamb, pawing the ground and straining, but I haven't the strength to help. For two pins, I'd join them under the hedge, lay my head on a ewe's side and stay here all night.

The sound of a car in the lane has my head snapping round. As it turns the corner, headlights blaze across the field and freeze me like a rabbit in the glare. The vehicle stops with its lights still on me, and I hear voices.

Two dark shapes run to climb over the hurdles and as I watch them struggle through the mud, all I can do is wonder who reported me to the animal police.

'What the bloody hell d'you think you're doing,' Jamie yells, 'and why didn't you ask us for help?' He's flaming anger when he reaches me. 'You're the most stubborn, pig-headed, awkward bugger I've ever met. Why won't you learn that we'd do anything for you, even break the law? All you have to do is ask and we'd be there, but no, you're a proud independent sod who'd rather…'

The other one interrupts. 'What's left to do?' It's Mike. I could hug them both.

They move quickly, once I've explained.

Together they lift all the live ewes across the field and load them into Jamie's pick-up and the back of the Land Rover.

Armed with torches they've brought we scour the hedgerows for strays. They carry the dead ewes and lambs over to a spot near the gate, for Jamie to pick up later, then he sets about clearing the straw off the road while Mike and I walk down through the trees after the rest of the flock. They've all found their way through and most are devouring the clean grass.

'Leave them here tonight, Julie,' Mike says, sweeping his powerful torch beam back and forth over the field. 'They'll all be on their feet tomorrow, just you see. We'll fix the fence at the top, then take those sick ones home.'

Zombie-like, I follow him back up the wood.

Jamie has dismantled the hurdles, and is turning his pick-up ready to go down to my yard.

Within half an hour, we have the sick ewes in the shed and I've been ordered indoors to change into dry clothes while they go back for the hurdles and my dead stock.

Dry again, and fairly clean, I light a raging fire, boil a kettle and curl up in my chair to wait for my rescuers.

Jamie has quit shouting. We all sit gazing into the flames, sipping tea and saying little.

Mike speaks first. 'You're a brave lady.'

I look round. 'Daft, more like. I thought I could manage myself, and it's not right to ask people to break the law.' I try a grin. 'Criminals are independent sods.'

Jamie snorts.

'What's criminal is letting sheep suffer like that. I've seen too many farmers who aren't allowed to get their flocks back home from rented land. I'd have helped, if only you'd asked.'

'Me too,' Mike says, 'and I'll be along tomorrow first thing to give you a hand. We'll get the ewes still in lamb off the field and into the shed.' He frowns. 'That's if you don't mind. Don't want to barge in where…'

'I'll be waiting, Mike, and thanks for everything.'

'No problem.' He finishes his tea and stands up. 'I'd best be off home now.'

'You can't go yet I haven't found out how on earth you knew what I was doing.'

He smiles. 'Think I wouldn't notice filthy sheep coming down out of your wood, and do you think there's anyone in this whole valley who didn't see? Wish I'd seen them sooner, but I was out breaking rules myself most of the day – I went over to see Davy. I know we've been told not to mix with other farmers but I haven't seen him for weeks. I only meant to stay an hour but they wouldn't let me come home till after the kids got back from school.' His smile widens into a grin. 'We had a grand time.'

Jamie laughs. 'Another lawbreaker? I'm beginning to feel left out.' Then he explains that he rang me every hour after he got back from his morning's visit. Worrying about where I'd been all day, he waited for Fiona to come home from school to look after the children, then drove over to find Mike in the lane staring at the mud-coloured ewes and lambs trickling out of the wood. 'I think I need a few lessons in spotting what my neighbours are up to,' he finishes.

'Just open your eyes,' Mike says.

At first light the next morning, Mike comes round as promised and we work together for two hours, mostly in silence, getting the pregnant thaives in the shed. As soon as he's gone, I hitch up the trailer to the quad bike and start ferrying fallen timber down from the wood to a patch of dead ground behind my buildings.

Ben always burned his casualties.

In normal times, most farmers send them off in the back of a knacker's lorry, or hire diggers to bury them on the farm but Ben liked the ceremony of a fire. I used to tease him about his sentimentality but he always asserted that the passing of his old ewes deserved recognition, and anyway, his father and grandfather had done it before him so who was he to change the old ways?

I carried on the tradition. The mother of Ellie's lambs went up in smoke, so did the lambs that didn't survive Phil's caesarean, and several others. Lambing means casualties – I'd soon learned that.

But I've ten dead thaives and fourteen lambs to burn and I want it done before the law descends in force, as I know it will, so I start building the fire as Ben taught me, hoping the smoke doesn't remind everyone in the valley of the pyres they've had to witness.

At midday, I return to the yard to see a car at my gate that screams officialdom. I march down to take whatever's due squarely on the chin, feeling strong, fortified by the sight of my thaives grazing contentedly on the back field and their lambs beginning to leap in play. Most of the ones in the shed are recovering too, and the ewe that started to lamb in the mud yesterday produced twins soon after Jamie and Mike left last night. Though weak, she was up and tending them within an hour, and I went to bed knowing that every back-breaking minute had been worth it.

One of the men at the gate says he's from Trading Standards and hands over his identity card.

'I have reason to believe you have flouted the current animal movement restrictions.'

'Yes.'

He stares; a small tidy man in a white paper boiler suit standing to attention as though practising for the parade ground.

'You don't deny it?'

'I have no regard for regulations that make animals suffer.'

'Then I must...'

'I'd like to say something first.'

'In your defence?'

'In criticism of your department.'

He shakes his head.

'If you want to make a formal complaint there are proper procedures, and appropriate channels to follow.'

I thought I was under control, but his officious manner stirs rage in me, a different sort, one with icicles hanging off it.

'And how long would that take?'

'I don't know – we're under pressure a bit at the moment.'

'I feel for you, I really do,' I say. 'Too many demands and not enough staff or resources to deal with an epidemic that's out of control.'

He stiffens. 'I wouldn't say that. We're coping as best we...'

That does it. I change feigned sympathy to sarcasm and let rip. 'Don't give me that old excuse – I'm tired of excuses, especially the one about time. You haven't had time to issue licences to farmers desperate to save their stock from diabolical welfare conditions, yet you've got time to come all the way from town to charge me with breaking a law that was killing my sheep! Where's the sense in that?'

He studies his feet for a moment then looks up.

'Rules are there for a reason...'

'Well this one doesn't apply to me – my sheep had no more than three yards of road to cross, a road that no one uses except me and my neighbour. It doesn't go anywhere, it isn't a rat run, it serves no function other than to sit along the hillside and soak up the sun or the rain. I ask you again, where's the sense in stopping my animals crossing it?'

He responds in exactly the way I expect, with a summons.

I've just been fined two thousand pounds by a magistrate who seemed fairly sympathetic at first, until I defied my solicitor's warning and coldly told the bench just what I thought of inflexible rulings that make no sense on the ground. I leave court with the distinct impression that I've been made an example of, a warning to other farmers who may be tempted to move their sheep without permission.

A reporter lurks outside.

'Anything to say, Mrs Sumner?''

'Only that my sheep will live because of what I did.'

'But you were risking spreading foot and mouth further.'

'In my case, there was no risk at all. I took every biosecurity precaution and acted purely for humanitarian reasons, and hundreds if not thousands of sheep will suffer and die if others don't do the same.'

'You mean every farmer should disregard the law?'

I know what he's on about, and that he'll probably distort the facts, but I don't care.

'Farmers know what's best for their own stock,' I say evenly. 'They're the ones looking after them, not some bureaucrat in London, so why shouldn't they be allowed to make sensible decisions about them?'

He thrusts his micro-recorder closer. 'Sounds like anarchy.'

I move closer, too. 'If democracy means senseless decisions from government, I'm for anarchy. Why aren't you reporting on the trauma farmers are going through instead of hanging round here like a vulture?'

'Not my job.'

'Well, it's time you made it your bloody job.'

Jamie grabs my arm and pulls me away to the car.

'You're exhausted,' he explains when he gets me inside.

'Don't mother me! It's quite enough to be slapped about by the State.'

'But why waste your icy words on reporters? Much better to save them for the pillocks at our gates.' He glances across at me.

'You've changed, or I'm seeing a part of you I haven't seen before? This cold iciness is much more scary than the old bossy tiger bit.'

'Good.'

We drive out of town in silence and I mull over what he said. I have changed.

Gone are the wild fluctuations of mood from desolation to rage, and the turmoil of fear and horror of the last two months, even my wild grief.

But Ben's gone, too.

He's not even pretending to be a line of pillows. All he's left me is his strength, and I'll use it.

CHAPTER TEN

My phone won't stop ringing. Most people in the valley and many beyond have read that reporter's piece in the local paper. They congratulate me, say they admire my courage then comment that they wouldn't dare do the same. I wonder why. Inflexible rules serve only to expose the inanity of the people who enforce them.

Between the lines of their admiration, I hear my neighbours' unasked questions of how I'm going to pay the fine. Two thousand pounds is a fortune to a small farmer, especially in these days of overdrafts. Nor is there the slightest chance of earning any money with the restriction on selling stock.

But I can use that fat cheque from the insurance company for my fine instead of a replacement tractor. I don't want another tractor. I can hardly bear to see tractors working on the inclines of my neighbours' fields. After the buckled tangle that became Ben's shroud, the sketchy plans I've dared to make for the future of the farm include the use of contractors for muck-spreading and harvesting hay, so I'll use some of the insurance money to pay the fine for saving my thaives and I hope it chokes the recipient. The rest of the cheque will help with my phone bills. After two weeks of hanging on the end of a phone waiting for distant officials who're never in their offices, my bill will be up a hundredfold.

Between calls from neighbours, I phone the local paper and ask the deputy editor if he'll forward a letter to one of his regular columnists, Dave Stringer, a Midlands farmer who has championed his industry for years, and uses his barbed wit to damn its critics. His words are a delight and a comfort, and these days they show me that Fiona, Jamie and I have at least one ally in our mission to defend the undefended.

I can almost hear the editor lick his pencil when I tell him who I am. My notoriety has spread. This could be useful.

Then I write to Dave Stringer and outline my cause, asking him to support it. I also ask him to tell his contacts in the media to stop reporting this god-awful epidemic as though it was neatly under control, and stop blaming farmers for spreading foot and mouth and costing the taxpayer millions with the compensation they receive. It's time, I write, to kick the media up off the floor where they've been licking the government's boots for too long.

Jamie rings when my pen and I have reached white heat.

'How's our criminal today?' There's laughter in his voice.

'My thaives are thriving.' I stab the table with my pen.

He pauses, as if aware of my mood. 'You're a lesson to us all.'

'Oh? Then why won't anyone learn? Why won't people who ring to congratulate me save their own animals? Why won't farmers defy cruel and senseless rules, instead of accepting them like a spell of rotten weather?'

Silence.

'Julie – are you okay?'

'No, I'm bloody not.' Flinging the pen away, I get up from the table and look out of the window to see Mike's clean-up team leaning against my gate, chatting and laughing as casually as if they're swapping tasteless jokes in a pub. As I'm sick of their stage whispers every time I pass Mike's gate, the innuendos about the dragon who lives across the lane, I want to go down and breathe fire in their ears.

'I need to see some protest,' I tell Jamie, 'some *useful* protest, and not just from the likes of you and me. I can't understand why no one has the guts either to report this mess truthfully or expose the Ministry for what it's doing to *people,* never mind animals. You've told me enough about the questionable biosecurity from Ministry officials and their total lack of response to farmers' despair, and I've read enough in the papers to know the media is either bound hand and foot or it's too idle to get out there and see for itself. What I want is an uprising, a bald refusal to comply with ridiculous policy.'

I pause to see the clean-up men now perched on my gate like a row of squawking gulls. 'Hang on a minute, Jamie.' Flinging the phone down, I wrench open the door and march down the drive only to see them fly away before I get there. Then I see that someone, probably one of them, has reversed into the gate at some time and broken one of the rails. Why didn't I notice before? I should have known – they're always using my entrance to turn.

Resolving to wind barbed wire over my gate as well as round their necks, I stomp back to the phone.

'And what's more,' I tell him, 'I'm sick of being cooped up with nothing to do but plague officials who neither come to the phone nor ring back. I'm coming with you on your next trip out.'

'But – '

I interrupt.

'Unlike the Ministry, I practise good biosecurity. Don't argue with me, Jamie. I need action, and I'm coming with you.'

Before I get in his car at the crossroads next morning, I've dug out Ben's overalls and his wellies for my visiting gear. They'll go through a bucket of disinfectant whenever I've been out, and I'll keep them securely bagged between visits.

We set off for a contiguous-cull farm ten miles west, and Jamie explains that though it's been through its preliminary disinfection, we'll go no further than the gate.

I stare through the windscreen, knowing from my mood that if any officials are around, they'd better watch their manner.

'Why this farmer?' I ask.

'I want to pat him on the back a bit. He tried to resist the cull because he knew his sheep were healthy – farmers are the first to know if any of their animals are sick because they see them every day, and he'd even kept empty fields between his stock and his neighbour's land.'

'And?'

'And he barricaded his gate and refused entry to the vet and his team.'

'At last, someone who's said no. I'll shake that man's hand, virus or not. So what happened?'

'The vet threatened him with the police,' Jamie snorts, 'then told him he'd have to pay for any court case, and his flock would still be culled. He also said that troublemakers don't get any compensation, so they won't be able to restock. What else could he do but sign the consent forms?'

'I'd *kill* the bastards.'

'No, Julie, you wouldn't.'

Wouldn't I?

I don't want to say any more, so look out instead at the empty countryside we're passing through. All I see is mile upon mile of empty fields, knots of vehicles in farm gateways, glimpses of red and yellow diggers in yards and a multitude of men in white boiler suits and white vans. Virtually every holding has been wiped out and I wonder how the farmers and their families are faring marooned behind their house walls. Do they still get up every morning before dawn and are the women still loading tables with food for their men? I doubt it. I see people without work, without a living, staring at each other in silence, their hearts and their kitchens as cold as Mike's after his cull.

Jamie parks a fair distance from the farm, and we walk up to the gate.

'You can't come in,' a man says.

I peer down at him and wonder why all these gate guardians are short in stature.

Jamie hangs on to his cool and says he has an important message for the owners and could they please come to the gate?

I recognise the look in the farmer's eyes and the greyness of his skin as he plods towards us, his wife at his side.

'So how's it going?' Jamie is saying.

'Not so bad,' the farmer says, standing back from the gate.

Not so bad. I shake my head, then try to smile as I feel the woman's gaze. 'Nice to see a cheery grin,' she says. Her forehead creases. 'Sure I've seen you before – I know, at the vet's. You used to work there, didn't you?'

I don't remember her, but smile. 'Yes, I left a year or so ago.'

'You got married, I recall now.' She's talking as though we've met in town on market day to chat about neighbourly things. Behind her, her life has been stamped out and yet she's interested in me, not her own problems. Maybe she's doing it to feel normal.

'Yes,' I say, 'I married a farmer.'

She laughs, takes a step forward to lean on the gate, and lowers her voice to a whisper.

'You've got your work cut out then, haven't you? They're not the easiest of men.'

I don't feel any pain, more a flash of pleasure, comfort even in the easy camaraderie and female conspiracy.

Jamie's leaning on the gate now too, telling the farmer about how many people and services are ready to help.

'Stan's not been too good,' she says to me. 'He can't bear to go in the sheds and fields any more. But we'll mend. Got to get up and get on with it otherwise they've won, haven't they? We'll fill the fields again, just you see.'

We leave them half an hour later and drive home in silence, me in awe of the woman's resilience and Jamie gripping the wheel as though his life depended on it.

'Bastards,' he mutters from time to time.

He drops me off at the bottom of my lane and watches as I tuck overall and wellies into an empty feed sack and tie its end securely with a length of baling twine.

'I'm glad you came, Julie.'

'The company's done me good,' I say, knowing it to be true. My mood of the last two days has lost its jagged edge.

'And your company's done those farmers good,' he says. 'Often it's all they need – a bit of human contact.'

Don't I bloody know it. What would I have done without contact from my friends and neighbours this last two months, and I haven't had the isolating process of the disease or the Ministry cutting a swathe of devastation through my yard.

I lean through the passenger window. 'Sorry for my temper, Jamie, and for swiping at our neighbours for not standing up for their stock. This morning's shown me their resilience.' I try a grin. 'You're a good mate, and what you're doing for people is...'

Something white is approaching from the village. I look down the road to see a convoy of three white vans speeding towards us. They slow then turn left up the lane towards Holly Farm.

Jamie's shouting. 'Please God, *no!*'

The vans pass Carol and Jim's gate and wind up the incline to the farm nestling in a hollow beneath the summit of the hill.

Even at this distance, I see the team of white-suited men move from the vans towards the buildings.

Jamie's out of the car, scanning the hillside.

When he turns to me, his face is white as a paper suit.

'It's the Bennett's. Their land touches my wood. We're contiguous.'

The fear in his voice freezes my soul. I shoot round to his side but can't find a word of encouragement or comfort. Nothing.

'No more,' he whispers. 'Not again.'

We watch in stunned silence, see the men emerge from the buildings and start rounding up sheep before Jamie snaps out of his trance and flings himself back in the car. 'Got to go – Ellie's lambs…' He starts the engine, his eyes wild.

'That website's full of terrible accounts of contiguous culling. They'll stop at nothing to track down every single animal on neighbouring land, even the ones that haven't set foot outside all year – even pets.' He grabs the door handle. 'Let me go, Julie. I've got to hide the lambs.'

'Shall I come with you?'

He yanks the door shut and hurls the car towards the village, and I hear the screech of tyres as he turns up his lane. All I can do is go home.

Mike's at his gate as I stumble past.

'You've seen?' He speaks in a monotone, not taking his eyes off the hill opposite. 'I've been watching – can't stop. Cars came first, then the army, now vans. The Bennett's place is rattling with men.' He turns to me and I see the pain of his own experience in his eyes, and intense sympathy for his neighbours. 'They'll be taking everyone out on that side of the road.' His voice fades almost to nothing. 'But then you'll know that.'

I do know. After a false start, the Ministry's now in much better gear. The army's in on the logistics side, and fleets of lorries are on standby to take thousands of contiguous carcases to rendering plants or vast burial sites. Mobile slaughter and disposal teams now move fast between outbreaks and the number of vets available nationwide has been swelled by hundreds of recruits from all over the world.

But farmers are in better gear, too. In the last two weeks, Jamie's kept me informed of all the news on the website, and we've even discussed rallying supporters to the gates of farmers who're trying to resist the culls when common sense coupled with generations of experience tell them their stock is healthy.

Jamie's given a name to the stringent contiguous culling – carnage by computer. He told me that the map reference of an infected farm is fed into the Ministry computer which then details all the neighbouring farms whose land touches. Within forty-eight hours, a vet, a valuer and a slaughter team arrive on these farms, the only warning being a phone call the previous night, sometimes early on the day. Animals are being slaughtered by the thousand, and most farmers end up signing the cull papers, despite their initial protests that their animals are not and could not be infected.

Conversation's difficult, even with Mike, so I stumble home to rally the troop of one. With Jamie holed up again, anything needing doing for my friends and neighbours is up to me. I won't drag anyone else in, not even Mike. He's done enough over the illegal movement of my thaives so I'll do it alone, and this time I won't stare in helpless fear like I did in the nine days Mike's stock were on death row, nor when the killing machine starts up again. I might not be able to save the animals but I'll do my utmost to help their keepers.

I phone Carol.

'I think we'll be all right.' Her voice is high with fear. 'The cattle haven't set foot outside this year yet and there's our wood between our sheep and the Bennett's, fifteen acres of it. There hasn't been an animal in there for years – it's far too overgrown.'

I look through the window at the broad strip of oaks and ash above Holly Farm, and wish I shared her confidence. The computer in charge of destroying the nation's flocks and herds doesn't have a clue about natural barriers, nor does it seem to listen to scientific opinion that the virus is spread mainly by nose to nose animal contact, and by people and vehicles. This bug doesn't rampage through ungrazed woodland or leap rivers, nor does it hitch a ride on a passing cloud to get to its next victim. I know – Jamie has briefed me well.

'Let me know what you need. I'm only two minutes away.'

'The children...' she begins.

A glance at the clock tells me it's an hour to the school bus.

'Shall bring them here?'

I hear Carol's breath funnelling out of her mouth. 'No,' she says firmly, 'not today. I want us all to be together until we know, but... if... oh, Julie, if they take us out, will you have the children? I can't have them see it.'

'Carol, listen to me – they can't take you out against your wishes. You can demand to be put on a 48-hour monitoring programme then get your own vet to do a blood test to prove your sheep are okay.'

'Can I?'

'It's your right,' I insist. 'James Casey and I have been doing tons of research and there are all sorts of things you can do if you're convinced your stock's healthy. I'll write them down and get them to you.'

I hear her sigh and know I'm blinding her with science. Shut up, Julie, and don't barge. Take this one step at a time.

'Don't worry, Carol,' I say as gently as I can. 'Go and find Jim now – be together. I'll ring again soon but don't forget that if you need an ally or an extra voice, I'll be there before you can blink.'

'You mustn't, Julie.' She sounds near tears. 'You've got to think of your sheep.'

'I *do* think of my sheep, Carol, but friends come first – don't ever forget that. Now, go and find Jim.'

Jamie phones. 'I panicked,' he says, his voice strange.

'Not surprised. Are the lambs in?'

'Yes.' He pauses. 'Listen – I'm going to deny I have any sheep when officials appear at my gate, as I know they will. I'm a woodsman with a few hens and geese. The Ministry can't force an entry to search my land so I'm going to padlock the gate and lie through my teeth.'

'And down to your boots, I hope,' I say, trying for banter.

Another pause. 'Got to go – the children will be home soon. What the hell will I tell them?'

'Tell them you're isolating the lambs, protecting them from the virus at the Bennett's.'

He doesn't say more. I offer my help, but he's not listening. When he says goodbye, I know he'll soon have his family home with him.

I feel totally useless, and alone.

Someone bangs on the kitchen door and I find a grey-faced Mike on the doorstep. He steps inside.

'D'you realise this is the first time I've defied that clean-up supervisor in broad daylight? He watched me come over.'

'Good – it'll give him something better to think about than stupid spring-cleaning of your buildings. Now, tea, coffee, or something stronger?' I know my tone is forced but I don't know what else to say. I know why he's here. 'I'm glad you came, Mike. I don't want to be alone.'

He settles into one of my tattered fireside chairs. 'Nor me.'

Quickly I make tea, take it over, and slump down opposite.

It's useless. We can't sit still. Though I resolve for Mike's sake not to be drawn to the window, he gets up first to open the door and step outside. We end up leaning on the yard wall staring across the valley, leaving our tea to go cold in the house.

I try a diversion. 'Want to see my thaives?'

Mike nods. We prise ourselves from the wall and go into the shed where I've got twenty or so left to lamb. They bleat their usual welcome, then shy away at the sight of a stranger. Mike goes over to a pen.

The first-time mother is nervous. She takes a step between Mike and her two-day old lamb. It's gawky, ears drooping, but it tries a small skip. I hear the wonderful sound of Mike's chuckle.

He turns and grins. 'Just what I needed,' he says, 'a bit of new life. You've done well, Julie, they all look grand – a bit different to when I last saw them covered in mud.' Taking a long look round the shed, he comes back to my side. 'After what you've learned, I'll be coming to you for advice when I restock!'

'Rubbish, Mike, you know everything about sheep.'

'Except how to keep them alive.'

Just for a moment, in the easy company of a neighbour, I forgot what's going on across the valley. Mike hasn't.

The spell broken, we return to the yard in silence.

Next morning, I see the mountain of dead sheep outside the Bennett's shed, a beached whale of a mound covered in black plastic. Then the diggers and loaders come, struggling up the lane to slash a long brown wound in the ripe green pasture of the Bennett's flattest field. The clank of the digger arms thuds through my frame and squeezes my heart and when I hear the grind of loaders ferrying sleepers and coal to the pyre site, I run for the lambing shed, hoping my ewes' bleats will blot out the din.

I thought I'd cope this time.

After Mike's cull, I assumed I'd have a bit more resistance to the mechanics of killing, but I don't. All I feel is useless.

'Ben! Where the bloody hell are you when I need you?'

The ewes flinch at my shout, so I clump out into the yard and hear the phone ringing.

It's Sarah, to tell me the Bennetts first found foot and mouth in some sheep still on a winter let on the other side of the far hill. The field touches three more farms on that side.

'So they're contiguous, as well as the five in this valley,' she whispers.

My mind spins into gear.

'But Sarah – the forestry land stretches right along the summit and it isn't used by stock. It means the farms on this side haven't had any contact.'

She sighs. 'Rob Bennett thinks he brought the disease in to his home farm. He had to visit his animals on remote fields – couldn't let them starve just because he couldn't bring them home.'

After that, waiting for the whole bloody business to start again, I go back to prowling, sapped of energy, mind a labyrinth.

I feel guilty that I live this side of the road.

Why should I escape because of a few yards of tarmac?

Why is the road a barrier, when it's had tyres of farm vehicles, vets' cars, disposal and clean-up teams all over it, day in day out, since the beginning of the epidemic? It's impregnated with mud and muck from farmsteads, and yet ungrazed woodland is deemed more of a risk.

The only thing to appease my guilt is the knowledge that the road means Sarah and Jack will escape the cull, too.

They finish the Bennett's pyre base at dusk, then the loaders start their grim task.

On and on they work, the vehicles' powerful lights flashing like looms from a bevy of drunken lighthouses.

I must turn away, I must not see the torching and generations of breeding and husbandry head for the skies in a wall of flame and boiling smoke. I will not look – Mike's pyre was more than enough for a lifetime.

But the wind's from the south carrying the eternal drone through my door. It's even louder when I ring Fiona and Jamie, coming down the phone as low-pitched background interference.

'Okay?'

'We can't see what's going on because of our wood,' Fiona says, 'but the noise is there all the time.'

I don't know what to say next.

'Don't worry, Julie, we're fine, and at least we can still go out this time. We need ordinary things – work to stop us thinking too much, friends and colleagues to chat to.'

She stops for a moment and I hear Jamie's voice in the background. 'Jamie says hello, and don't worry, but will the lambs suffer from being shut up?'

'Not a bit,' I mutter, wanting to drive over there, whirl little Dan round my head, park my feet on the Rayburn, let them pour beer down me, listen to precocious Ellie, rake up another tale for her from veterinary nursing days about a courageous dog or accident-prone cat on its tenth life.

I want friends and colleagues. I want laughter, teasing and joking…and Ben.

When I ring off, I straighten my back, go to check the ewes without a glance across the valley, then take to my bed though its too early to sleep.

After ramming cotton wool tufts in my ears, I find a book and try to read until I discover it's upside down.

Then I'm up, pacing, prowling, crying.

'Where are you, Ben? I need you, now. How could you leave – don't you care about me or your farm any more?'

Prowl, pace, prowl, pace, and I'm ransacking my innermost depths for something he left me, something to hold, even the grief, the haunting, bruising grinding of my insides I've had until recently. I'd sell my soul at this moment for the company of the numbed blankness the week after he died, when neighbours called by and stood in the shadows round the room, when Fiona rushed in to hold me in her arms and cry, when the undertaker's morbid expression made me want to punch him, and when Phil lurched in to stare at me, mouth open, eyes brimming before he buckled and sobbed as though he'd also lost the one he loved.

I watched them as though from a distance, saw them make gallon after gallon of tea and coffee, bring cakes for the funeral, serve dainty sandwiches that Ben would have laughed at before grabbing a fistful to fill his mouth.

But none of them are here now, they can't be.

They're all out there saving their own lives, or slumped together in cold kitchens scared at the fear in each other's faces.

I want you here, Ben. I need your eyes to watch over me, your arms to keep the world out, your voice.

CHAPTER ELEVEN

I must have slept, but it wasn't for long enough. Something's wrong, different. Flinging aside the curtains, I see the horrible majesty of the Bennett's pyre. This time Fiona won't ring because the orange light bouncing off the sky, filling the fields and searching the woods will have her cowering in Jamie's arms. Maybe they'll have the children, too, all huddled up together, and she'll be singing quiet songs to stop them being too afraid.

But I'm alone.

Self pity doesn't help so I go down to spend the rest of the night with the thaives in the lambing shed. With mindless music playing on the radio in there, I fluff out new straw in an empty pen and curl up under my jacket to listen to the ewes' murmuring bleats and the lambs' responses. Having all the lights on stops the orange glow from across the valley invading my bed, and I sleep until dawn and get up with the sheep.

But when I leave the shed, all hell is breaking loose.

White vans and army Land Rovers are everywhere, zipping along the road from the village and whining up the hill opposite.

Squinting along the hillside, I see clusters of white vans, sheep being rounded up in tens of fields, hordes of men, some on quad bikes, others running.

Shouts and engine noise bombard the still air. Mass killing has begun on all the farms adjoining the Bennett's land.

Now there are trucks, fleets of them, lining the main road from the village to well past my crossroads in a nose-to-bumper crocodile.

They're waiting for the signal to move onto farms to pick up their cargoes of carcases to be taken away to a vast and anonymous tip in someone else's countryside. They are not blood-tested – so how does the Ministry know if foot and mouth was incubating on any particular farm? Don't they want to know for the future, to help plot the spread of the disease, to help draw up a plan to cope with the next epidemic? Maybe they don't care.

Maybe they're so engrossed with slash and burn they can't see further than the end of their gun barrels.

The truck drivers are standing in a group near the crossroads and sometimes their laughter drifts up to me. I wonder how they can drive away a load of dead and probably disease-free animals without wanting to weep. Do their children ask what they hauled at work today, and what do they tell them?

I go in to grab the phone and dial Jamie's number. 'Talk to me,' I demand, then let all my frustration and loneliness splurge out. 'Sorry, Jamie,' I finish, 'but I'm rattling around doing nothing over here – how are you all?'

'Fine – we're okay.'

He sounds too cheerful, even though his emotional wires must be twanging, but he still hasn't had a visit from the Ministry.

'I keep telling you, Julie, we're going to miss all this. We're not a registered holding so we're not on the Ministry computer – don't know why I didn't realise, before I panicked the other day.'

'There's a convoy of trucks lining the road,' I say, unable to change the sole topic of conversation.

'I've seen them. Let's hope they're cleaner than the ones I've read about on that website – leaking old crates dripping blood and gunge all the way to the burial pit.'

Jamie doesn't sound angry any more and I feel as though I've lost an ally, but I suppose protecting his family and Ellie's lambs is taking all his attention and energy – when it comes to self-preservation, the rest of the world can go hang. I know that from bitter experience.

'By the way,' he says, 'we met Carol at our boundary. She and Jim are going to resist the cull – they know their stock's healthy.' His tone is conversational, as though he's telling me he's been out to buy new socks.

'But Jamie, that's brilliant!'

'Something you said, apparently, about her right to demand monitoring. I've printed tons of stuff for her about action she can take, the legal side too, and she's persuaded Jim. Can't quite see from here but there'll be things going on at their gate soon. I daren't leave this place unguarded but you could keep an eye – even telepathic support across the valley is better than none.'

When he's gone, I look through the window to see something large blocking Carol's gateway. It looks very much like their tractor and muck spreader. There's also a line of cars and white vans in the lane. Why didn't I notice before, why didn't Carol phone, and why have I let my own gloom obliterate my neighbours' needs?

When I dial Carol's number, I get her mother.

'Hello?' She's fearful.

'It's okay, Mrs Grundy, it's only me – Julie.'

'They've just arrived,' she breathes. 'We got the call about six this morning – just getting light, it was.'

'Can I speak to Carol?'

'No – she and Jim have gone to meet them. She shouldn't be troubling herself – it's not good for the baby.' She turns away to say something and I hear the children's voices. 'Carol tried to phone you early this morning,' she says when she comes back, 'but you must have been out with your sheep.'

No, I was rolling in the hay with self-pity for a bedfellow. God, Julie, you're pathetic.

'Carol told me to stay inside with the children,' she's saying. 'They haven't gone to school, of course.'

'I'm coming over this minute, Mrs Grundy. I'll be at the gate with them, and stay all day if necessary.'

'Oh, Julie, that's good – they need someone with them, someone like you who won't stand any nonsense. I'll breathe easier now...but what about your place? Can you leave it?'

'Of course – I'll ask Mike Corley to keep an eye on the lambing shed if I'm not back in a couple of hours.'

'Poor Mr Corley – he's already been through all this and...so did I, back in the sixties. It's too...' She's wandering now, desperately in need of someone to talk to but I must go. Deciding to get Mike to phone her, I say goodbye as kindly as I can, then I'm diving for the door and running for my bag of visiting gear.

In too-big overalls and wellies, I charge down the lane to Mike's, cross his yard, batter on the door.

No answer, no time to wait, so I belt for the crossroads.

The truckers stop talking and watch my progress.

'Shouldn't go there, love,' one says, 'No place for a woman.'

'Don't you *love* me,' I shoot back, ducking between two of their towering forty-tonners before they can patronise me again.

Carol's gate is barely two hundred yards up the narrow lane where the traffic's aiming for M25 density. Cars and vans whizz past me but an army Land Rover slows enough to let me direct a scowl straight between the driver's eyes. Passing a chipped yellow loader and parked vans full of men, I race up the last few yards and slither to a halt on the mat of disinfected straw to face three white-suited men and an army sergeant. On the other side of the gate is Jim's barricade, his tractor and muck spreader leaning oddly with some of the tyres flat. Carol and Jim are standing by it, dwarfed by their machines, and my heart goes out to them when I see their grey faces and clouds of fear in their eyes.

'Julie,' Carol says. Her hands rest on her belly as though protecting the baby. 'Thank God you've come.' She grabs Jim's arm and looks up into his face but he's doing his best to stare out the officials.

One of the men peers up. 'Who are you?'

'A neighbour. Who are you?'

He ignores me and turns to speak in his colleague's ear.

'I asked who you were.'

'What business is that of yours? Mr and Mrs White are friends, I'm here to support them, and I insist on your names.'

'Don't you know this is an infected area?'

'I'll start first. My name is Julie Sumner, and I farm on the other side of the road. Now, will you please have the courtesy to introduce yourself and your colleagues.'

He stares beyond me, no doubt looking for my farm, but I've had enough. 'You're the Ministry vet, aren't you? Why is it so hard to tell me that?' I turn to one of the other men who's holding a clipboard. 'And you must be the valuer. Local auctioneers?'

He's nervous, but nods.

'So you've probably sold some of Mr White's animals at market. And mine. How does it feel – betraying your clients?'

He looks anywhere but at me.

'Now look,' the vet says, 'this is no business of yours…'

'I don't think there's anything to stop me standing at my neighbour's gate, unless Parliament passed a law last night.'

He sighs and nods to the sergeant, who braces his shoulders and takes two marching steps towards me. I have to stifle a laugh because he looks like one of little Dan's toy Action Men.

'Look, Ma'am,' he says, chin down and chest out, 'this is serious business and you're in the way. Please go home.'

I ignore him and walk over to the gate to be nearer Carol. She looks ready to weep. 'Don't worry,' I whisper, 'you've got this far – just keep strong. I'll be quiet now, unless you need me to speak.'

'Mr White,' the vet says to Jim, 'I told you on the phone that it is vital your stock is culled today. Now please let us enter.'

Jim shakes his head. 'Nothing wrong with my animals.'

The vet's mouth tightens and he points up the hill towards the Bennetts. 'Your land lies adjacent to infected premises, therefore your animals have been exposed to infection.'

'No, they haven't. My cattle are still housed, and fifteen acres of ungrazed woodland are between my sheep and Bennett's land.'

The vet glances up to the sky, and the others shift their feet.

'Mr White, I must be allowed in.'

Jim shakes his head, his eyes still fixed ahead. 'You do not have my permission,' he states in a monotone.

'I don't need your permission.'

'My stock's not been exposed to foot and mouth.'

The vet looks at his watch. More sighs. 'I have the authority to enter your land to inspect them and I insist on doing so.'

Jim's wavering, I can see that. Don't, Jim, I try to signal with my eyes, don't give an inch – they'll take it, and everything else.

When Carol grabs my arm through the gate and holds tightly, I say to the vet, 'What exactly does your inspection mean?'

He ignores me and persists with Jim. 'Mr White, please open the gate and let me in otherwise I may have to employ the police to help me enforce my powers of entry.'

'Go ahead.'

The vet runs his hands through his hair, then speaks in a softer tone. 'Look, Mr White, you may be an excellent farmer but you don't have expert scientific knowledge.'

Jim lifts his chin. 'I know when any of my animals are ill, or even off colour. Mine are healthy – all of them.'

'This is hard to spot, especially in sheep. Think how you'd feel if they came down with the virus tomorrow, or the day after.'

'They won't. There's been no contact with Bennett stock.'

'So you watch every animal, all the time?'

Jim shakes his head. 'Don't be stupid, I've got a hundred and fifty cattle and three times that many sheep.'

'So how do you know one hasn't been tripping through your wood to the Bennett's land?'

'Because my fencing's good.'

'Ah, but lambs have a remarkable talent for squeezing under the tightest fence.'

Jim's head plummets, and I step in, interfering old bugger that I am. 'I asked you a question. What does your inspection entail?'

Authority is back in his voice in a flash. 'This is nothing to do with you, Mrs…so please stop interfering.'

'Mr White is entitled to more information than you've given. Tell him what your inspection means. Does it include blood tests? Do you check every animal? Are you prepared to put this farm on a 48 hour monitoring programme so that a proper scientific decision can be made about whether his stock is incubating foot and mouth, and not just because some remote computer says so?'

He turns to the sergeant who's examining his boots. The valuer has sloped off to talk to the men in one of the vans.

'Look,' I say coldly, 'Mr and Mrs White's living is on the line here. They have the right to demand veterinary monitoring for 48 hours.' Turning to Carol and Jim, I ask if that's what they want.

'Yes,' they say in unison.

'There. I don't think their wishes could be any clearer.'

The veins in his neck twitch and his eyes cloud with anger. I half expect him to hit me, and wouldn't that be good?

He says at last to Jim, 'I'll arrange that, but to start the monitoring, I have to see the stock today, so open the gate and move that tractor.'

Jim's hackles shoot up.

'Why? If there's only you coming on, I don't need to move it.' He isn't grey now, more the colour of stewed plums. 'Think you can fool me? If I open the gate and move the tractor, you lot will barge in and wipe me out.'

He grips the gate, and lowers his voice. 'So round up your men and get the hell out of here. I'm going to phone my own vet, so I can guarantee proper blood tests and inspection, then I'm contacting my solicitor and my MP. I'll also write to the Ministry today about my decision, and remind them of my rights.' He takes Carol's arm, grins at me, then fixes the vet with a defiant stare.

'Magnificent,' I say, when the vet gives up and walks off.

Jim gives a shaky laugh. 'Never thought I'd manage it. I nearly lost it back then, but thanks to you…'

'I didn't do anything.'

'You bloody did, Julie. Ben would be proud of you.'

Carol nudges him and his face freezes, but I laugh it off.

'It's okay to talk about Ben – I won't go weepy.' But I ache.

'I'll phone Phil Carding now,' Jim says, 'then I don't know what happens next. Wait, I suppose.'

'A vast mug of tea is what happens next,' Carol laughs. 'Shall I bring one out?' She frowns. 'Comes to something when I can't invite a neighbour in, doesn't it? Mum's right when she says this virus spoils more than the animals.'

'No thanks, Carol. I'm going, but not until that lot's gone. Wouldn't trust them as far as I could lob that muck spreader.'

She's trembling now, Jim too. 'Go on in,' I urge, 'your mother must be frantic. I'll stay here a bit.'

'Sure?'

'Absolutely, and you've got to think of the baby – go on.'

At the mention of his fourth child, Jim takes Carol's arm and leads her away, shooting a wide smile over his shoulder for me.

'And leave the tractor where it is,' I call.

'Couldn't move it if I wanted – my air pump's out of action too, can't think why!'

I watch them out of sight then stand in the middle of the entrance, arms akimbo, until every last anonymous man jack of the killers has gone. Only then do I walk down the lane with legs like jelly and one thought in my head, that Carol and Jim think the battle's over. I know that's as likely as making hay in winter.

CHAPTER TWELVE

Needing company, anything to stop me shaking to bits, I call in to see if Mike's home and find a couple of lads in his yard, the last two left of his clean-up team hired to burn off every bit of fleece clinging to the miles of his fences. They're sitting in the warm spring sunshine, shirts off, idle blow-torches at their feet, doing sod all. They don't even flinch when they see me and my anger finds a vent. 'Haven't you got any work to do?'

'Plenty, thanks.'

I hear the distinct aside that the old dragon's back.

I could do with a fight, but I bang on Mike's door instead.

'He's out,' calls one of the lads. 'Must've seen you coming.'

That's it. I'm at their feet in seconds. 'Say that again.'

I stoop for one of their blow torches, turn the gas on, rummage in my pocket for non-existent matches. 'I said say that again.'

Finding enormous pleasure in watching them run for cover, I switch the gas off and leave the yard, to let down every tyre on their battered old car parked outside. It all helps.

After I've checked the thaives and made a mug of tea, I take a kitchen chair outside so I can keep an eye on Carol and Jim's gate for the rest of the morning, the rest of the day if necessary. If a car even slows at their gate, I'll be over there.

The trucks are in action now, lumbering up the hill to all the other farms for their bloody loads and inching back down, air brakes hissing. The day winds on and no one slows at Carol's gate but I won't stop my vigil.

The phone rings in the afternoon, and I take it to the window.

'Julie Sumner?'

'Yes.'

'Dave Stringer here – thanks for your letter. Not the sort of fan mail I usually get.' His voice is low-pitched, almost gruff.

'What sort do you get?'

'Anything from pats on the back to irate townies commenting on how we farmers pollute the countryside.'

'I'm a townie.'

'The editor says you're a sheep farmer now, and there's none so righteous as the converted. What can I do for you? I've heard you're one of the few standing up to the anonymous mighty.'

'Come over here right now and help me kill the bastards – they're swarming everywhere, droves of them.'

I hear him take a sharp breath.

'You're near the county's latest outbreak then.'

'I'm on the opposite side of the valley, saved only by the B-road that runs along the bottom, but they're taking out at least seven farms as I speak. I was at my neighbour's gate early this morning helping him resist a contiguous cull.'

'You want a reporter,' he says after a pause, 'not an old gone-to-seed columnist like me.'

'And what would a reporter do apart from distort the facts, or write what the editor insists on? I had one of them pestering me outside the magistrate's court and I don't want some hack telling the world how old I am or what colour my hair is. I want an ally, someone from outside this hellhole who knows what they're talking about, someone with connections.'

He gives a short laugh. 'And you pick me?'

'You're a farmer, aren't you?'

'So are all your neighbours.'

'But they're not working for the press. He doesn't see – how can I make him see? 'Look, Dave – can I call you Dave?'

'Most people do.'

'Why did you ring? You must have thought I was some weirdo.'

He's considering this, I can tell. 'Curiosity,' he decides at last. 'Not many of us have the… nerve to stand up to what's really our boss. We're all in the Ministry's pay what with subsidies and such like, and we're all scared out of our wits by this epidemic. It takes guts to take on a faceless power – there isn't a nose to punch.'

'I tried this morning – it's amazing how easy it is to wind up uniforms on legs.'

'Wish I'd been there.'

'Come on over here, then – no, don't. I wouldn't wish this on my worst enemy.'

'Can't anyway. I'm way north of you and we haven't got the virus round us and no one wants to bring it in. Don't go out much, apart from the village to post off my column.'

'Exactly! We're all marooned, either by foot and mouth or by the fear of it.' And I go on to encourage him in his efforts to tell his readers exactly what's going on, and what isn't. 'Both you and I know there isn't enough accurate information put out, either for farmers or for poor urban Joe Public, who's only been fed stark images of burning animals or the scandal of exorbitant sums paid out in compensation.'

'You think I'm not trying now?' He gives a grim laugh. 'My editor's got the biggest blue pencil in the world.'

'You could tell him you've got a local source right in the thick of it, someone who's prepared to feed you facts about what it really means to live in an infected area, and not just to those who're culled out.'

He considers this but I haven't finished. 'With your writing skills, Dave, and my straight-from-the-horse's-mouth information, your column could help stock owners even more. We could start an uprising between us, a demand for better action, more information, more credit for our knowledge and experience, and maybe we'd get more non-farmers rallying to our side instead of criticising us. Then we could...'

'Hey, hang on a minute,' he says, stopping me dead. 'Give me a moment to speak. I'm whole-heartedly behind you in this. All I have to do is persuade the editor about reporting from the front, so to speak.'

'You will? You'll use your brilliant style of wrapping up words in lengths of rusty barbed wire to show the world what's really going on?'

'Don't know about the world,' he laughs, 'it's a local newspaper.'

'So what information do I give you for your next column?'

He's roaring with laughter now. 'I like nothing better than straight-between-the-eyes directness.'

'Not even the truth?'

Now I've got something to get my teeth into. Dave and I go on to discuss different aspects of the epidemic, deciding on the fear of people in rural communities, whether farmers or not, as the theme for his next column, then arrange to keep in touch every few days. I put the phone down and go back to my vigil feeling as though my steam valve isn't set quite so low. I'm under no illusions that his column will wave a magic wand over the whole damned situation, but it might help, and what more can I do?

Nothing's happened at Carol and Jim's by late afternoon. Desperate for action, I drive down past the remaining few parked trucks to the village for bread and milk. There's no knot of people outside, today. The shop's deserted too, the owner looking as if she's running on empty.

'It's not right,' she says, hollow-eyed.

'It's wicked, Sue, a wicked waste.'

Then we hear a whine of tyres outside the open door.

'The army,' Sue whispers. 'There's no mistaking the sound.'

At the crunch of boots, we turn to watch a young private march in. He stops and stares at us.

'Can I help?' Sue is suddenly brisk.

The squaddie scratches his baby-fine stubble. His nerves are showing.

'Um...twenty Marlboro, please.'

I can't stop myself. 'You old enough to smoke?'

He colours up. 'They're for the sarge.'

'They'll kill him.'

At that, he turns green.

'Why pick on him, Julie? He's only there to answer the radio phone, guard the Land Rover and fetch fags for his boss.'

'Bit of a boring job,' I say.

'Don't mind, really.'

'You must mind what's going on, though.'

'Nothing to do with me – just keep quiet, do me job.'

'Bet it upsets you, being so close to all the killing.'

His face fades from green to ivory.

'It's got to be done.'

'Who told you that?'

He gives me a blank stare, but I can't stop.

'Come on, who told you that?'

'Officers – in our briefing.'

'And did they tell you what happens when the farmers and their families know their animals *haven't* got the virus? Can't you imagine – don't you even think about it?'

Fear flashes in his eyes but he rallies. 'I'm not paid to think.'

'More's the pity.'

Sue's hand is on my arm. 'Leave the lad, it's not his fault.'

'That's the trouble – it's nobody's fault. No one thinks, no one takes responsibility, no one stops the carnage. Well, I will!'

Sue holds out the cigarettes between me and the squaddie and I want to knock the packet to floor and grind the life out of it. How dare she protect him? But he grabs it, throws money down, and escapes, no doubt to tell his sergeant there's a loopy woman in the village. As he whines off, Sue looks at me and sighs.

'If only they were all like you.'

'Who – farmers?'

She nods. 'I'm an incomer too, and we're different, more used to town ways – standing up to officialdom, fighting for our rights, opposing our neighbours when their hedges get too big or they build extensions across our view. But we came here for a feeling of community. Mind you, I don't know how long we'll last.'

My rage subsides a couple of millimetres. 'Trade bad?'

'Our regulars only drop in for basics, like you today.'

'Sorry.'

She attempts a smile. 'It's not your fault, Julie – everyone seems to be living out of their store cupboards, or maybe they're not eating so much. But it's not only that, we don't get passing trade any more, no visitors, nor any holiday cottage people. Sometimes it feels as though we've bought a shop on an island but the ferry service has been scrapped.' She leans on the counter and sighs. 'Most of our trade this week is from that lot swarming over the hill – Ministry teams, the drivers, truckers, army and…the slaughtermen.' She shudders. 'I can't get used to that, serving customers who've just slaughtered hundreds of animals, coming in here to buy a sandwich. How can they eat?'

I shake my head, but she hasn't finished.

'Ironic, isn't it? We came here for a quiet life away from the hordes of town and see what we get.'

I came here when I married Ben.

Now, I'm neither local nor an incomer; not a proper farmer, nor a veterinary nurse. A spare part.

I go home, wondering why she kept saying nothing was anyone's fault. Much as I like her, I can't be doing with such a wishy-washy approach. In my book, everyone's accountable for their actions, and the higher up the system they are, the more responsibility they should have. That vet, for instance. Didn't the over-educated idiot see what he was doing to Carol and Jim? Couldn't he feel their fear? I cannot picture a vet like that tending a kitten's paws or the canine victim of a traffic accident, so he must be a failed practitioner, a bureaucrat bandaging his bruised ego with miles of paper and an officious manner.

I phone Carol. They haven't got hold of Phil, and the other vets in the practice are too busy. They left messages on all recording devices and mobile numbers available, then battened down the hatches.

Back to pacing for me, into the night, diving for the window occasionally to scowl at the crimson glow of the Bennett's pyre, squint in the direction of Carol's gate in case some little bastard thinks he can sneak back after dark. But I can't see into this moonless night so I sleep in the chair by the empty fireplace, refusing to go to bed for what I might find there, or not. But sleep comes in small doses and I'm at the window again and again, trying not to look at the dying pyre so that my eyes adjust to the dark. What's that light over there – is it the beam of a torch, a visitor in the small hours, or only Jim checking the heavy chain and padlock on his gate?

I didn't set any alarm so what the hell is that noise? Leaping from the chair I see by the clock that I've slept through the dawn and it's nine o'clock. I'm out the door in a trice searching the opposite hill. Nothing, so why are my ears resounding with that goddam din?

It stops.

'Julie – get down here!'

It's Phil at my gate. Joy washes through me and I'm tearing down the drive, forcing the sleep out of my legs, desperate to get to him.

But he stands back from the gate as I lunge for it. 'I've had my hand on the horn for at least ten minutes,' he says with a scowl. 'Farmers take lie-ins now, do they?'

'Phil, brilliant to see you – come on in.'

'Can't – I'm not clean.'

'Do I care?' I fumble with the catch.

'Don't, Julie – I'm not clean and I'm not coming in.'

Then I understand, and a wave of misery swamps the joy. Then anger. 'Have you any bloody idea how pleased I am to see you, how much I need to see a friendly face?' I point at the opposite hill where machinery and vehicles still groan. 'They're wiping out that side of the valley and you turn up to tell me you won't come in.' Fighting back hot tears, I lean over the gate. 'And standing two paces back makes it worse.'

'Don't, Julie, it's bad enough without you yelling. I spent yesterday dealing with an outbreak so I won't come on the land because of your sheep, not you. It's three days until I'm clear to go anywhere near healthy stock.'

I thump the gate. 'So you should be at home getting clean, even though showers can't remedy what you lot are doing.'

I hear him sigh and I hate my anguish and its petulance.

'Julie,' he says patiently, 'you're lonely, terrified, angry…and I hear you've been bossing the Ministry around.'

'So?'

'That's the woman I know, who kept my clients in order.'

A hint of a grin lights his wonderful face, and a trace of the man I knew shimmers between lines of fatigue, and it's enough.

I relax an inch. 'Good to see you, Phil.'

'And wonderful to see you.'

'Tea?'

'Love one. Bring it down – I'll wait in the car for it.'

'So I'm a drive-in tea shop, now.'

He chuckles and I clump back to the house to put the kettle on, then stare into space thinking about the good old days with Phil, the time when I was content enough – before I met Ben and became a farmer, before the hell of foot and mouth.

I go over to the fireside chair where Ben used to sit. It looks bereft, too. I stroke the arm, lift a cushion and bury my face.

'Tell me how to live without you,' I say.

When I take the tea down to Phil he's asleep; head back, mouth open, skin grey with fatigue and one arm hanging out of the open door, and I see what he's been through in the last weeks.

I've heard that Phil has been taken on as temporary veterinary inspector by the Ministry, to cope with the upsurge of cases in this area. Poles apart from the pillock at Jim's gate, I know that Phil will have been sympathetic. Though brusque and impatient, he'll never bully or patronise. He may call some animal owners stupid, but never when their livelihood is on the line.

I let him sleep, watch over the gate, see the twitches of his eyelids, the pump of blood in his neck.

He wakes with a jump. Seeing me, he sinks back.

'Bit knackered,' he says.

'This tea's cold – shall I make another?'

'No.' He sits up and examines my face. 'How are you?'

'Not so bad.'

He laughs. 'That's what all farmers say.'

'What about Jim White – if you're not clean, who's doing his inspection?'

'One of the vets in charge round here at the moment. They won't finish all the contiguous premises for a couple of days so they're on tap, so to speak.'

'Not the one from Friday? He's a sly, officious bastard,' I say.

Phil looks up at me, his mouth hard. 'There's an emergency on, Julie – they're tackling it the only way they can.'

Anger flies out of my mouth. 'Don't start defending them!'

'They're doing a job, which has to be done quickly and efficiently. And I know what it's like, more's the pity.' He hangs his head again.

'Okay, it's a bloody awful job, but that vet was no more than a cog in a killing machine. He showed no more empathy or humanity than he would poised over a dandelion with weedkiller.'

'That's how he copes. And I've done it too – shut everything out so I can actually do the job, even though it goes against everything we learned at veterinary school and since.'

'I don't believe this, Phil!' I shout. 'If it's so bloody unethical, why do it? Why not stick to mending people's pets?'

He puts his head in his hands. 'I thought I could make it better,' he mumbles. 'I heard terrible things, so I went in like a crusader for all the farmers in this part of the county, a lot of them my clients. Don't go on, Julie – I can't take it.'

'Then put yourself out to grass, like you've been threatening to for years.'

I grip the gate and stare at my crumpled boss, unable to fathom his reasoning.

'Do you know what, Phil? Defying idiotic rules and the authorities that enforce them is liberating. Once you see that governing powers are riddled with flaws and you stop believing they're always right, you find strength you didn't know you had.'

He looks up again, devastation in his eyes. 'Do you think I want to destroy people?'

I'll hit him in a minute.

That Phil, the one who taught me so much, should turn round and mumble some miserable excuse is completely beyond me.

Then I realise his crusading spirit must have been sucked out of him and obliterated by the exhaustion of long hours and little return for his input apart from thirty pieces of silver.

And he's an old friend as well as an employer, and I can't bear to see him so knackered and crushed.

'Right,' I say, opening the gate, 'get out of that car, find a clean paper suit and come up to the house with me. You look as though you need a bit of TLC.'

He shakes his head.

'Do I have to drag you up, Phil? You've been a day off-farm, there's a bucket of disinfectant right there for your boots, and I need company. So do you, by the look of it.'

I get him up to the house.

We don't talk about the epidemic but recall the years I worked for him, the string of trainee nurses and young vets, and his clients. We remember the old lady with the hypochondriac tabby, and the smallholder whose sick goose caused hissing mayhem in the waiting room, terrifying dogs and hamsters.

I stuff a tray of sausages in the oven and butter slices of bread neither of us will get through.

And I forget my vigil for a couple of hours.

He leaves a new man, less hunched as he walks to the gate.

Then he's frowning across the valley.

Following his gaze, I see white-suited men herding the tail end of Carol and Jim's flock of sheep into one of their sheds.

Jim's tractor has been moved and white vans and yellow loaders crowd the driveway to the buildings and more are parked outside the gate.

Phil lays a hand on my arm. 'It'll be the first inspection.'

Either he's lying, or more fool than I thought.

I fly down the lane, but he catches up and grabs me.

'Don't go, Julie. You can't stop it.'

Wrenching my arm out of his grasp, I manage to stand still long enough to shout at him that he *knew* it would happen, that he kept me talking for hours so I couldn't keep watch for my friends.

'That's not true.'

'I don't know what's true,' I spit. 'I don't know who to trust. One by one, all my neighbours, my friends, are being wiped out, and it's enough to make me think we're on a hit list.'

Then I'm off again.

I'm running up the lane to find a guard on Carol's gate and the heartrending sound of cattle bellowing and stampeding in the sheds.

'Let me past!'

'No – you can't go in.'

I have a police officer on each arm and their grip hurts.

Someone's weeping.

They look too fierce for tears so it must be me.

CHAPTER THIRTEEN

Phil walks me back down the lane, one arm round my shoulders, the other across my stomach as though I'm going to escape. He doesn't say anything, just leads me home and pushes me gently down into Ben's chair. Sitting down, he stares at me in silence.

I wish he'd sod off.

Then Mike comes, walking through the door as though not sure he's welcome. He pulls a chair over and sits down across from Phil. I see them talking with their eyes.

'I've just heard what you tried to do for the Whites, Julie,' Mike says at last, 'but maybe this is for the best.'

Phil puts his pennyworth in. 'You can't take the world on by yourself.'

Why not? And who else is there to help protect my friends? I refuse to look at them and stare instead at the cold ash and charred lumps of wood in the grate.

'And don't forget you're still…'

I'm still grieving, Phil. Go on, say it.

'You're still raw, Julie, and your thinking's a bit…it's upside down, so let people make their own decisions. There's plenty of time to help them when this is all over – they'll need someone like you then, someone with a big heart, someone who…' His voice trails away.

'Like you did for me back in March,' Mike says. 'I wouldn't have come out of it so well without you.'

When I don't respond, Phil sighs and goes to put the kettle on. Mike digs out the mugs. Neither ask if I want tea. Nor did any of those people who crowded my kitchen in January. While they fiddle with tea, I leap up and head for the door. They run after me but I reach the shed door and dive inside to be with my sheep, the only living beings who won't tell me what not to do.

Mike stays in the doorway but Phil follows me down the length of the shed, so I spin round and glare.

'Please go away – I have work to do.'

I haul straw to an empty pen, cut twine, fluff out new bedding.

'These the ewes you rescued? They look good.'

I say nothing.

'You're all right now?'

Busying myself works, and after a few minutes of watching me fiddle with straw and buckets, he saunters back to the door.

'You know where I am, Julie. Ring if you want me – you've got my mobile number.'

At last they leave, shutting the shed door quietly, and their conversation fades to nothing as they walk away. I peer through a crack between the boards. They reach his car, and I can see from Phil's expression that he's worried about me. As we've spent years peering over animals on his examination table, he can probably read my every last frown or flinch or smile, but I won't let him read me today, not after he deliberately kept me from my vigil for Carol and Jim.

Patience, Julie. Patience. They'll go soon.

But it's ages.

At last Mike shakes Phil's hand and heads for his own gate then Phil takes a long look at my shed before he sinks into the car and drives away.

It's a long wait until dark, hours of messing around, first in the shed, then in the kitchen. Into the bin go the sausages I cooked for Phil together with the tin and its lake of mushy fat. I pick up the mug I got out for him this morning and deliberately loosen my hold so it slips through my fingers to the floor. When it bounces, I boot it across the kitchen and hear the satisfying crack as it hits the edge of the tiled hearth.

I'm back in Ben's chair holding on tight to a cushion when the first rifle crack thuds across the valley.

So, Ben, do you think we're next? And what are you going to do about it? Nothing? You're obviously like everyone else round here, taking annihilation on the nose as though it's your due. It's your bloody farm, for Christ's sake! The one your grandfather started from nothing that your father loved, and you kept it going in lean times, shared it with me. And what about your neighbours? Where are you, when we need you more than ever?

The shots at Jim's won't stop, and when they do it'll be the noise of the loaders shovelling his living into trucks. But I haven't heard any trucks arrive. Maybe they're waiting for dawn to load.

At last it's dark, so I can go outside to wait. No one will see me, not even Mike, though I bet Phil told him to spy on me.

Across the valley, there's a light on in Carol's kitchen. I'd like some binoculars so I can see how they all are.

It's all gone quiet. Everything finished an hour ago. I watched every vehicle leave, then waited some more, just in case.

After pulling on Ben's overalls and boots, I walk down my front field, through the ewes, trying not to disturb them. Mike won't see me – in dark blue overalls, I don't stand out, not like the Ministry men. There's something almost luminescent about their white suits.

I walk to the bottom and struggle over the hedge, across the road and up Carol's front field. As I round the corner of a shed into their yard, the smell of blood and disinfectant smacks me across the face.

A woman shrieks when I knock on the kitchen door.

'It's only me,' I call, 'Julie.'

Jim flings the door back. 'Jesus…'

'Not Jesus, just a neighbour.'

He's frozen, one hand on the door, the other clamped to the lower part of his face.

'Am I allowed in?'

He opens the door wider and I see that the kitchen isn't like Mike's after his cull. Lights are on everywhere and it's immaculate – a cloth on the table that looks as though it's just been ironed, a small stack of plates on it, cutlery in a bundle ready to be laid out. But there's no food, no sign of it, no pans on the cooker, not an onion or slice of bread to spoil the gleaming worktop.

Carol's huddled with Amy. Her eldest, Jason, is on the floor by her legs, holding on tight. Mrs Grundy's opposite with the middle child on her lap. They stare, trying to see through to the marrow of my bones.

'I came to see if you're all right.'

'No,' Carol whispers. A tear inches down her cheek. Amy reaches up to wipe it away.

'I thought I'd make a meal but…' Mrs Grundy begins.

Jim's holding my arm, gently urging me in so he can shut the door on the night. He pulls out a chair by the table for me then sits down on the opposite side. 'You shouldn't be here,' he says in a monotone.

'I needed to be here.'

'We didn't have the virus, so you should be all right.'

'I don't care about the virus.'

Carol's eyes are wild. 'The children,' she mumbles, 'they wouldn't let me get them away, said there wasn't time.'

'It's better we're here, Mum,' Jason says, 'best to be at home when things are bad.' How like Jim he sounds, even at ten years old, and he's being strong for his mother, despite what he's seen and heard.

But why am I here? What possessed me to intrude on this closed family scene when they're all in shock and only needing each other, when hell exists outside their kitchen and they desperately need to keep every bit of it out.

'Can I do anything to help?' Please, God, stop me uttering such inanities.

'I'm going to sleep in Mummy and Daddy's bed,' Amy announces.

'And me and Andy are keeping Nan company,' Jason adds. 'Dad's going to get the camp beds out of the attic for us.'

I look at Jim. 'Can I help you do that?'

He stares at me, his eyes vacant until the shutters lift. Heaving himself upright, he heads for the stairs.

We get the beds set up in silence and Jim slumps down onto one. 'The only thing that's all right in this,' he mutters, 'is that your stock will be fine now.'

'We've got the road between us, Jim.'

'Yes, but it wasn't wide enough to save you.' He looks up. 'They came back to tell me that if they didn't make a firebreak out of my front field, you'd be next on their list, then Sarah and Jack.'

This I don't believe. 'That's blackmail,' is all I can get out.

'No – they said there was a new rule about roads only being

barriers when they're so many metres wide. I had to sign – I couldn't put your sheep at risk, not after you losing Ben and everything.'

Just for a second I'm in danger of losing my stuffing as well as Ben, but I daren't say a word in case Jim drowns in the outflow. Bastards, conniving bastards, lying about road widths and manipulating Jim's concern as a neighbour for their own ends. And I know what those are – even if they don't include a perverse wish to rid the countryside of livestock, they still involve a blindness, a slavish adherence to rules issued by leaders who haven't a clue how to control the epidemic except in blind panic. Bastards. I'll show them what they've done to these friends of mine.

I go downstairs with Jim then leave them to their grief. They don't want an outsider hovering at the edge of the room, like those in my kitchen when Ben died. Hoping they get some sleep, I walk out into the stinking night.

But there's fire in my boots now. After the cull lorries leave Jim's the next day, I charge up to Fiona and Jamie's. Ellie comes out of the barn and sees me parked at the gate.

'Julie,' she screeches, running towards me. Her voice drops. 'Have you come to see the lambs?'

'Why are we whispering?'

'So no one knows we've got them.' She struggles with the gate catch.

'Wait, Ellie – go and find your mum and dad. I'll stay here.'

She frowns, then runs to the house, leaving me praying that my friends won't mind a mini biosecurity breach.

A minute later, the whole family is rushing towards me. I climb out of the Land Rover as Jamie opens the gate then Fiona dives into my arms. 'You came,' she breathes into my chest. 'I hoped you would.'

Jamie thumps me on the shoulder. 'You're a true mate,' he says. 'Calling on neighbours is only for the brave these days. Fiona, will you please let go of Julie so I can have a hug too.'

We go towards the barn but I stay at the door to watch the lambs charge out from behind a bale of straw and leap around the floor as though they've been switched on. They've grown so much I hardly recognise them. Then we make for the kitchen where Jamie opens the bottom oven door of the Rayburn. Falling into the chair, I park my feet and sigh with the nearest thing to pleasure I've had for weeks.

'You don't think I'm a health hazard, then?'

Jamie snorts. 'Don't start me on that, Julie. I'm more likely to pick up the bug from the road than from you. And considering Rob Bennett only had one infected animal, I doubt it's in the valley at all.' His eyes flash in rage. 'Nor does it stand much chance, not with every farm on this side taken out.'

Fiona hands me a mug of coffee. 'It's you who's got to be careful, and Sarah and Jack. You're the only ones left.'

Do I need reminding? Not knowing what to say, I look round their cosy shambles of a kitchen and recall the chill neatness of Carol's. I must have shuddered, for Fiona comes up to me. Her hand's on my shoulder. I lean my cheek against it.

'You know about Carol and Jim?'

'I heard in the shop this morning,' Jamie says.

'The vet lied to them.'

'I'm not surprised.' He gives me a sharp look, then turns. 'Right, kids – half an hour grown-up time. Off you go.'

'Dad!'

'You know the rules. Go and give the lambs some clean straw, then chuck some corn to the hens and geese.' He helps them on with wellies, ushers them outside. Then he's back, in the chair opposite, leaning towards me. 'You know something I don't.'

And I ruin their day in the telling.

Fiona has tears in her eyes. 'You tried though, Julie. You can't do any more than that.'

'I bloody can, and I will. One of the reasons I'm here is to pump Jamie for the names and numbers of contacts in the press, radio and television. I'm going to expose some of the things that have gone on round here, then I'm going to find out who that vet was and tell the world what it means to be hunted down and lied to before being wiped out.'

I see their stunned faces and stop.

Fiona takes a quick look at Jamie before she speaks to me.

'You mustn't.'

'Why?'

'Because you're…'

'I'm what?' Anger's got hold of my voice again. 'Bloody-minded, vindictive, bonkers? Probably, but someone's got to stop men like that, or least teach them a bit of humanity.'

'I didn't mean that,' she says, 'and you're right to be angry. No, Julie, I meant you're not thinking…you're still raw from losing Ben and…isn't it better to protect your farm, your living, care for the sheep? They need you.'

She doesn't understand. Don't I give my sheep everything they need already? Didn't I save them from a muddy end? My boots and car are squeaky clean from constant dowsing in disinfectant and I wear protective gear whenever I approach anyone else's gate. My biosecurity is off the scale of thoroughness, a hundred times better than the most hygienic Ministry man. I tell her as much. 'It's the arrogant assumption that they can do what they like to other people's land and lives,' I finish, 'and they're all protected by the great white suit of anonymity.' I pause for breath but don't look at them. 'There are two lads on Mike's land who don't give a shit about anything but their suntan and there's a vet out there playing God without His permission. In the name of something I can't quite fathom, they're invading people's lives and hearts with no more regard for their feelings than a rapist.'

Jamie gets up to pace the kitchen and I see his distress. He's torn between being out there with me and protecting his family.

'No, Jamie, you can't help me. Until everything calms down, you two must hole up for the sake of Ellie's lambs, but I'm free to yell this from the rooftops, and yell I bloody will.'

Fiona's weeping now. I've pulled the plug from her dam of tension and it's bucketing out. 'I'm afraid for you,' she mutters, clutching my hand. 'I don't want you to be hurt any more.'

I've said more than I should. I've let my rage show and I wanted to keep it all to myself. No one can help and nor do I want them to.

There's a loud bang on the door. 'You've had nearly half an hour,' Ellie yells from the other side. 'Can we come in now?'

Jamie opens the door and they charge forward, only to stop at the sight of their mother's face. It's time I went.

Jamie gave me what I wanted before I left, a file stuffed full of media contacts. When I got home I rooted out a page-a-day desk diary, an unused freebie from some agricultural supplier, and it's now my battle book. I might have abandoned Jamie's initial crusade but I'm taking it up again, this time determined to expose individuals to the media instead of leave a string of unanswered complaints in remote offices. There's a lot of time to make up so I work into the night to enter all Jamie's names and numbers in the addresses section then rack my brains to remember events and write them in roughly the appropriate dates. It's three in the morning and the pages from the beginning of March to this first week in May are full.

After checking the thaives, I snatch an hour's sleep in the chair then stick my nose back in the diary. Reading through, I see it's a catalogue of mishandled disasters, right from Mike's interminable wait for a slaughter team in March to the events of this week. My court case is in there too, and details about the pillock at Mike's gate, even the blowtorching duo. What I have to do now is find out the names of individuals behind the Ministry mask.

I've got hours to wait for the world to man its phones so I charge down to Mike's at seven.

He opens the door with a furrow between his eyes.

'Hi, Mike, how's things?' Stupid question. 'Has the clean-up finished?'

'Just about, then I'm off for a couple of weeks.'

'Anywhere nice?'

He stares at me as though I've accused him of bunking off to the Bahamas. 'Just to Davy's. They've offered me a bed as soon as I've had my final inspection and I can leave the farm without wondering what'll go missing next.'

Poor man.

My heart flips at what he must face every morning when he gets up to a wasteland. And I've neglected him since he helped rescue my thaives. Some neighbour you are, Julie, forgetting he'd have sod all to do except keep an eye on those men.

‘They’ve been here almost two months,’ I say, wondering where the weeks have gone, yet feeling them to be the sum total of my life.

‘Too long,’ he growls, ‘especially when I wasn’t infected. I’ve never known such time-wasters. Blooming waste of money, if you ask me.’

‘I’ll miss you, Mike.’

He tries a smile. ‘You’re a good neighbour.’

‘You too, but going to Davy’s will be a break for you, and you’ll have the grandchildren spoiling you and your daughter-in-law feeding you up!’ I’m trying to make light of his departure but I know he feels he’s deserting his ship. The captain’s last off, after the rats.

Rats. That reminds me. ‘What’s the name of your clean-up contractors?’

‘Why?’

‘I want to take something up with them – one of their vehicles reversed into my gate and broke a rail.’

‘Sorry about that.’

‘For goodness’ sake, Mike, it’s not your fault!’ I must have shouted because he flinched. ‘Sorry,’ I say, ‘my nerves are sharp.’

‘Not surprising with you trying to save everyone.’ He shakes his head. ‘You can’t beat this, Julie.’

Why is everyone trying to stop me? I turn my eyes away so I don’t shout again. ‘When’s your inspection?’

‘This week sometime.’

Good. I’ll be watching. I need the inspector’s registration number – any form of ID is better than none.

I leave him with an invitation to come over for toad in the hole and a few jars before he leaves for Davy’s, then go home to note down the name of the contractors. I’ll be taking up more than a piddling broken rail with them.

Then it’s time to check the thaives again, wait for the clock hands to reach nine o’clock then pick up the phone and dial the Ministry’s regional office.

‘I want to make a formal complaint.’

‘Um,’ says the girl, ‘just a moment.’ The line goes dead for a few minutes then she’s back, trying to be helpful. ‘I can’t find out if there's a form to fill in for complaints but I could ask the office manager to phone you back when he gets in.'

'How long have you worked there?'

'Only a week – I'm temporary staff. There's a bit of a crisis on at the…'

'Poor you.'

'Pardon?'

'Never mind.' I refuse to pick a fight with a temp, or start a wait for someone who never will phone me back. 'Look, please do me a favour by writing a message down in very large capital letters. Are you allowed to do that?'

'I suppose so.'

'Then I want you to put it in on your office manager's desk. Still okay?'

'Um, yes.'

'Right – here it is.' And word by slow word, I give her my name then dictate details of the date of the outbreak and the addresses of the Bennett's infected premises, Jim's contiguous farm and mine. Then I spell out a statement about the behaviour of Jim and Carol's vet and the lies he told about road widths.

'Got it so far?'

'Yes,' she chirrups. 'I wish everyone would leave such clear messages.'

I know I'm being patronising but it's working. 'Good, now put on the bottom that I will ring the office manager every day because a formal complaint demands a response.'

'Done that,' she says a while later.

I get the name of the office manager to put in my book then thank her for listening to me.

Dave Stringer's turn next. I compliment him on his weekend column, though it didn't have the caustic edge I'd expected, then I give him a very detailed account of Jim's cull; from our protest at the gate all the way to the stack of dead stock in the yard.

He doesn't speak for a moment.

'Dave?'

'I'm here, just thinking. There's no way the editor will print anything remotely like that. He'll quote the Official Secrets Act at me or give some such excuse like a press blackout or something.'

'Is there one?'

'Don't think so.'

'So why don't they want the truth?'

He sighs. 'An editor's job is to inform and entertain his readers, full stop. Anything too gory or with the slightest risk of a libel suit has him sticking to the village pump for gossip and news. His job's on the line, don't forget – the owners of the paper can eject him from office faster than you or I can pick up a bacon butty. '

'Fine – I'll find another way.' I'm calm, so calm.

'Hang on – I do have contacts, other columnists, not many but there's one who writes for a national paper. Maybe I'll give him a bell later. By the way, my column ended up a bit soft, didn't it?'

I don't want to chat. Dave can't help so I'm itching to get off the phone. 'It certainly wasn't your usual style,' I say.

'It got the big blue pencil – all the best bits!'

He's sussed my mood because he apologises and reiterates that his hands were tied by the bloody blue pencil. I've had enough of his excuses, and if he refers to any colour of pencil again it'll be hard not to send the phone skidding across the floor to the same end as Phil's mug.

By the end of the morning, by being nice to young people on switchboards, I've entered the names of a lot of important people in my battle book. At least they have names. By teatime, not that I want to eat, I've got an aching hand and a reasonable pile of letters detailing the treatment of Jim and Carol and a lot of the other injustices perpetrated round here since March. Halfway through the afternoon, I want to rush over to Jamie's to get him to type it out on his computer then just print hundreds of the damn things, but I won't involve him. This is my battle, and if it takes weeks to write to every top reporter and producer in the media, and to all the government bigwigs, then so be it.

For a break, I ring Fiona.

'Hello, sunshine,' I say with a smile plastered on my face, 'sorry about yesterday. Overtiredness makes me angry, but never mind that – how are you all?'

'Fine. Ellie did a smashing painting of the lambs, and Dan's grown an inch since Christmas. But what about you, Julie?'

'Plodding on – still three more thaives to lamb but maybe they're loving their life of Riley in the shed so much they're indulging in phantom pregnancies.'

She laughs. 'Don't blame them.'

I think she's fooled. She must be fooled. I don't want them to worry about me. I'll go my own way without being fussed over or shadowed.

I write on for the rest of the week with hardly an interruption apart from a dash to the postbox for the last collection every day. On the day Mike has his final inspection, I take a break and stroll down to the lane to take the registration number of the car at his gate. I've already taken the blow-torchers' number but I nose round this car and scan the mess of papers on the passenger seat for any clue to the inspector's identity. There it is, neatly typed on an opened envelope. Silly man for letting the mask slip.

It's memorised and in my book within five minutes, then I ring Mike to ask him over.

He comes on Friday and I cook too much for a pair of picky eaters and wish I'd got a dog to polish off the leftovers.

Mike's quiet.

'Bet you feel funny about taking time off,' I say when we've moved over to the fireside chairs and settled. 'We small farmers aren't used to that.'

He glances at me, but his eyes show he's miles away. 'Not a lot for me to do round here. I'll be better helping Davy out a bit. They might have escaped the disease but they've been on a Form D restriction for months now, like you, and Jack and Sarah.' He shakes his head. 'Davy's got no money coming in at all from the sheep so my pension will help out a bit. Can't do more than that.'

The poor man's depressed, I can see every sign – he has no energy or interest and he's talking too quietly, all wrapped up in his thoughts and not able to focus on much beyond them.

'Sarah phoned the other day,' he says. 'Asked me round to tea for a bit of company but I got a shock when I saw Jack – he's bad. He always was a bit of a dweller on things but he thinks this mess is the end. If it wasn't for the work he's put into his pedigree herd, I think he'd rather have been culled out.'

I can't believe it. How could anyone want annihilation?

'He can't see any future, that's his problem,' Mike's saying.

'But he's still got his stock!' I hear my voice gathering like a storm and can't squash it. 'His herd is the result of years of patient breeding and good farming – it should be precious to him.'

'Not when the milk doesn't fetch tuppence and he can't sell his young stock,' Mike says. 'His farm supports two families. How, with nothing coming in and the cows still housed inside and fed, because he daren't let them out for fear of getting the bug?'

'So he'd rather lose his herd and get a fat compensation cheque? I don't believe that, Mike.'

'Well, I wouldn't wish an empty farm on anyone.'

I can't stop irritation spiking my voice, so I shut up. Half of me wants Mike to take all this somewhere else. I've got more important things than Jack's self-indulgent mood. Why doesn't Sarah give him a clip round the ear, and tell him to buck up?

'Sarah's scared,' Mike's saying. 'Jack's taking more and more time off just to walk the fields. Takes his shotgun with him – says it's for vermin.'

My attention whips back. 'Oh, God – it's that bad?' I've heard reports of increased suicide among farmers, not only those who've lost their livings but the ones who can't cope with increasing debt and a dark horizon of a future. And I remember how good to me they were when Ben died, doing their bit to fill a small corner of my empty world with cakes and pies and company. Jack even plodded over one day to help Mike move my sheep when Fiona told them I couldn't get out of my slurry pit of agony. Isn't that what Mike's in now, and isn't Jack heading for one in top gear by the sound of it? You insensitive sod, Julie Sumner.

I'm instantly contrite and I hear Ben's chuckle. It always made him laugh, the way my blue skies could cloud over in the space of a blink, the way I'd listen patiently to a delivery driver's woes over a mug of coffee then give him a rollicking for reversing his truck carelessly. They usually ran for their lives.

But Mike's a mate. Change of approach needed.

'Mike, you know I'll keep an eye on your land and buildings while you're away but can I do anything else?'

He sort of smiles.

‘Not really. I’m getting contractors in to make hay and silage, then I’ll sell it. But that’s not till later, and I’ll be back well before then. What I don’t want…’ He looks at me shyly. ‘I’ve said it before, but here it comes again. I don’t want to come home and find you doing time for beating up a Ministry man.’

‘Would I do that?’

Maybe the vet who abused Carol and Jim, maybe the pillock at Mike’s gate, for not keeping his troops in order, maybe that squaddie for being a brainless uniformed wimp, maybe the…I laugh, but it’s a harsh sound and I know it doesn’t fool Mike.

‘Right,’ he says, heaving himself up. ‘Thanks for tea – best be off now to pack. I’m going tomorrow.’

The minute he leaves, I’m back in the diary, and writing.

CHAPTER FOURTEEN

It's barely dawn on the day I post the last of my letters in the village. They've left me with an odd feeling, as though I've turned a few stones and inspected the low life beneath.

The village is empty, not like the sky which promises rain. We could do with it. The grass, though leaping up in spring growth, looks dusty. It hasn't had a rinse for weeks, nor have the bloodstained yards round here.

By the time I'm home, the heavens are making up for it. I stand outside and let the rain drive through my mucky clothes. It's better than a wash, and there's nothing like feeling cold for getting me up in the morning, even though I haven't been to bed for ages. Can't be doing with wasting time there.

I squelch to the shed to inspect the last thaives and threaten them with the great outdoors if they don't get on and do something. One of them is so enormous she's either having triplets or she's been eating enough for the three of them. Then it's back outside to check the rest of the flock in the back fields. I moved them there at the end of April to leave the front fields to grow on for hay. Heaven knows how I'll do the hay harvest, me with no tractor and the bug making me reluctant to get contractors in. Don't want to think about that.

Walking up the slope I see some of the January lambs would soon be ready for market if there was one, if it wasn't standing disinfected and empty, if there wasn't a ban on movement or sale of animals, if I hadn't had restrictions slapped on me after the Holmes' cull and extended this week because of the Bennett's. Stupid bits of official paper have informed those left with stock that we'd better watch our p's and q's and wash our wellies and not let anyone on the farm and certainly not congregate with other farmers. You are hereby ordered to fill the moat with stinking disinfectant, pull up the drawbridge, repel all friends and bloody well don't breathe until we pass a law to let you. Bastards.

I go up to the wood and try to walk through the brambles but a frenzy of spring growth is crowding the path I cleared for the thaives in April. I haven't the energy to clear it again. My letter project has wiped me out. Leaning against a tree I see I can't even spend an idle moment gazing across the valley – the view's been wiped out by grumbling low cloud and undulating curtains of rain.

Back in the house, I light a fire. I'm cold to the bone, bereft of work, lonely. And knackered. But I won't sleep.

Then I'm up and pacing again but a quick look out the window shows me the weather's made even more of a prisoner of me. The cloud is so low I can't even see Mike's buildings, not that he's there. Has everyone left me?

I can't stand this. Grabbing the Land Rover keys, I belt across the yard and kick the old brute into life then head for Jamie's. I need his Rayburn, his kitchen, his company. Maybe he's been forced out of his wood by the weather and is doing something interesting in his workshop. Maybe he needs a hand. I'll do anything – sharpen a chisel, mop his kitchen floor, make coffee.

When I sound the horn at his gate, he waves from the back door and beckons me over. He's in shirt sleeves and slippers and he seems pleased to see me, God knows why, odd friend that I am.

He takes me through the kitchen to their sitting room. By the look of it, they don't use it for sitting – it's chill, and a shambles. Papers lie on every chair, they're stacked up on the windowsill and the coffee table is piled high with books and bulging files. A whirring computer squats on a folding garden table.

'I've interrupted you.'

'No, Julie,' he says with a smile and a scratch at his stubble. 'I'm getting back to the front, if you see what I mean. Back in the fight. Look at this.' He sits down and points at the screen. 'It's that site I told you about. Someone's posted evidence of a whole catalogue of biosecurity breaches by Ministry officials, slaughtermen, contractors and truck drivers – they're not putting their boots anywhere near a bucket of disinfectant, nor are they bothering to take off their protective clothing or clean their vehicles properly before leaving a site.'

Someone's hammering on the back door.

'That'll be Sam,' Jamie says with a grin, 'a mate of mine from the old days. He phoned to say he was passing through today and was I in? Brilliant – haven't seen him for yonks.'

'Shall I leave you two to saunter down memory lane then?'

'Certainly not! You'll like him – he's one of us ex-townies.' He charges for the door. 'Mustn't keep the poor man waiting in the rain.'

I sit down and peer at the alien screen but I'm kicking the chair back and tearing for the kitchen the second I hear Jamie's cry. It's something between the bay of a hound and the screech of a wounded rabbit.

My soul freezes over when I see the white-suited man, the same Trading Standards official who came to my gate to caution me about saving my thaives. He's sodden, and the rain has flattened his hair and ruined what careful combing he made over his bald spot. He looks like a bedraggled monk in silly clothes.

He frowns at me but speaks to Jamie. 'Please answer my question. Do you keep animals?'

'Yes – hens and geese.'

'No sheep?'

'No.'

A muscle lying over the man's jawbone flicks. 'Sure?'

Jamie's hackles are rising. 'Look, mate,' he says slowly, 'I live here, have done for two years. Surely I know what animals I've got.'

'We've heard you keep sheep, two of them.'

'So you've got nothing better to do than listen to rumours?' His hackles are upright now. 'I thought you had a crisis on – maybe you should be out there checking on cruelty to animals rather than snooping round my place. And who gave you permission to enter my land? I want you to go, now, or I'll make a citizen's arrest for trespass.'

The official sighs but he doesn't move. His first mistake.

Jamie gets to full spate inside a nanosecond. 'You think I'm some hillbilly that you can walk all over, don't you? If you must know, I left the big bad urban world to live a quiet, honest life here. I do not want cold callers from town on my doorstep and I certainly don't want you. Now clear off.'

The man shakes his head and makes his second mistake. He starts to walk towards Jamie's barn.

'Don't you bloody dare!' Jamie dives into the rain in his slippers. I charge forward, not to stop Jamie but to use my long stride to leap ahead of the official and stand in front of him. That's when we all hear one of the lambs bleat.

'I think Mr Casey asked you to leave,' I say icily.

'This has nothing to do with you,' he mutters, 'and shouldn't you be home minding your own business? You are not helping matters.'

'Jamie – what would you like me to do with this trespasser?'

He takes the man's arm and tries to turn him saying, 'I'm allowed to use reasonable force to eject you.'

I take the other arm and that's when he gives in.

Jamie collapses when he's gone. Gently, I coax him back to the house and park him by the Rayburn then make hot sweet tea. He splutters over it, puts the mug down on the floor and doubles up in sobs.

I kneel by his chair and hug him while weeks of incarceration and valour and fear pour out of him to soak my clothes more thoroughly than the rain ever could.

''They'll be back,' he's saying, 'they'll be back in force, all of them – vets, police, guns.'

'We'll stop them, sunshine,' I croon. 'I'll stay to help keep them out.'

He sits bolt upright. 'The children! What shall I do?'

'Do you want them home?'

'Yes. No, I don't know.' He takes a deep breath. 'Yes, I'll get them all home, we've always shared everything – I'll ring Fi at school.' And he's charging for the phone to ask the school secretary to get Fiona out of class, this minute – yes, it's an emergency, please find her *now,* and no, he doesn't want her to phone back and he'll hold on and block the line all day if necessary.

He looks across to me while he's waiting but he doesn't see me, then he fires words down the phone again. 'Fi, please go and get Ellie and Dan and come home.' He replaces the receiver almost immediately. They must have prepared for this.

'What do you want me to do, Jamie?'

'Stay, please, just in case.' He strides back to the Rayburn and thumps it. 'How do you think they found out? I can't imagine anyone…no – it's probably via the children, quite unintentional. Word's just got round and…'

'Don't think about that,' I say. 'Now, how would you like a dragon guarding the lambs?'

'You? No, Julie. What if they're incubating foot and mouth?'

'They aren't, Jamie. They haven't had the slightest contact with the Bennett's flock and anyway, the outbreak was almost a fortnight ago.'

'But I don't *know* that for sure, not without blood testing. And airborne spread hasn't been completely disproved.'

I've got to stop his mind whirling for it'll lift off in a minute at the rate he's panicking. 'Stop it, Jamie,' I insist, grabbing his shoulders, 'just calm down!'

I've shouted but it works. He hangs his head.

'Practical things,' he mutters. 'Fi and I decided to resist if ever they came. I've got chains and padlocks for the gate and barn, and we've planned for a long siege – food in, freezer full of stuff, pounds of flour and dried yeast, those sort of things. There's sacks of lamb pellets and corn for the hens and geese but I'm nearly out of hay for the lambs.'

'You don't need hay. Why not put them out on grass?'

'In this rain?'

'Jamie, they're sheep, not puppies. They've got that shelter you built in the field for them and you don't have to hide them any more now the Ministry knows you've got them. Just get them in the barn every night.'

'Good thinking – I'll do it now.' He's halfway across the yard before he realises he's still in his slippers. Turning, he gives a small grin. 'Glad you're here, Julie.'

'Everyone needs someone.'

He comes back to find his coat and boots then together we go for the lambs. While they're blinking at the light, we grab them and carry them to the field.

It's a sight for sore eyes watching them charge round the grass. Then they leap too near the geese who've recently hatched a fleet of goslings. An indignant gander goes into low-flying attack and the lambs are running for their lives.

'Milk,' Jamie says when they calm down and start grazing, well away from the gander. 'We've got everything but fresh milk – can you get some from the shop? Fiona won't think to stop and I daren't leave.'

'Good as done,' I say.

'Thanks, Julie, you're a star.'

I head for the shop and buy a fridgeful of milk and pounds of fresh fruit and veg too, anything to make their life feel normal whilst under siege. Rushing back, I feel useful, an ally, someone to fetch and carry, or take an official firmly by the arm. I'll stay another hour then go home just to check the thaives, then come back to do what I can for them. I'll sleep in the Land Rover outside their gate if necessary.

But when Fiona gets home, I'm hovering in the shadows, feeling a spare part as the family reunites and rallies to meet the enemy.

She remembers me. 'Thanks for everything, Julie, but we're fine now. You must go home and see to your sheep. I promise I'll ring the minute we need you.'

She must have seen my face fall for she's instantly contrite. 'I didn't mean we don't want you here – Jamie couldn't have managed without you this morning – no, it's that we're going to batten down the hatches and see this out. You'll be more help on the outside.'

You don't need me, I think sourly on the way home. Sam, Jamie's old friend arrived just as I was leaving, after Jamie had chained up the gate to keep me out. I watched their reunion and felt even more like a satellite out of orbit.

My house is dead. It's cold, bereft and lonely and I don't know what to do with myself. I can't keep an eye on Fiona's gate for the low cloud obscuring the hill but nor can I do nothing. My muscles ache when I sit, my stomach rebels when I eat, and my mind won't stop churning in self-pity. Shambling out through the rain to the shed, I see the fat thaive is fine, thank you very much.

It's dark when Jamie rings.

'The vet's just been to the gate,' he says in a flat tone, 'but he's gone now. Fiona was magnificent – cool and calm, demanding to see his authorisation and quietly picking holes in his argument for culling the lambs just because we're contiguous to the Bennett's land.'

I've heard it all before, at Jim's gate, and look what happened the next day.

'He recited something,' Jamie's saying, 'about how the lambs are a health risk to other animals round here, then about how we were liable to legal proceedings because we hadn't told anyone we'd got sheep *and* because we were obstructing a Ministry vet, but Fiona just kept repeating the laws about right of entry. She's done her homework, all right. We're working on a letter to the Ministry at the moment to say we're arranging a blood test with our own vet and that we refuse them entry until the results are through.'

'How are the children?'

'Scared, but we faced him as a family. We're not letting each other out of sight – it helps. You mustn't worry.'

How can I not worry when I wouldn't trust a Ministry man any more than a stranger with a knife at night.

'What did the vet look like, Jamie?'

He thinks a moment. 'Can't remember – he was just a man in a white suit. God, I was scared. Mind you, he was nervous – it showed in his stutter, and he kept staring at the children as though they were aliens.'

'I expect he thought you should have kept them out of things.'

'I'm sure he did, but the lambs are theirs. Their opinions count – Ellie told me as much.'

I've got envy streaking through me – their family unity compounds my raw and lonely state, and though I try to control them, slashes of pain are shooting through me. I don't want to be here in a bereft house with only a pile of cold memories for company, and I want Jamie to understand that without me telling him.

'I'll phone first thing, Julie,' he's saying. 'Better go now – we're going to try and eat.'

'Okay.'

He hesitates. 'Sure you're all right? You don't sound that good.'

‘Just tired.’

‘It’s all that battling for me this morning. Don’t know what I’d have done without you.’

‘Ask me over,’ I yell into the phone when he’s gone. ‘Include me, adopt me, hire me as live-in shepherd, cook or bottle-washer. Give me a blanket by the Rayburn to sleep on and let me belong to someone.’

I leave my miserable kitchen and go to bed for the first time in days to hug a line of cold pillows.

When Fiona phones the following evening, I’ve just lit another fire and stared into it, wondering where the day went. Rain’s scrabbled at the windows since dawn.

‘Please, Julie, please come now.’

I hear a child crying before she puts the phone down then I’m running for the Land Rover and screaming through the village towards their lane.

There are two cars parked by their gate.

One’s a police car with its radio crackling gobbledegook. The other is an estate with its rear door gaping. The boot’s full of plastic crates and packets and bottles. I know a vet’s car when I see one. But there’s no one about.

The only sign of life is a light on in the yard and one streaming through the open back door. I fly over the gate to the house and find two uniformed police officers standing inside with their backs to me, blocking the rest of the room. The woman officer turns as I charge in and lets me see between them.

Jamie’s standing up to them, and Fiona’s at his side holding onto the children’s hands. Dan hiccups, his face wet with tears.

‘Julie,’ Jamie says, voice icy, ‘these officers are trespassing – they ignored my locked gate and say they’re here to make sure there’s no breach of the peace when the vet comes. They say he’s got a right to come on to inspect the lambs.’

Words trickle out of my mouth. ‘But he’s already here.’

And Jamie’s charging towards me as though there aren’t two police officers in the way.

They grab him but he’s an writhing eel in their grasp. I lunge for one of his hands and pull hard.

They're no match for the strength of our dread, and we're free, running out into the rain to the barn where a faint light glimmers through the crack round the door.

The police catch up with us when Jamie yanks the door open, and I hear the baying, haunted cry he made yesterday.

Two white-suited men crouch in the straw. They look up, their faces eerie in the torchlight and one has a hypodermic in his hand. But the lambs are dead, their legs twitching and shuddering, their heads curled round as though they're trying to see what's behind them. Even the police officers freeze at the sight.

'You murdering bastards,' Jamie roars. He lunges forward but the police grab him.

'Inspection, my fucking eye,' he spits as he's dragged out. 'I'll be waiting for all you vets in hell and I'll bloody well make sure you get what you deserve.'

I can't move, and I can't understand how the vet could give the lambs a lethal injection when it was obvious they were healthy. I bet they rushed to meet him when he entered. I bet they skipped and pranced and bucked for him.

The policewoman's hand comes round my upper arm but I shake it off. 'Don't touch me,' I whisper.

'We don't want any more trouble.'

'You call it trouble? How would you feel if someone broke into your house and killed your pet?'

'Come, come, now – that's not the same.'

I stare at her, resisting the temptation to sink my teeth into her silly pink face.

'These lambs were pets, for Christ's sake! Can you imagine what would happen if the government started killing dogs, cats, hamsters and budgies? We wouldn't just have trouble, we'd have a bloody uprising.'

The men are moving. One of them has put the lambs in a plastic sack and the other's putting the needle into a box. He snaps the lid shut and stands up, looking everywhere but at me.

'You're an insult to veterinarians,' I snarl.'Why couldn't you inspect the lambs, and test them? They're not a threat because you lot have already killed all the sheep round here. Why couldn't you let two children enjoy the responsibility of looking after them?'

He tries to move past me but I block his path. He's looking at me, but biting his lip.

'I know you prefer to stay anonymous to protect your precious safety,' I fling at him, straight between the eyes, 'but don't you have a voice either? I'm asking you perfectly straightforward questions and you don't say a word.'

The policewoman grips my arm again. 'That's enough – back to the house now,' she insists, pulling me to one side to let the men pass. They head for the gate with their awful swag.

Fiona and the children aren't in the kitchen, only Jamie pacing the room, the policeman watching his every step.

'Julie,' he says when he sees me, his face a mask of putty with empty holes for eyes. 'Oh, Julie.'

I shrug the woman off, and go to hold him. From upstairs, a child's crying throbs through the floorboards.

'I think you'd better go,' I say over my shoulder to the police.

'I have to caution Mr Casey first,' the man says, 'about his attempted assault on the vet.'

'Well, get the hell on and do it, then clear off and leave this poor family alone.'

Jamie is duly cautioned, given a stern finger wag by the policeman and told not to do it again, naughty boy. I hang on to my anger then see them off Jamie's land, laughing in furious glee when the policeman slips off the wet gate and bruises his dignity.

Then I go back in to send Jamie up to be with his family. I stoke up the Rayburn and sit by it until all's quiet upstairs, then leaving all the lights on and a note on the table for them, I go home to sit by my dead fire and berate myself for not grabbing the needle off the vet to give him a taste of his own medicine.

CHAPTER FIFTEEN

Next morning, I go back to the Caseys . Fiona's reading a story to Dan. Jamie has Ellie on his knee, just holding her. They all look up at me blankly.

Ellie's the first to speak. 'We're not going to school today,' she says, in a matter-of-fact voice despite the wobble in her chin, 'and if it stops raining we're going up to the wood to find a place to build a tree-house.'

'I'm going to hide the hens in it,' Dan adds, 'then no one will get them. We're not sure about the geese, though. The gander's hard to catch.'

I say a tree house will be good for adventures, when the summer comes properly.

Ellie looks hard at me, as if she knows I'm talking for the sake of it. 'When I grow up,' she says, 'I'm going to be a vet teacher because they need showing how to look after animals.'

It's not long before I leave – they don't want someone hovering in their shadows. But I don't want to go home yet, so I head for Holly Farm – and find the White family much the same.

Now I'm wandering around my own lonely patch, occasionally shouting at the fat thaive to get on with labour or I'll sharpen my carving knife and open her up myself.

I can't sleep or be bothered to change my clothes or eat, and I'm spending most of my time sitting by an empty grate wondering where my anger and its energy went.

The vacant faces of my friends fill my mind. Okay, they're pretending to be resilient, carrying on, hiding the pain in useless activity or losing themselves in work, but Carol's not well. She's too thin for advanced pregnancy and her smile of welcome when I called was slight. And her mother's on a baking-fest. She showed me her freezer packed full of neatly labelled bags of pies and cakes and fancy bread as though she's hoping all that food will bring their appetites back.

I drop in on Jamie and Fiona every evening, to find Fiona researching enough plays to keep her drama students happy for a century, and hear from her that Jamie's spending most of his time up in his wood. I wonder if he works up there, or if he's sitting on a fallen bole plotting a revolution.

Worse, the children look at me with something bordering on suspicion. Maybe because I'm an adult.

Sarah's more than nervous. I hear on the grapevine that Jack's becoming increasingly depressed and has taken to wandering off at all times of the day and night. Alan, their son, is drinking too much, buying it in the shop since his Young Farmers' group stopped meeting in the pub back in March for fear of picking up or passing on the virus. It's rumoured too that he's thinking of giving up farming for the sake of his wife and baby, maybe even leave the area and everything he's ever known to get a job outside farming and earn proper money.

Gloom hangs over us, a despondency reinforced by constant low cloud and a sodden landscape.

No one goes out except me, the shop's sombre as a graveyard, the bleats from my flock echo emptily round the valley. The phone doesn't ring and the postman doesn't bring any response to my letters. Even the media seem to have gone on holiday. Nothing happens, the days grind on, and by mid-May, I've examined my own navel enough to write an essay on it.

Then the Ministry rings.

'Mrs Sumner, my name's Frank Phipps. I need to fix up a date to inspect your stock.'

'Are you a vet?'

'I am.'

'Are you clean?'

He doesn't reply for a moment then gives a short laugh. 'Are you asking if I showered this morning?'

'Don't be facile.'

What a prat, making light of his boring day by being flippant with some clod of a farmer. I heard Sarah and Jack had their veterinary inspection last week, the one required of all farmers still with stock in infected areas. Jack couldn't face him and slunk off somewhere so Alan had to show a white-suited and clean-booted man into the cowshed to let him peer in mouths and inspect hooves. God, why are they so trusting? I'm not going to let them through the gate.

The vet's voice assumes a wisp of authority. 'I'll be in your area this afternoon. Would three o'clock be convenient?'

'No.'

'What about tomorrow?'

'No.'

'Mrs Sumner, because you are in an infected area, I am required by law to inspect your sheep so you will please co-operate.'

I'm winding him up beautifully – there's a twitch in his voice now. I bet the muscles in his face are jumping too.

'Mrs Sumner?'

'I said no.'

He arrives at three o'clock on the dot with a policeman who has the temerity to summon me with a short burst of his siren. I walk outside, look straight at the two cars then go back in. One of them sounds his horn. And again. And again. Something about their insistence dissipates my gloom and flames start dancing in my head. Now I'm ready to do battle.

'Would you please stop disturbing the peace,' I say after I've marched to the gate.

The vet is nervous. 'Thought you might have forgotten I'm coming.'

'I told you on the phone I'm not letting you in. You're too much of a biosecurity risk.'

'But you must.'

'Who says?'

'Er – it's all down on your Form D Restrictive Notice.'

'Don't you quote official-speak to me.'

He swallows hard. 'You're in an infected area and I have to inspect your sheep for signs of foot and mouth.'

'They haven't got it.'

'With respect, I don't think you're in any position to say that.'

Who does the professional idiot think he is? 'I'm the owner,' I assert, 'the one who sees them every day, the one who'd be the first to spot a sheep that's off-colour or off its feet.'

He takes a deep breath. 'I meant…as a layman, you don't know what you're looking for.'

'Oh,' I say with a supreme effort to look wide-eyed and ignorant, 'you mean I'm not qualified to notice when a sheep's temperature is above normal, or that it has blisters on its hooves, or even that its gums are sore?'

I go on to recite every one of the symptoms of foot and mouth and the scientific evidence for its transmission that I've committed to memory for my own information, as well as to compete with such pedants as these. And I knew he'd try to persuade me he was a better judge than I am. Well here's my expertise, I gloat to myself, watching him gape wider than a landed fish as I lob chunks he couldn't get his teeth round in a month of Sundays.

'But I still have to inspect them,' he says when I finish.

'You will not.'

The policeman, who's obviously been told not to interfere unless absolutely necessary, stops writing in his notebook and waggles his pen at me. 'You must comply, Mrs Sumner.'

I smile icily at him. 'I won't, and don't threaten me with that pen or I'll report you for using an offensive weapon.'

His hands drop to his side so I turn back to the vet and give him my best grin. 'Now what? You going to have me arrested?'

He mumbles into his chest and tries another tack. 'Please be reasonable, and remember that if your flock is incubating the virus you're putting your neighbours' animals at risk.'

'Oh, God, not that old chestnut. There's hardly an animal left round here to infect.' I stare at him until his gaze drops. 'And I'm not letting you anywhere near my sheep because you're the biggest risk of all to them. I asked if you were clean yesterday and you didn't tell me.'

Probably a mild-mannered fellow at the best of the times, he's struggling with irritation now. His head comes up and he braces his shoulders. 'I insist on inspecting your sheep.'

'Prove that you're clean, that you haven't been looking down any animal's throat in the last week, tell me you've come equipped with full biosecurity gear, including a respiratory facemask, and I might, just might let you on.'

He doesn't say a word.

'Your silence is evidence enough,' I say. 'Did you know, for instance, the virus can live in the human throat for three days?'

I've had enough of his blank face. 'No? Then just go away and take some time to digest some of the scientific opinion I've read since the start of the epidemic and you might improve the Ministry's sloppy standards of biosecurity.'

I've started to turn away but the policeman stops me with his best authoritative voice.

'You are stopping a government official going about his duty. That's obstruction.'

I spin back and laugh in his face.

'Ooh, another offence! If you swotted up on me before coming here, you'll know I'm already a criminal for trying to save my sheep from starving and drowning in mud. Will I end up in front of the magistrates again? Will I have a record? Will I go to jail?'

'Er, no, but Mr Phipps can apply for a court injunction to enter your land and inspect your sheep, as is his right as an officer of the government.'

'More threats, heh?' I feign a yawn. 'So boring. Just get your silly bit of legal paper, and then try and get on my land. I'll tell you now, it won't work. I will resist, with force if necessary.'

'Is that a threat, Mrs Sumner?'

'No, it's a promise, now sod off and leave me to do what I do best – look after my sheep.'

I stride up into the lambing shed where I watch them through a crack until they get back in their cars and go. And good riddance.

I've had an official at my gate demanding to come in. I've shared some of what my friends and neighbours have been through and like them I'm going to fight the Ministry.

Unlike them, I'm going to use everything I've got to resist entry, to the last ounce of air in my lungs.

I'm preparing for invasion now, filling the moat and pulling up the drawbridge. I can't run to vats of boiling oil but I won't hesitate to wave a pitchfork at any unclean official who wants to bring the bug onto my soil. *My* soil, no longer Ben's, *mine*, and I have a duty to protect it because he left it in my care.

Better than the sunniest day for dissolving the clouds of lethargy I've wallowed in, a resolve to fight to the death has put back the kick in my boots. The gate is chained and padlocked and I've wound barbed wire round its every rail to stop anyone shinning over it when I'm not looking. This is war and I'm going to buckle down and abandon my telephone and paper campaign as a waste of time and effort for it brought no response – even Dave Stringer's columns are feeble. I'll ignore the big bad world and get on with looking after my land and protecting my sheep.

Next day, I make a decision. Time for those last three thaives to hit the big wide world. Enough of this lounging round – even the fat one can take her chances outside. I'll keep an eye on her, of course, but a continual watch for signs of labour is like waiting for snow in summer.

At first light, I squelch through the rain to the shed to move them out to join the rest of the flock. Pushing the door wide open, I march in. 'Right ladies – this way.'

They start towards me but the fat one is walking three-legged, her left front hoof dragging through the straw. I shut the door to keep them all in then grab her, hold her against the wall and lift her foot to remove what's hindering her, probably a thorn that's been scooped up with the straw by the baler. What I see makes me relax my hold on her and she struggles, bleating angrily.

'Stand still,' I hiss, too scared to bawl at her and too terrified to look at the hoof again. It can't be. Please don't let it be. Then I'm howling at God. 'Don't give me this, not now, not after everything else. You took Ben from me, you've made prisoners of all my friends and now you want my sheep!'

I find enough strength to steer the thaive into a pen, before slumping against the wall wondering where my stomach went for there's a bloody great gaping chasm where it used to be. Sliding down the wall, I crouch in the straw, defeated and wrecked by an image of an army of paper-suited men bursting into my stronghold to murder my sheep.

'Ben, where are you? Please, Ben, help me.'

He's here. I can feel his hands, those beef-red slabs of his on my shoulders. Now he's pulling me upright and holding me, soothing my tears and stroking my hair. 'Come on, Julie, come with me.' He's leading me towards the ewe. 'Look again,' he's saying, 'just look again.'

I manage to lay the ewe down on her side. Holding her down with my knee, I reach for her foreleg. Her hoof is inflamed, raw, and two small blisters lie between the cloven sections.

'Look again, Julie,' Ben's saying, 'check everything.'

Quickly now, I inspect her other hooves. They're sore too but with no blisters. I look in her mouth and find it clear. Then I'm out of the pen and running for the door. The driving rain outside cools me and Ben's thumping along beside me to keep me on track. Diving for the bookcase, I grab my old veterinary manual and flick to the pages on foot and mouth, re-scanning the pictures and symptoms I learned off by heart but now as though my life depended on it. But it does.

'Right,' I say to Ben, 'where's the thermometer?' Racing to the cupboard in the pantry where we keep our animal medicines and equipment, I rummage through the crowd of bottles of penicillin and hypodermics, boxes of castration rings, foot rot sprays and iodine. There's no thermometer.

I hear him chuckle. 'Once a veterinary nurse, always a veterinary nurse. When did we ever take a sheep's temperature?'

We didn't, and I'm a fool to think Ben would adopt such poncy clinical measures. The book in his head told him that a sheep's healthy if it's on its feet and grazing. It's ill if it's not eating or it can't get up, so we put it in a shed, treat what we can and keep an eye on it. What good does it do to take it's temperature?

'Okay, okay,' I shout, 'but foot and mouth's a virus and that has the temperature rocketing, just like flu in people.' I force myself to stand still and try to stop my mind spiralling out of control, try to think what to do, what not to do, who to call.

I'm up the stairs, two at a time and racing for his mother's bedroom hoping against hope she had a thermometer for Ben's childhood ailments.

Yes! It's there, lurking at the back of her dressing table drawer in a box of curling photographs and a clutch of hairpins. Thank God she and Ben never threw anything away.

'It's not foot and mouth,' I say out loud as I streak back across the yard. 'She been eating enough for three. She's only lame. It's not foot and mouth. It's not...' Repeating the mantra over and over again, I charge into the shed and push the thermometer up the poor animal's rectum. She flinches and turns to blink at me.

It's the longest minute of my life, longer than the time it took me to tear across the fields after Ben's runaway tractor. Stay with me, Ben, I say now as I said then. Stay with me, don't go.

I don't know whether to cry or dance when I see her temperature is virtually normal but all I can do is close my eyes and thank God and my lucky stars, whoever's listening.

'It's not foot and mouth. It's not…' Then I'm dancing, forcing my legs out of the immobility of fear and kicking up the straw like a child in a pile of autumn leaves. But I'm frightening the ewes – stop it, Julie, calm down.

Taking a deep breath, I examine the thaive's raw foot again and commit what I see to memory. Then I give her a bowl of feed and stuff more hay in the rack just to see if she's the slightest bit off her food. She isn't – the greedy pig turns her disgruntled back on me and eats.

Back in the house, I can't work out what she's got. The vet book is vague. I need advice.

Dialling Phil's mobile number, I get the voicemail service and leave a message asking him to ring me as soon as he can.

He doesn't phone back within the hour so I leave another message. Another hour and still no response. Rumbling at the back of my mind is the Ministerial admonition that it's an offence not to inform the Regional Office of the slightest suspicion of a notifiable disease. But I won't set that machine going, not even to save my own skin.

I phone the surgery instead.

'Hi, Julie!' It's Becky, a nurse I trained years ago, a competent but nosy woman. She sounds ready for a good long chat about the old days but I have to cut through it, trying to keep my voice even. 'Do you know where Phil is?'

'He's not in much these days – he does more Ministry work than private stuff. The other partners are a bit overworked because of it, us nurses too, but I suppose…'

'It's important, Becky.' I loose my cool, 'I must speak to him.'

I can almost see her brain cells prick at my abruptness. She takes a sharp breath and I know I've been sussed. 'Oh God, Julie,' she squeaks, 'not you as well, not after…you've been through enough, losing Ben…it's not fair.'

I've got buckets of tears behind my eyes again and it's hard not to blub down the phone. 'Becky,' I splutter, 'I *haven't got foot and mouth*, if that's what you're thinking. I haven't got it but I need to speak to Phil. Please tell me where he is.'

'Honestly don't know, love. Shall I ask one of the partners?'

'No!'

'Sure? Phil might have phoned when I was busy with a client.'

I can't handle this, nor can I put the phone down. She'll go running to one of the partners to tell him poor old Julie's got the bug and isn't it a crying shame and you'd think she'd had more than enough, wouldn't you?

'Becky!' I can't help my voice rising. 'Please listen to me. I need to speak to Phil and Phil only. Find out where he is and phone me back.'

She says nothing. Is she too busy signalling to someone else to come and hear this juicy snippet of news? Is she holding the phone out so one of the vets can hear what this distraught ex-employee and client has to say?

I slam the phone down and kick the leg of the table. Then I kick it again.

I don't know what to do. It's an hour since I phoned the practice and Phil still hasn't rung. I've phoned his home and got no reply. I've scoured the manual again for other causes of sore feet and found all sorts of ills from foot rot to laminitis and dermatitis. I'm not a vet so how do I know which is what? God, what shall I do now? Just do something. Leaping away from the book, I phone Phil again then tear back to the shed to inspect the other two ewes. Nothing.

Someone's breathing harshly – me. I'm panicking and can't stop. I'm terrified – and alone. There's no one to talk to and Ben won't listen any more. Is he standing back and waiting for me to decide, just like he used to, watching me with that wonderful lopsided grin of his, just waiting until I calm down all by myself?

The phone ringing blasts every thought out of my head.

'Phil – at last!'

'It's not Phil, it's Greg Howarth. Remember me from the practice? Julie – speak to me.'

'No offence, Greg,' I say carefully, 'but it's Phil I need. Any idea where he is?'

'Who knows these days? He's doing so much Ministry work we hardly see him.' He laughs, but it's forced. Silly boy, trying to be light-hearted and pleasant when I can read his every thought.

Wasn't it me who helped him stumble and grope through his traineeship?

Does he think I don't know what he'll say next?

I'm not fooled by this exercise in client liaison. He's up to something, and I've a bloody good idea that if I don't say much he'll blurt it out.

'Er, Becky said you had a problem – can I help?'

'No.'

'Sure? It's just that Becky said you sounded a bit upset.'

Becky said this, Becky said that – why can't she mind her own sodding business?

I can hear him regrouping. Get ready, Julie.

'So how's things these days? Farming going all right?'

I let all my breath out in one swoop, and say yes.

'You've got quite a flock, I hear. All healthy? Sheep afflictions are quite hard to spot, you know.'

Can't he come up with any better tactic than that? He's more fool than I remember. I don't say a word.

'Right then,' he says at long last, 'better get back to work – too much of it now Phil's elsewhere. I'll leave a message for him to phone you – okay?'

He's gone, thank the Lord, back to his dogs and pussycats and nurses who like to mother him.

I go back to the thaive who's eaten all her grain, every scrap of hay in the rack and is now devouring a stalk of straw as though she hasn't eaten for days.

By the end of the afternoon, the cage I'm in has become so small I can't move let alone prowl. I've panicked so much I'm limp and all I can do is curl up in my chair and feel totally abandoned and alone. When someone hoots at the gate, I can't get there fast enough.

Phil's even greyer in the face than before.

'What's all this fuss then, and why so many cryptic messages? My mobile's hot enough these days without you demanding to be heard.' He's irritable, more than usual, and I shrink but he sees my expression and hangs his head. 'Sorry – today's been hell and I don't want to play any more.'

'I've got a problem, Phil,' I blurt out before he gets impatient again. 'One of the thaives – she's very lame…but she's not off her food and her temperature's normal.'

He stares blankly, a frown deepening across his forehead.

'What the hell are you saying?'

'I want you to look at her.'

He slumps as though someone has stolen his bones. 'I don't believe you, Julie, you of all people. Why the hell haven't you phoned the practice? You know I can't come on.'

'I didn't know you weren't clean.'

'What do you think I do all day – stroke ponies and deliver chickens?' He's shouting now. 'For God's sake, there's a bloody crisis on!'

Don't lose it, Julie. Don't cry, don't shout back, don't sympathise with his lot, and don't tell him he's making you feel the last person in the world is deserting you. Say nothing and when he calms down, he'll turn back into the big-hearted grump you used to know and love.

But he doesn't. 'What's wrong with this bloody ewe, then?'

'It's got sore feet and blisters in one of its hooves.'

'Oh, God.' His eyes close, and I think he's crying. All I can do is stare, watch his hands come up to cover his face, and his shoulders heave.

'Phil, it *isn't* foot and mouth – I'm convinced of that.'

He drops his hands. 'And how would you know? Have you ever seen it before? God, Julie – lameness is one of the signs.'

'What about foot rot, or fungal dermatitis? She's been on damp straw for weeks.'

He's crying again and I see it's not for me but for himself, an overload of exhaustion and fear and being pushed beyond his limits by the work he's doing. If I'm patient, he'll see I'm right.

But he stiffens.

‘If you won’t report this to the police or the Regional Office,’ he says in a voice I don’t remember him ever using with me, ‘then go and phone the practice. They, not you, will decide whether or not to report a suspected case. Go and do it now. I’m going home for a shower and then I’ll ring the practice to see if you’ve been sensible and law-abiding.’ He gets in his car and drives away without looking at me again and the bottom falls out of my world.

CHAPTER SIXTEEN

It isn't foot and mouth. Phil can't be thinking, with all the pressure he's under. If only he'd come on he'd see that the thaive's obesity is too much for her dainty little feet. I'll starve her, that's what I'll do. I'll spray her hooves with iodine then feed her straw stalks until her weight comes down and stops making her feet sore.

But what if Phil reports me? Maybe he hasn't gone straight home. Maybe he's parked in the village phoning the Ministry this very minute, telling them to get the mob out to break down the gate, and…

I run for the Land Rover, start it up and drive down to park it across the gate. It's not big enough to block the whole width so I take it back to the livestock trailer, hook that up and take it down too. It doesn't take long to position them and let every single tyre down. No one's coming through my gate except Phil and he'll be back, full of contrition about his bad mood and I'll smile my best understanding smile and maybe have a joke or two about how well I know his moods. Then he'll take one look at the thaive and tell me I was right, after all.

The night is so long, hour upon hour of watching the road, waiting for Phil to come back. I've left all the yard lights on to welcome him, and those in the sheds. I've got the wire cutters ready too, so I can snip through the cat's cradle of barbed wire on the gate. It won't take a tick to let him in.

But he doesn't come. Is he too tired? Be patient, Julie, and let him sleep his mood away. At first light, he'll bounce out of bed and pull on his clothes, not able to waste a minute on breakfast or a cup of tea because of his need to reassure me that I haven't got foot and mouth.

There's a car coming out of the village now, its headlights beating a path, but it drives past the end of the lane. I'm not dismayed. Phil hasn't had enough sleep yet to be properly rational and accurate in his diagnosis. No, he's waiting until his brain cells are rested. Sleep, Phil, sleep, and I'll just curl up in my chair and be patient. Better still, I'll pull my chair away from the hearth and park it in the open doorway so I can see his lights turn into the lane. Then I'll be down at the gate snipping the wire before he's even past Mike's gate.

Mike. I wonder how he's getting on at Davy's. Bet he's loving having the grandchildren around, and his daughter-in-law to fuss over him, and her parents to chat to about the good old days. His days will be so full now that he won't look grey round the gills any more. Poor Mike, to suffer that cull on his own.

I'm on my own too but I'm lucky because Phil's out there rooting for me and Ben will be back whenever I need him, like yesterday morning. If I can feel his hands on my shoulders, he can't have gone.

The night is so dark. All those leaden clouds hanging over us like army-surplus blankets, but at least it's stopped raining and I can see lights on across the valley.

It's way past dawn but there's his car now, darker than I remember but the clouds make the light bad even this far into the day. Time for action, Julie.

Down at the gate, I see the car isn't his.

A thin man in a white suit gets out. He's got a nervous smile, like Frank Phipps had yesterday. 'Mrs Sumner?'

I don't say a word. I'm not talking to anyone but Phil.

He smiles again, a bit of a fixed one but I don't give a fuck whether he laughs or cries. Then he walks up to the gate and holds out his bit of plastic. There's a blur of a photograph on it and some words I can't be bothered to read.

'Mrs Sumner,' he says, formal now, 'I'm a veterinary inspector. I'm informed that you have a sick ewe. May I come in to inspect it?'

I'll only talk to Phil, but I stay where I am in case this person tries to climb the gate. He looks at his feet as though searching for what to say next but he won't find any words there, silly sod.

'Mrs Sumner, I'll ask you one more time. Will you let me in?'

He asks me three more times, then tells me he'll be back later.

When he goes, I know what I must do. Phil's obviously been held up so I'd better make his job easier for him when he does arrive. I'll take blood samples for testing and that way he can just nip in for a quick look at Fatso, take the samples to send to the lab then go about his other important business.

Back in the house, I go through cupboards and find a tiny jar of mint sauce, one of mustard, and an old bottle of aspirin. The mint sauce looks neglected but I haven't had roast lamb for months, not since Ben left. What's the point in cooking roast dinners? I rinse the jars, put all three and their lids into a pan of cold water on the cooker, then watch for an age until it comes to a full rolling boil. The labels come off and twist round and round in the water like waving banners, but I don't have time for silly games. I fish the labels out and chuck them.

Now I wait for the thing to cool down by itself. No cheating allowed, no running cold water in the pan, for the jars won't be sterile, and I mustn't have a single microbe in them, not if Phil's going to persuade the authorities I know what I'm talking about.

I go outside and force myself to walk up and down until the pan's cool enough to handle. It does give me a bit of time to reflect on how good I was as a veterinary nurse and remember how one of my major tasks was bossing young nurses into preparing scrupulously clean instruments and vessels for the vets. Funny I don't mind a mucky house, but Ben showed me life's too short to sweep floors or wash dishes as soon as they've been used.

At last. It's cool enough to pour the water away and screw the lids back on. Then I fetch three new hypodermics from the medicine cupboard and head for the thaives. Still munching happily on straw, the fat one's easy to grab and I've got the strength of Hercules this morning. My brain and hands take over, and all those years of practice swing into action. I've found a vein and taken a good sample of her blood almost before she's noticed.

Injected into the jar, it looks like cloudy redcurrant jelly but it's far more precious even than rubies so I stow it safely in my pocket ready to give Phil for testing. Then I catch the other two and take their blood.

Now show me I'm wrong, I think as I go back to the house to label the jars and put them in the fridge. Then it's out to the flock. As a responsible sheep owner, I'll check every hour until dark, just to confirm they're all healthy. Phil will need this information when he comes.

They're fine, I knew they would be. Every single ewe is walking well. The lambs are skipping or feeding, the older ones in gangs race round the perimeter of the field. They wouldn't do that if they were ill.

Then it's back to the house to wait for Phil.

He must be very busy for its not until the afternoon that he sends three cars. One's a police car.

But I know two of the five men at the gate. One's the Trading Standards official who arrested me for moving my thaives, and the other… how dare Phil send him!

'We're here to inspect your sick ewe, Mrs Sumner,' he says, holding out his identity card. 'I'm John Reed.'

I know very well who you are – the murdering bastard from Jim and Carol's gate, the one who lied that I'd be next on the list if he didn't cull their sheep. You shouldn't have believed them, Jim, because he wants to kill mine anyway.

A ball of something is unfolding inside. It feels like those jar labels coiling through boiling water and I resent it. I've had a peaceful morning blood-testing the thaives in the shed and checking the rest every hour. In between, I've been sitting in my doorway watching the valley go about its business. The sun barged through the clouds too and warmed me enough to shed the old jacket I've been in for days.

The tangle's reaching for my throat but I mustn't let it out. I must be sensible and calm.

'Someone's made a mistake,' I say to John Reed. 'Phil Carding wouldn't send you if you were the last vet in the world.'

The man frowns. 'Who's Phil Carding?'

'My vet and my friend.'

He sighs. 'You're not making any sense.'

'And you're wasting your time. I know my ewe hasn't got foot and mouth.'

He bristles. 'I decide that, and I insist on coming on now.'

'No.'

He's got a tangle too, except his is waving from his eyes. It doesn't frighten me. If he gets angry, he'll lose his authority and I'll have won.

He changes tack. 'Do you know there's a bulging file on you at Regional Office?'

'And what does it hold? Evidence of my obstruction, not only at my gate but at Jim White's and James Casey's? Oh, I nearly forgot – it must also have a bundle of papers from Trading Standards about my illegal movement of sheep back in April. Aren't I being a naughty girl, stopping all you important people from dealing with a crisis?' I lean forward and grin. 'Do you think I give a fig about what's in my file?'

'Well, it may affect your future as a stock owner.'

I glare. 'Do you have any idea how transparent you are? This blackmail of yours is as subtle as a kick in the groin.'

I don't wait for an answer but turn to the policeman. 'Constable – tell this man that he has no right to come in if I don't want him to. I believe that would be forcing an entry.'

The policeman steps forward. 'I'm an inspector, actually, not a constable, and I'm convinced Mr Reed has every right of entry to inspect your sheep. Under Animal Health laws...'

'Don't give me that,' I put in. 'You police have little to do with the laws on animal health – it's all in the hands of butchers like these. And why aren't you protecting my property rights?'

The vet butts in and by the look of his face, he's not going to give an inch. 'If you don't let me on, I will apply for a court injunction to enter and inspect your sheep. Should you resist then, you will be in contempt of court and that will mean an arrest.'

I've had enough. If I don't walk away from him, I'll be over that gate to wrap my beefy mitts round his throat, but if I do I'll be carted off then there's no one to protect my sheep.

'Good day,' I say, and turn to go but there's a screech of tyres on the road then I see a battered red Marina careering up the lane.

'Julie, you should have phoned,' Fiona says when she reaches the gate. She didn't run from her car, merely got out, pulled herself up to her full five feet two and walked straight through the bank of officials.

I reach for one of her hands through the bars and squeeze it. 'I'm okay, apart from this lot wasting my time.'

She stares at me, searching my very soul and seeing every thought and fear writ large.

'Let me in,' she says.

'Best not.'

She pulls her hand away and starts to climb the gate, ignoring the barbed wire tugging and tearing her skirt. The police inspector reaches towards her to pull her back.

'Don't lay a finger on her,' I snarl. 'I'll have you for assault.'

He pulls his hands back but John Reed grabs a piece of paper from one of the others and pushes it through the gate. 'You have a suspect animal so I am placing this farm under Form A restrictions. This means no movement of animals or people on or off the premises.'

But Fiona's already over the top of the gate so I grab the paper and tear it to shreds. 'That's what I think of your silly restrictions, especially when Mrs Casey was already on my land. As you aren't, I can't see how you can eject her.'

Fiona shoots me a grin then struggles down to my side and we face the officials together.

She's so thin and cold and pale I want to wrap her up in my arms to warm her but I daren't take my eyes off the men for long. They're heads together, up to something. Now Reed's talking into his mobile phone, his free hand lifting and falling and waving in a weird one-armed semaphore. The policeman has retired to his vehicle and I can hear the radio crackling. There's another sound too, a whine of tyres.

An Army Land Rover whips up the lane from the road and a sergeant and a private run towards us. The squaddie is holding a pair of heavy-duty wire-cutters. He doesn't look at me.

'Don't you dare,' I shout at him.

He pauses only a second, still not looking at me, snips effortlessly through a strand of barbed wire, then another, and another, working his way along the gate and decimating the cobweb I've spent hours spinning. I try to reach through the gate but he's too quick at dodging.

'Don't worry, Julie,' Fiona says calmly from behind, 'this'll do the trick.' I turn to see her pulling a video camera out of her pocket. When she starts filming, the squaddie stops work and looks wide-eyed at his sergeant who also seems uncertain.

Reed marches forward, brandishing another piece of paper.

'As I said before, these premises are under Form A restrictions which give me the right to come in and inspect your sheep.'

'A wonder they don't get tired, saying the same old thing over and over again,' I tell Fiona, behind the whirring camera.

'And you, miss,' Reed growls, 'are defying government restrictions by being that side of the gate. May I have your name?'

'You bloody may not,' I shout, 'and I'm another one who'll never get tired of saying the same old thing again and again. I will not let you on – not today, nor tomorrow, nor next year. Please leave my gate and go back under the official stone you crawled out from. Now!'

He stands his ground, examines the Form A then looks at me. I'm sure there are wisps of steam spiralling from his ears.

I won't stop. 'That soldier stopped cutting the wire on my gate when we started filming and it confirms you have no right to make a forced entry. I told you to go, now please do it.'

They're backing off, at long bloody last.

'I'll be back later,' he says, chin down, 'with a court injunction.'

'You need to go home,' I say to Fiona, after they've all gone, and I've told her about Fatso. I've also lit the kitchen fire to try and stop her shivering.

'No.'

'Please, Fiona, you look so tired.'

Not just tired, she's wrecked, destroyed. Her children are emotionally wounded, she's been trampled on by the Ministry and she looks brittle enough to snap in a strong breeze.

'I'm not going home,' she says, straight at me. 'You need help resisting that lot, and they'll be back, mob-handed next time. You don't stand a chance without me.' She hands me her car keys. 'Now go and park it across the gate on the other side. Put it in reverse gear then lock it up.'

As I take the keys, the phone shrills.

'Julie! I've been watching from here with binoculars. Why didn't you phone us?'

'Don't start, Jamie. I've had that non-stop from Fiona.'

'Where is she?'

'Sitting by my fire.'

I hand the phone to Fiona and go out to move her car and check the sheep for I don't want to overhear what plans they've got for me.

This is my battle and I'd prefer not to drag anyone in, especially not Fiona. She has enough of her own problems without mine as well. What sort of friend would I be to wreck her further?

Crossing the yard, I see Jim and Carol at the gate.

'We saw the mob,' Carol says when I reach them.

'I have a lame ewe but it's not foot and mouth.'

'And you're not letting the Ministry in?' Jim's as pale as Fiona and it's written all over his face that he wishes he'd stuck to his guns at his own gate.

'No, I'm not letting them in. The ewe will get better with my treatment.'

'Good for you,' Carol says, hands across her belly, shielding her child from a world full of bastards. 'When are they coming back?'

'God knows.'

'We'll watch for them then come down and help you.'

'No, Carol, I don't want you to,' I say, my voice too strong, almost a shout. I struggle to temper it. 'I don't want to put you through any more aggro – you've had more than enough to last a lifetime and you must think of your baby.'

She frowns. 'But you helped us.'

'Fat lot of good it did you,' I almost spit.

'Now come on,' Jim says, trying to appear strong when the shadows under his eyes proclaim that he's not. 'You did help, more than you know, and we want to help you tomorrow.'

Do they know something I don't know?

Why tomorrow?

Why not at midnight, or even in half an hour?

I wouldn't put it past the Ministry to be lurking in the village this very minute, regrouping, amassing more men and a squad of armed police.

Maybe all they're waiting for is a Centurion tank with a four-inch cannon on the front. That's the only thing that would shift my Land Rover.

I send them home with the biggest smile I can muster and as many forced assurances I can dredge up. I tell them their children and Carol's mother need them calm and at home instead of being hassled by the police for interfering with a precious vet.

They go eventually, take a few steps then look back at me as though they're deserting me.

'Go on,' I call. 'Thanks for coming, and I'll be up to see you when it's all over.'

Fiona won't go home, either. She just sits, watching me, grey eyes boring holes through my chain mail, and I have to keep getting up to do things so she doesn't turn me into a colander. First I check the blood samples in the fridge and wish I'd given them to Jim to pass on to Phil, then I prowl back and forth past the window just in case the mob's arrived without me hearing. Then I go out to the woodshed for another load because even a banked up inferno doesn't seem to warm her up.

On another escape from her gaze, I fetch blankets from upstairs to drape round her. I make her tea, find biscuits we won't eat, fry some bacon for sandwiches that neither of us touch.

'Sit down, Julie,' she orders.

I perch on the edge of the chair, and risk her gaze.

'You're trembling,' she says.

'So what? You look like a jelly.'

And we laugh.

Our mouths split, and I hear a cross between a chuckle and a gasp from her throat and a strangled choke from mine.

We laugh until we cry. Tears pump down our faces then turn to sobs and she at last crumples up under the blankets, hugging herself with her skinny little arms. My heart cracks.

I reach over and pull her onto my lap to hold her warm and safe, and she weeps and sobs and wails into my chest while my tears soak her hair. Then I'm rocking her and crooning, telling her it'll be all right even though I know it won't, and she says I mustn't be alone and she'll stay forever and bring Jamie and the children down so we can all hold each other through the long days and weeks and years and even longer nights.

Now she's sleeping, probably for the first time since their

lambs were killed. The fire's died, but we're warm holding each other and I don't want to let go of her to stoke it up because she needs to sleep to make her own hell go away.

I don't know what time it is, but judging by the lack of traffic on the road, well into the small hours. Fiona still sleeps in my arms, hardly stirring apart from the occasional twitch. I'm her guardian, her gatekeeper, and I won't let anything disturb her until she's rested. She hardly weighs a thing, but I still had pins and needles in my thighs earlier. They're gone now – I forced them away by concentrating hard on keeping watch over her. She's done that for me from the moment Ben died, kept an eye on me, stopped me dying from the bruising ache inside me, coaxed me out of troughs and brought me down from the clouds of bewilderment. For that I will protect her to the end of my strength and my courage.

It's still sort of dark, that funny grey hour before the true dawn, and I can hear engines. Fiona hears, too. She's instantly awake, pushing hair out of her eyes – then leaping for the window.

'They're back, Julie. Put the yard lights on.' Grabbing her jacket and the video camera, she's out of the door before I can knead a bit of life back in my legs. I hit the light switches then stagger after her.

She's at the gate being lanced by strobing blue lights radiating from two police cars blocking the road end of the lane. I rush down to protect her but there's no one on the other side.

We wait, but not for long.

The army Land Rover comes first, stopping at the road block then whining through it and up the lane to park above my gate. Then three police officers stroll up and start talking to the army personnel.

No one looks at us.

Fiona stops filming it all while we wait for the vets and she talks to me quietly, explains that she doesn't think the Ministry could get a court injunction in less than twenty-four hours. She's brimming with legal information about our siege and she tells me to stay calm. And I feel on the periphery of it all and want to go and check the thaives and the rest of the flock and just leave this lot to their machinations.

We stand there for more than a hour, until the sun flicks orange arrows over the hill to compete with the police lights. It's then I see Jamie racing down the White's lane towards the road, his jacket flying out in wings and something like sparks shooting from his boots. He reaches the road block and I hear him cursing and shouting at the officers stationed there. Then it goes deathly quiet.

'He said he'd come,' Fiona whispers to me with pride in her smile, 'and he'll find a way through, don't you worry. Nothing stops Jamie when he's on a crusade.'

'But the children…' I begin, worried for them.

'Looks like he's taken them to Carol's on the way over. I bet he's been up all night watching, just waiting for the time to grab his sword and ferry the children to Holly Farm.' She's grinning now and I envy her Jamie, someone to ride to her side at the wink of a blue bulb.

'Sleep's done you good,' is all I can think of to say.

'Thanks for that.' She looks me full in the face. 'None of us want to be without you, Julie, and that's why I'm here, to see you're not carted off.'

'I won't be.' I might sound confident but I'm not. What chance have two women got against the mob that's coming? But I can't stand here doing nothing. 'I'll go check on the thaives,' I whisper. 'The fat one needs more stuff on her feet.'

'Okay,' she says.

It would be easier without Fiona, I admit to myself on the way to the shed. My concern is for her and I feel torn, dithering, not worrying about the sheep enough because all my energy and thoughts are involved in seeing she comes to no harm.

After seeing that the fat thaive's improving, I take a swift look over the back field. There are my ladies, healthy and munching away, oblivious to what's going on, then shouts from the gate have my uncertainty falling away faster than rain down a gully and I'm running, gasping, yelling too. They must have got Fiona. Those bastards have leapt over and grabbed her and I'm not there.

It's not Fiona in danger, it's Jamie. He's loping across my front field and it's the police who're shouting. One's trying to negotiate the gate but I get there before Fiona has to do anything.

'Get off my land,' I growl at him.

He stares at me; a bull-necked fellow I haven't seen before. Nor did I notice before that all the police are wearing flak jackets. Do they think I'll dig out the 12-bore and start shooting? Maybe there are even more officers lurking in the shadows, their gun sights trained on me already, just waiting for their senior officer to flick an eyebrow before they fill me full of holes.

All this for one sheep and two women.

'I said get off my land.'

He hesitates.

'You have no warrant to enter my premises and you're being filmed. Do you want to end up in court?'

The police inspector comes up behind him.

'Get down, Parkes, on this side.'

The constable leaps down and walks away, his back alive with indignation. Poor dear. I think he wanted to show off by capturing the villains of me, Fiona and Jamie, and now he's had his hand slapped by a senior officer.

I glare at the inspector, not the same one as yesterday. 'I'm right, aren't I? You have no warrant. Only the vet can force an entry *if* he's managed to get a court injunction at such short notice.'

He turns away.

Jamie's over the front field gate and at the top of the yard now. Fiona stops filming, rushes up to him, and I feel another stab of envy. They're together again, his arms tell her he loves her. I can't look.

But I go to meet them as they walk down to me and we're in a huddle and it feels like a warm blanket. 'Now I've got two people on my land who shouldn't be here,' I say with a grin. 'Don't you know I'm a Form A premises, you naughty people?'

Jamie tugs his forelock. 'Uh, what's one of those, guv?'

'I can't think of a better pair of criminals than you,' I say feeling tears massing, just when I don't want them.

When Fiona reaches for my hand and Jamie leans over and gives me an awkward kiss, my taps lose their washers. I can't help it, even though I felt I cried myself empty last night with Fiona.

'Courage, Julie,' Fiona whispers.

'Hah, there's plenty more where that came from.' Straightening my back, I tower above her.

Our heads whip round as one when the convoy rumbles out of the village – three cars, another army Land Rover and, oh God, a fleet of white vans.

We watch in silence as the cars move slowly up the lane from the road block and park higher than my gate. The vans and their occupants stay down on the road, nose to tail, lights out and silent, unopened, sinister.

'They're going to kill my sheep.'

'No, Julie,' Fiona says as strongly as she can with that funny catch in her voice.

'They bloody won't,' Jamie croaks, 'not if I've got anything to do with it. It's intimidation, that's all.' He grabs my hand and strides towards the gate to do battle.

John Reed is waiting for us with five men banked round him.

'Good morning, Mrs Sumner.'

His eyes tell me he slept well. They're pale green, not the colour of thunder I remember in them yesterday and at Jim's gate.

Ignoring Jamie and Fiona, he introduces me to the men as though we've just met at a business meeting. Then he explains what will happen once I let them all in.

'But you're not coming in,' I state.

'We've been through all that,' he says patiently, 'so just open the gate and tell me where your suspect ewe is.'

'No.'

He sighs one of his best, and turns to a man who hands a piece of paper over.

'This is your copy of a High Court injunction,' he says, staring, 'which allows me to inspect your ewe.'

I grab for it, ready to tear it into confetti, but Fiona gets there first.

'It is not for you, miss,' Reed protests, 'only for Mrs Sumner.'

'I'm her legal advisor,' Fiona says calmly, 'here to brief Mrs Sumner properly. You will not do anything until I've done so.' She leads me out of earshot, to the top of the yard. Battered and raw, I comply, and hope Jamie's okay for a moment on his own.

When she reads it, I see her face empty of what little colour was there. I snatch it from her hand. 'It's a proper one, isn't it?' But I can't focus on the words. Either it's a poor copy or the print is on the loose, leaping through the flashes of coloured light zipping round me.

'You can't stop them,' she whispers, 'and if you try, you'll be arrested and taken away for contempt of a court order. Don't let that happen – your sheep haven't got foot and mouth and they need you here. Please, Julie.'

A noise from the gate has my attention. Jamie's arguing with a squaddie in big gloves who's tearing away the last of the barbed wire. Another is snipping through the padlock hasp with a hefty pair of red bolt-cutters. Then I'm running when the gate opens and Jamie tries to resist the barrage of men, but that young police officer has pinned his arms before I can get halfway there.

A cow's bellow comes from my mouth. 'Let him go!'

Jamie's mouth is working but I can't hear what he's saying so I lunge for him. I'll save him, just like I did when the police grabbed him in his own kitchen. But the young officer is too much for me, and the other two drag me off.

The inspector cautions me then arrests me to prevent a breach of the peace. 'And one step in the vet's direction and I'll have you for contempt of a court order.'

Fiona has naked fear in her eyes.

CHAPTER SEVENTEEN

Jamie's been led to the police cars at the road block and I'm confined to the house with two police officers. Fiona's with me, looking out for me, even though she's terrified for Jamie. She looks haunted yet she watches their every move, but when she tries to speak, nothing comes out, not until the policewoman saunters round my kitchen peering at the small and silly things that are part of me as well as my home.

'I suggest you stop snooping,' Fiona manages in her best sharp tone. 'The injunction doesn't give you any right to go through Mrs Sumner's personal possessions, even with your eyes.'

The policewoman has such disdain on her face I want to sit on it but I can't, not with the inspector guarding me like a criminal.

Steady, Julie, you need to be icy calm to rescue Jamie.

Struggling for a reasonable tone, I face the inspector. 'What will happen to Mr Casey?'

'He'll be arrested and taken to the police station for entering Form A restricted premises without permission.'

'But who'll look after his children?'

'He should have thought about that before,' he says.

Fiona takes a step forward. 'So it's more important to enforce a ridiculous law than show a bit of humanity towards my children.'

'Oh, so you *are* his wife? Where are the children?'

'With a neighbour.'

'And there they'll have to stay because you're not allowed off this farm until the vet says so. Wouldn't it have been more sensible to have thought of that before you tried to help Mrs Sumner defy the law?'

'You *are* a bastard,' I mutter.

He whips round at me. 'I've been lenient with you so far but one more word of abuse and you'll be down at the police station as well.'

I have to be calm. I must not make this unholy mess any

worse. Haven't Ellie and Dan been through enough without the authorities depriving them of their parents too? *Why oh why* did Jamie and Fiona barge in? It's hardly more than a week since their lambs were killed so why didn't they stay at home and let me fight my own battle. Then they wouldn't have added to their problems.

I face the inspector as icily as I can, resisting the urge to bash some colour into his urban skin. I know he's urban – he's as pale and lumpy as an uncooked apple pie.

'If I promise to behave myself, will you let Mrs Casey leave?'

Fiona steps forward but I stop her by raising a hand. 'Don't argue with me, Fiona. I don't want Ellie and Dan to be without you, especially after last week.'

'I have no authority to let Mrs Casey leave these premises,' the inspector recites. 'You'll have to speak to the vet in charge.'

'Right,' I say, all set to go and find him.

'But not yet,' he insists.

'Why?'

'Because you'll cause trouble.'

'What if I promise not to?'

He turns away but I move round him to make him look at me. The policewoman's instantly on the alert.

'Please don't ignore me,' I insist calmly, even though rage is boiling a hair's width beneath my skin, 'I've been arrested to prevent a breach of the peace. Does that mean house arrest?'

'Well no, not exactly.'

'Not exactly? Tell me exactly.'

'It means I have to stop you breaching the peace.'

'So why have I been confined to the house? Because it's easier for you?'

'Yes, and no.'

'Explain the law to me – every word of it,' I demand, struggling to keep my voice low.

He takes a deep breath. 'We must watch you the whole time.'

'Where?'

'Everywhere.'

'So am I free to walk about my own land as long as you supervise me and I don't swear at anyone, or stick two fingers up at the vet?'

‘Yes, but if you interfere with the vet in any way, it’s an obstruction and you’d be arrested for contempt of the court order.’

‘Right,’ I say, thinking I’d sell my soul for the chance to interfere with that vet, ‘I promise to smile sweetly and not swear, and I also promise not to hinder Mr Reed in any way. Now take me to him.’ I flash a grin at Fiona, who’s frowning. Trust me, I say with my eyes.

The inspector’s beaten, but he nods to the policewoman. She moves to my side. I walk between them to the door.

They’re like a couple of miscast shadows on each side of me, all the way across the deserted yard to the shed. I open the door, take a step in and stop, just so they can keep to my side. I can feel Fiona behind, my ally, my hero, my friend, and though I know she’d say the children will survive without her and Jamie for a while, I’m not having that.

‘Mr Reed,’ I call across to the pen where he’s peering into the fat ewe’s mouth, ‘I would like you to let Mrs Casey leave this farm. She has two young children to take care of.’

He doesn’t glance up. ‘Not now, Mrs Sumner.’

‘Please,’ I say in a steady tone, ‘it’s very important.’

‘I said not now.’

I shut up, even though I want to grab the man by his balls and whirl him round my head. That’d get his attention.

My ewe is struggling in distress, but he’s not taking the slightest notice. I mustn’t lose it. Getting Fiona home with Ellie and Dan is the most important thing I’ve ever had to do. My mouth shut, I wait until he’s finished examining the ewe, but he still doesn’t look at me, just walks over to inspect the other two thaives, then he goes to huddle with the men.

‘Excuse me,’ I call, ‘but may I hear your verdict about the sheep? They are mine, after all.’

He’s still ignoring me and my fists are so tightly balled my nails are slashing my palms. I open my fingers and try to relax. ‘Mr Reed, I insist on hearing your opinion.’

Fiona’s got her hands on my hips from behind. Is she willing me to go on to the end? Will I wreck her chances of going home?

But I can’t stand the tension. ‘Inspector,’ I say, ‘I want to talk to Mr Reed. May I move closer?’

He's looking to Reed for an answer but the sod's too busy with his own arrogant importance to notice. I take a small step forward.

No one stops me. My shadows move with me; Fiona, too.

'Mr Reed, I am entitled to know about my sheep. Please tell me what you think of their condition.'

Someone's screaming inside my head, yelling for Reed's blood. I want his guts too, preferably in my hands so I can stuff them down his officious little throat.

'As Mrs Sumner's legal adviser,' Fiona says through the small space at my side, 'I must insist you answer her question. She is entitled to know the fate of her stock.'

Reed loses it then, as I knew he would, and he's marching over, his pale face angular with shadows.

'I'm not sure what's wrong with the ewe,' he says, thin-lipped, gaze fixed somewhere over our heads, 'and as I'm just about to phone Head Office to ask for an opinion, I'd be grateful for less interruption.' He finds his mobile phone and stabs at the buttons.

'You haven't answered my original question,' I persist. 'I want you to let Mrs Casey leave.'

'No,' Fiona says behind me, 'I won't go, not now.'

'Yes, you will,' I say in a stage whisper.

Reed's had enough of us. He lowers the phone and comes back to me in such fury that even the inspector stiffens.

'For God's sake,' he spits, 'get that woman out of here!'

I'm winning. 'Do you mean me, or Mrs Casey?'

'Both of you!' His chin will touch mine if it juts any further.

'But you said *woman*,' I say earnestly, 'not *women*, and as it's quite obvious, to me anyway, that Mrs Casey and I are both of the female species, which one of us do you mean?'

'*Get them out,*' he yells to the inspector.

'Sorry,' I say. 'This is my shed, and according to the inspector I've every right to be here, so long as I make no trouble.'

Now I've got his gaze, and I see in his eyes that he's near his limit. Exhausted. Something else, too, sits hidden within those cabbage-watery depths – he doesn't want to be here any more than I want him here. He'd rather be home tending roses, or delivering kittens at his practice.

Time for my trump card. I slap it down. 'I insist Mrs Casey is allowed to go. She's not my solicitor and her children need her. Please give her permission.' Once she's safely away, I can kill the bastard.

'*Julie, stop it*,' Fiona shrieks behind me.

This is the last straw for Reed. He sags. 'Get her…get Mrs Casey off these premises,' he sighs to the inspector, 'then take Mrs Sumner out of my sight.'

'I have a right to stay here with a police escort,' I insist, 'and I will not obstruct you in your duties provided you perform them correctly. All I ask is that you credit me with a little intelligence, respect my concern for my animals and let me in on any decisions you make about them. I know enough about the legal side of all this to demand you do so, and I have witnesses in these two officers if you do not. Make no mistake, if you continue to disregard my rights, I will devote the rest of my life to exposing you and your kind to the media and taking you through every court in the land.'

He closes his eyes and I know I've won. Turning, I hug a wilting Fiona then let the policewoman take her outside.

'Give Ellie and Dan a kiss,' I call after her. 'See you soon!'

The door closes. She's safe. Now I can fight my bloody battle.

Reed walks to the far end of the shed and turns his back while he phones HQ. I wait patiently, willing my legs and arms to stop twitching. I can't hear what he's saying and there are long silences when he shuffles his feet or straightens his shoulders.

'Right,' he says at last, starting back, 'as I'm not sure…'

'Then you need a second opinion. If that means another vet, may I have my own here?'

'There's no need. Head Office has decided…' He's halfway down the shed, passing the fat thaive who's chewing on a stalk with dreamy eyes. Shards of fear form in my veins.

He walks past her. 'This valley is already an infected area,' he says, not looking at me, 'and because there's been no outbreak north of your land, Head Office has decided not to risk letting the disease spread any further than your boundaries.'

'So I'm to be a firebreak cull,' I say, my voice even, 'and because one of my ewes has sore feet, you kill my whole flock.'

He doesn't respond.

'How can anyone make a clinical examination down a phone?'

'They are experienced…' he begins.

'Experienced what? Are they practising vets? Or virologists? Are they old enough to have actually seen foot and mouth during the last epidemic? Or are they just tin gods who want this plague stopped for political reasons even if it means killing every animal in the country?'

He stops, his gaze fixed ahead, but I've got his attention.

'I demand to know if *you* think it's foot and mouth. I want *your* opinion. You're the only one who's examined that ewe.'

'HQ have made the decision. It's out of my hands, now.'

I close my eyes, see skeins of red across the back of my eyelids, but I will not scream.

'Please, Mr Reed,' I say as steadily as I can, 'tell me what you think. I worked for thirty years as a veterinary nurse in a rural practice and though I haven't actually seen foot and mouth, I know more than most what the symptoms are. All I want is a reasonable discussion with you about what could be wrong with her. Personally, I think she has some form of digital dermatitis. I thought she was in lamb a month ago but now I know she's just vastly overweight and has spent too long on the damp straw in here. Her feet are raw, but not from foot and mouth.'

He doesn't seem to be breathing. Am I getting through? Have I touched a remote nerve somewhere that shrieks at him to honour the oath he made at vet school to preserve life? Can I touch a human part of him that's longing to shrug off the nightmare of this epidemic and escape to a friendly chat with me about the ridiculous price of veterinary antibiotics or the entertaining ailments of old Mrs So and So and her chocolate-stuffed Chihuahua?

We're all holding our breath now, the police too.

'Mr Reed?'

He exhales a long pursed stream of air then snaps into gear. 'It's out of my hands, Mrs Sumner.'

I can't move.

If I do, I'll crumble.

But I must speak for my ewe.

'Are you going to kill her for nothing?'

His silence is my answer.

'What about the other two? They don't have any symptoms at all and…' I don't know who's speaking. It doesn't sound like me. '…and there's been no contact for weeks between these three and the rest of my flock, and...'

He turns, and looks at me as a person for the first time rather than an irritation or block to authority. His eyes have changed colour again, too. Somewhere in that soupy green are flecks of…what? Regret? If so, he's a proper vet and no bureaucrat. Before this plague dragged him under and gummed up his principles with too many edicts, I bet he worked in a practice full of worried clients and spoilt pets.

I must find out who he is.

'I want to see your identification,' I say.

He sighs, back in officious mode. 'I showed you yesterday.'

'I'd like to see it again.'

He reaches into his white suit to bring out his licence to ignore his principles. Scanning it, I ignore the fuzzy photograph, the signature and the Ministerial claptrap, searching for clues to his real identity. It's there – writ small, but once I focus on them the words might as well be on a hoarding – *John Reed, Temporary Veterinary Inspector*.

'So you are a proper vet,' I say looking up at him. 'Are you part of a practice? Do you have nurses like me working for you?'

He doesn't respond, nor does he move.

'I suppose you volunteered,' I persist, 'like my vet, who rallied to the call to fill the depleted ranks of state vets and save the country from doom. Like you, he's still out there, getting his ethics buried in mud and gore. You'd get on well with him – he betrayed me, too.'

He plucks the plastic card out of my hand, braces up and walks out of the door, and I know I've lost.

'Come on now,' the inspector says, taking my arm.

'Don't touch me,' I hiss, taking take a long look at my thaives.

'We'll go to the house,' the policewoman tries. 'You don't …'

'I am not going to the house.'

And I will not break down or sob.

‘All my animals are about to be killed and I’m going to watch. I’ve not misbehaved, I have not obstructed the vet in any way and I want to witness everything. It’s the least I can do for my sheep.’

Mike watched everything when the killers came and so will I – every moment, every man, every vehicle, every single one of my three hundred and fifty sheep and all those lambs I brought single-handed into the world.

I’m glad he’s not home to see his neighbour dragged down the same road.

‘I’m going outside now.’

They fall in beside me.

Standing just outside the shed with my back to the door, I see Reed by the gate, directing his troops.

He’s back in command of himself and following orders from on high to the letter, punctilious in authority. But I’ve seen his Achilles heel. Maybe I’m the only one who has.

Soldiers have pushed my Land Rover and stock trailer out of the gateway and now a shiny new model drives through towing a trailer stacked high with hurdles.

It zooms past me towards the entrance to my back fields and three men in blue waterproofs start to build their grown-up meccano set into a prison for my sheep. More blue men run back and forth and the police officers’ heads are on swivels.

One of the stockmen races up, hot and sweating in his oilskins, his face as crimson as a dawn sky before foul weather. ‘Can we use your quad bike to round up the flock?’

I can’t speak. I won’t speak.

He frowns as though I’m refusing to join in a game, then runs back to the others to lift his hands and shoulders in bewilderment.

They set off on foot into my back field, and the sheep run up the hill towards the wood but can’t get in.

Just like Mike’s last round-up, the lambs think it’s fun, and the older ones break off but when they reach the top and double back they aren’t skipping, they’re running for their lives.

Down on the road, a blue cloud of diesel smoke eddies across the sun as the white vans start up. Black-windowed, they turn into the lane and park along the verge near my gate. Men in jeans and open-necked shirts leap out and buzz round the vehicles. I see them dressing up in white suits. I hear laughter. I see them strapping black belts round their waists and now there are bulging holsters slung over their genitals and I wonder why they need to draw attention to their manhood.

More laughter, until they're all zipped up in white and presenting themselves for duty to Reed. His head and hands and fists and fingers are telling them things but they're not really looking at him.

Now he's leading them up the yard. Their holsters swing in time with their steps and when they draw near, not one of them looks at me.

Reed does. He's wearing his plain green eyes again and there's a muscle keeping time near his jaw. He says something about the man standing next to him who has a clipboard and a blue biro and I wonder what he's going to write.

'I suggest you go in the house,' Reed states.

I will not speak.

The policewoman takes my arm, gently pulls me sideways so Reed can open the shed door. I order my legs to follow the two white suits he takes in with him. The second is a big man, broad verging on fat. The sun streaming through a gap in the walls catches hairs on the back of his neck. Strange how some mousy hair glints auburn in the sun.

My shadows are so close I can feel their fear, especially the inspector's. He is so stiff he'll break if I touch him. Why don't they turn away, or are they mesmerised? I'm trying to work it out when the two white suits climb into Fatso's pen. Reed watches.

The big man reaches into his holster with one hand and into his pocket with the other then fits a sleek capsule into the top of the gun. I hear the policewoman gulp. I don't suppose she's ever seen what goes on inside the farms she's policed.

The other white suit grabs Fatso, who's still eating, and holds her steady. She's annoyed. She lifts her bad foreleg to stamp her indignation but keeps it aloft as though she's remembered it hurts.

They don't give her time to reconsider.

The thud of the captive bolt jerks through my bones. The ewe slumps and there's the gut-wrenching sound of the inspector losing his breakfast all over the straw.

Reed frowns across at him. 'Out!'

My shadows desert their posts. The policewoman pulls her boss out of the door as though she's got to be somewhere by yesterday. Reed must realise I couldn't move if my life depended on it because he ignores me and turns back to supervise the necessary killing of the other two thaives.

I don't know how I got outside the shed but I'm standing by the straining clanking hurdles that hold the rest of my flock. The sheep are there by magic. I didn't see or hear them come down off the field and only now are they bleating. Blue men and white men are lifting the lambs out, one by one, passing them into a separate pen where Reed is waiting with a hypodermic. He looks at me briefly then turns away to plunge the needle into his first victim but he's not broad enough to shield me from what he's doing. I've seen the effects of fatal injections all too often when I worked for Phil, that slow sinking of the head and flutter of the limbs as life left the bodies of old dogs and sick cats. Lambs do the same.

The police officers don't return for hours, eternities of thuds and bleats and cries and ewes calling for their lambs to their last breaths. And now there's a misshapen and bloody pile of fleeces and legs and noses. I'm watching over them.

Most of the blue and white men have gone. They holstered their guns, laughed as they loaded up their hurdles, and joked some more before they hightailed it out of the valley. The police are still here, the inspector and his female prop standing near the gate looking wan. There's an army sergeant and his squaddie too, talking to Reed. I catch Reed's eyes when he turns. Apart from the policewoman, he's still the only one who looks at me.

I must need that contact, for I watch him constantly, only moving my eyes away when the growl of another engine rumbles out of the village. It turns into the lane and trudges up, its clean yellow paint marred only by slashes of rust, bucket tucked under its chin, large tyres bouncing comically.

Masses of diesel horsepower push the loader through the gate, and I glimpse the driver.

He bounces too, amid a forest of wheels and knobs and levers, but he doesn't look at me, either. He has a job to do, an important job, a well-paid job. I wonder if he ever talks about his work.

More grinds and groans.

The bucket rears then lowers its head to forage along the concrete into my pile of sheep. It scoops and judders and eats at the edges then lifts its neck to disgorge them into the centre. In so few minutes, it makes a mountain out of a low mound and there is blood on the yard, lakes of it, and limbs too, torn off by the greedy monster then spat out and abandoned until it comes back for them.

There is nothing in me apart from silent tears and they are pouring out in such streams that I wonder why I'm not dry.

Yet more come, when Fatso and her cohorts are thrown out of the shed onto the heap, and when the few blue men left spray the mountain of my life with foul-smelling disinfectant then swill down my yard, yet more when they drape the heap in black plastic, and when Reed approaches me with something to sign and mumbles on about when the deliveries for the pyre should start.

In his green gaze, I have a vague memory of vowing to tear him apart, but I must have been in another world for I haven't the strength now to pull the wings off a midge.

'I've taken blood samples,' he says, 'and will let you know the results the minute they come through. Should be in a few days.'

I see those flecks in his eyes again, those fragments of humanity. I know he's a real vet.

He's staring intently at me now, and his mouth is opening slowly. He begins to speak.

'I'm sorry, Mrs Sumner, it was out of my hands.'

He shouldn't have said that.

I could have floated on this safe and flat calm sea of tears if he hadn't said that. I look down at the scarred and rough implements of my hands and see them flex and lift and curve.

The policewoman appears from nowhere to force my arms back. It doesn't hurt, though her grip is so tight my tendons and skin are stretched to tearing point.

'No,' Reed says to her, 'she didn't touch me, let her go.'

The policewoman escorts me across the yard instead, back to the inspector whose face is as green as Reed's eyes.

We stand together and watch everyone take off their white suits, hose down their boots and cars, then climb in and drive away. Reed doesn't look at me again before he leaves.

Now the inspector mumbles something about me not representing a threat to the peace any longer, so he's de-arresting me. He mumbles something else, as he walks unsteadily through the gate and closes it.

I stand perfectly still as they all drive away without a glimmer of a blue light, and I wonder what they'll do with the rest of their day. There's a breeze, the sort that feels like rustling silk on your skin. I can feel it in my hair too, sliding between every follicle.

They've tied a white board on the gate with string. I go to see what it says.

Infected Premises. Keep out.

Good. That means I'm alone. I can't cope with any more people.

CHAPTER EIGHTEEN

I suppose I'd better go in the house. There's nothing to do out here, now that my sheep are dead.

The phone's ringing when I get near but it's easy to ignore the clamour. I just have to pull down the shutters in my ears and get on with things. The sink's a mile high with mugs and plates and on the draining board is a frying pan with cold stiff strips of bacon embedded in solid fat. What am I supposed to do with it? I don't want to work it out so I'll sit down in my chair by the dead grate. There's a piece of paper on the arm. Reading it, I get a vague idea that some judge or other is ordering that sheep must be inspected, and culled if found infected. I can't remember what I've read the minute I turn away so I don't know why I bothered looking at it.

Leaning back, I close my eyes until the phone rings again. It's persistent, punching holes in my shutters, so I get up and wander into the hall then up the stairs, one enormously high step at a time. The phone stops when I'm halfway up but starts again the minute I'm lying on my bed. It's making my bedside table vibrate and the lamp wobble. I'm up again, trying to find somewhere, anywhere I can't hear the phone, and I'm halfway across the yard before I realise I could have pulled the phone plugs from the sockets but I'm too tired to go back.

I am so very tired.

I walk towards the stinking black shiny mountain then turn into the lambing shed. It's empty and quiet but it takes all my strength to slice open a new bale of straw and pull it apart to make my bed. I like the smell of straw. I like the smell of sheep in here. Curled up in my nest, I watch the light between the wall slats fade and turn black.

Sometime in the night, I wake to see a steady blue light lancing through the shed, but it can't be more police cars because their blue lights flicker.

The moon must be up. Moonlight is blue, not silvery – all those poets and songwriters are wrong.

I wake up again and again, and every time the blue beams have changed position. One of them is now shining into the fat thaive's pen. The stalks she left in the rack make shadows like a spider's legs.

I wonder where she is.

When I wake again, the moonlight's gone. The gaps are grey and I can hear distant voices.

'Julie,' calls a baritone. 'Julie! Where are you?'

I'm safe tucked in here. No one will come through the gate because of the notice. No one will find me. The phone won't ring in here. I can sleep.

Now I've got yellow beams jutting through the shed. The sun must be high, but it's too bright. The night's better.

'Julie!'

Lots of voices all saying the same thing – a tenor, the baritone's still there too, and a woman, but they're too far away to bother answering and anyway I need to sleep. I want to sleep for a long time and maybe when I wake up the world will have stopped revolving and I can float up into space and drift round the satellites. They don't have phones or voices.

But the noise hasn't stopped when I wake again. I know that because the squeak of the gate opening woke me and now there are running footsteps as well as the voices. They go past the shed and sound to be heading for the house. Then it goes quiet. Then they come out and start making their noise again.

One's coming too near the shed. I've got to be quick if I don't want to be found and I have to climb over the bale stack because I have no strength to make a cave in it. There's a narrow gap on the other side, and some loose straw. I lie down and pull it over me.

Just in time. Someone's outside the door.

'Oh, God,' the woman says, 'those are her sheep.'

The door crashes open.

'She's not here, Fi.'

'Sure? Look properly.'

Now the tenor starts again. 'I've searched all the outbuildings. Shall I go up to the wood?'

'Please, Jim. We must find her.'

Why must you find me, when you'll just make me do things? Please go away, all of you. Search the house and the outbuildings and the wood if you must, then leave me alone. I don't want to be fussed over. I don't want to talk. I don't want to eat or sit by my fire. I want to be nothing.

I realise eighty acres of wood and pasture and hedgerow are hard to search but it takes such a long time for them to reassemble in the yard and decide I'm not here. The woman's crying and it tugs at me a bit but I haven't any energy to look after her.

At last they go. The car coughs, starts, and grumbles into the distance. I stay in my narrow bed until it gets dark again.

The moon's not here tonight but I know every foot of this place. I could walk it blindfolded. Ignoring lights on across the valley, I creep out of the shed, along the wall, over to the house.

I'm thirsty.

Fumbling in the dark for a mug in the sink I knock a pile of plates over and the clatter hurts my head. But I find the tap and turn it. Water sprays everywhere.

Calm down, Julie. Do it slowly. There's time.

No, there isn't time. They'll be back. I know what voices do. Steady now, start again, feel for the mug's rim with one hand, find the tap's mouth with the other. Hold them together, now turn the handle. Turn slowly, hear the drips, turn more for a stream to fill it. Drink, open your throat, fill the mug again, drink more.

A bottle, I need a bottle. Find the cupboard where you keep fizzy drinks for the children, and empty it carefully down the sink or they'll be back snooping and working out why there are sticky pools all over the floor.

Steady, Julie, there's time.

The relief when I've got a plastic bottle full of water has me almost singing but I mustn't or they'll hear me. Quietly now, and get a loaf from the freezer. Stuff everything in a bag. Now find blankets. May nights can be cold.

I'm ready. I've been upstairs for blankets and draped them round my shoulders. One more thing then I'm off.

Back out into the yard to hug the shed wall then down to the gate and the Land Rover. There's an ancient tarpaulin in the back, one I use to lie on under the car. And the tow rope – I'll need that.

Got them. Don't look across the valley – the lights are watching eyes. If I don't look they won't see me.

The only way through to the back field is past the black shiny mountain. It stinks but I mustn't be sick. Hold your stomach but don't drop the tarp or you'll never find it again.

I'm through to the field. I must rest, just for a moment, find my breath. Up the hill now, one step at a time, push hard. Rest again, up again.

The wood rustles and hisses. It's alive but no phones ring, no voices intrude. There's my oak tree just inside, the one with horizontal branches too low for the tree's good. I've been meaning to lop them to stop the oak tearing itself apart in a gale but I haven't and I'm pleased because I want them for my home. I'll use that grey hour before dawn to scavenge some fallen boughs, and I'll make myself a tree house. Ben would laugh.

I don't want to think about Ben. Don't want to think about anything. Sleep now. Make a cocoon of blankets and the tarp and curl up.

Sleep.

Noises. Not voices. Engines.

Yellow diggers and loaders are down in the lane, and a big red excavator. More white suits. And yellow jackets with shiny white strips on their backs that glisten through this murky light.

They can't see me in my hiding place. I'm safe, and no one will come because the tenor voice searched up here yesterday. I'm free to sleep, or watch the men and the diggers.

Drink first. Then I'll go up the wood to see if I can fill my bottle from the spring. It's rained a lot, so there should be plenty. Coming back, I'll scout for branches to make my new home.

Back into bed now. I've seen some branches. I'll fetch them when I wake next. Another drink then snuggle down. The diggers' noise is a sort of music, and my eyes are heavy.

Now there's an army bloke at the bottom of the field below me and he's pointing at the grass and talking to a yellow suit. The diggers rumble through and start to shave off the turf so the excavator can dig properly. Its arm dips and digs and lifts and clanks, so sleep is out of the question. Never mind. Get those fallen branches and make a nest.

It doesn't take long to bridge the gap between two of the oak's sweeping limbs. A few turns of the rope and it's done, steady and safe, and now I've a good view of my back field.

The sun's high and they've dug quite a deep hole already. It's long and narrow like Ben's grave. Trucks have dumped piles of timber and coal and someone's emptied my Dutch barn of straw and hay – the bales lie like fallen dominoes.

I want to sleep for years but the noise won't let me. Still, I snatch time between the biggest clanks. Maybe at dusk they'll all go home.

They don't. It's dark and they're still working back and forth between the black mountain and the pyre and their headlight beams are searching the field. They can't find me though. I'd like them to stop now but on and on they go, back and forth, grinding and clanking. I get to spot the difference between them – one of the drivers rattles his bucket three times to empty it of sheep, not two like everyone else.

I must have slept again. I didn't see or hear them go but it's quiet and moonless, black down there. What's that though – a torch beam? Two beams. That means two people. Maybe they're the soprano and the baritone looking for me again. Keep your head down, Julie.

But there are flames flicking and flashing where the torch beams were. They dip and lift, dip and lift as they move across the field leaving more flames behind them. These are small but they're growing, reaching, joining together. Black stick legs run back and forth in front of the fiery wall and now the sky is a forest of flames. A black cloud boils above me.

The orange sky shines bright enough for the voices to see me, so I've covered my face in the blanket because I must keep hidden. Specks of bright light twinkle through the blanket weave. When I move they skip and hop and jump about, just like my lambs once did.

At dawn, I want to watch the flames but people are around still and machines are cleaning the yard. I must wait until they go.

They stay all day and more arrive the next day. That red car keeps coming up the lane, too – I've seen it before, lots of times, but the barn hides the gateway so I don't see the driver.

So very tired. Thirsty, too. I don't have the energy to go again to fill my bottle at the spring. And I need something sweet. The bread turns into sweet pap if I chew it long enough, but I get impatient, and can't get chocolate biscuits out of my head. Those velvety discs are waiting for me. Everything's gone quiet, so I'm going home to dive into the biscuit tin, submerge myself, coat my teeth in chocolate and drown in crumbs and sugar.

On the way home, the fire entices me towards it. Diggers came back at dusk to push in the edges of the fire and send clouds of sparks tumbling through the air like a swarm of fireflies. They're the souls of my sheep.

It's too warm by the fire. Only the centre's alight, more of a glow than flames, and the smoke has changed from black to white, curling wisps drifting up into the sky. I'd like to go up with them.

When I turn the corner of the shed, I see a light in my kitchen. How dare someone break in! Creeping along the house wall to look in the window I find the curtains are drawn.

Maybe it's a burglar.

He's rifling through my things and making my shoulder blades hurt, and the muscles over my jawbone. A harsh noise is pumping through my ears, too. I step towards the door, reach for the handle. Slowly, slowly, lean gently, open the door a whisker at a time so it doesn't squeak.

I get it open wide enough to see the sink but my stack of dirty dishes has gone. Everything's been washed, dried, and put away. I've never seen the draining board gleam like that. I didn't know burglars washed up.

I ease the door further open.

'Thank God, Julie,' a quiet voice says. 'We were…'

He doesn't finish because I crash the door back against the wall, just in case he's behind it. I miss. Phil steps into view.

'What the bloody hell are you doing here?'

'We were worried about you.'

'We? Who's we? And it's a funny time to be worried about me now, you – you bastard. Didn't you see the fire out there?

Maybe you thought I was getting rid of rubbish or something, but a fire that size needs more than a bit of rubbish.' I can't stop the words pouring out. 'And where were you when I *really needed you*? Patting some poor sod of a farmer on the back because you murdered his animals? I hope it made you feel better.'

I fling myself across the kitchen, yank a cupboard door open, find the tin, and ram a chocolate biscuit into my mouth. If I don't turn round, he might go.

'Julie, listen...'

'No, *you listen.*' I spin to face him, spraying crumbs. 'You betrayed me, Phil. You ignored me when I needed you most. You made some lame excuse about not being clean and *you walked away from me. Worse, you didn't come back.*'

'I couldn't...'

'Couldn't *what?* Find disinfectant and a nice clean white suit? You've done it before. You sat in here a few weeks ago when you weren't clean, so why couldn't you come in to see my thaive?'

The words must have dammed up while I was in the wood and I've got to let them all out or I'll explode in a cloud of biscuit crumbs. 'I wanted *you* to look at her, I needed *you* to tell me she didn't have foot and mouth. You'd have seen straight away that she didn't, but instead you let that incompetent, arrogant, officious bastard Reed bring his mob to *wipe me out. Why?*'

I don't want to hear his answer, his excuse, so I open another cupboard for beer. Water's not enough to put out the fire in my mouth. Beer's what I need, gallons of it. Flicking the tops off two bottles and still facing the wall, I down them one after the other.

He's quiet at last. Maybe he's gone.

He hasn't. He's slumped in one of the fireside chairs. How do I convince him that I don't want him here? Do I have to slice open his thick skull and shout into his brain that I never want to see him again and be reminded of his betrayal?

Now he's head in hands and sobbing. Rage soars up through my stomach and threatens to blow my head off.

'And don't try that with me,' I shout. 'There's enough misery in this place without a load of self-indulgent tears. Go home, Phil, now! I *don't want you here.*'

He stands up, takes a deep breath and tries to stare me out.

'You're out of your mind with grief, Julie,' he says softly. 'First Ben, now your sheep – it's too much. Let me help.'

I can't take this. I'd rather he yelled than tried to reason. At least then I'd have something to attack. And who does he think he is, telling me how I feel? How does he know what it's like not to have Ben. No one knows what Ben and I made together. No one knows what it's like to be half of something whole. No one.

'Get out before I throw you out,' I hiss.

Haggard, head bent, he walks out of the door, letting me go back to my chocolate biscuits and beer, but not before I've watched him drive towards the village. It must be late – there aren't any other headlights on the road – but I don't see his car come out on the other side of the village, the only headlights are climbing the lane to…Is he going to Fiona's?

Is he reporting in, and will they tell Carol and Jim as well, so everyone can invade my home again?

I don't want anyone, not even Ellie and Dan. I don't want to be reminded of any of the good old days of pantomimes and veterinary nursing and woodland management and Rayburns with their lower doors open for my boots. I will not be reminded. After all, if Jamie hadn't been so stupid as to defy the police at my gate, I wouldn't have been so worried for Fiona when Reed came. If she hadn't been on my mind, I'd have been able to scratch his fucking eyes out and feed them to my sheep. My sheep. Ben's sheep. They've gone.

The phone isn't ringing any more. I've yanked the plugs from their sockets and it's quiet again. I need peace. I need to work things out. I need to sort out the jumble in my mind, then sleep more and sort some more. First though, I've got to stop the voices coming in, so I use the night to reassemble the barbed wire cobweb round and over my gate. I've managed to chain it up again as well, though it took a long time to find another padlock. Then I pushed the Land Rover, flat tyres and all, back from where the police and army left it. I can't manage the trailer. It's too heavy even though the biscuits and beer have given me the strength to shift a mountain.

A mountain.

A mountain of sheep turned into a cloud of fireflies.

All the lights are out in the house and the darkness is comforting. I've lit a candle in the kitchen, just one, and I'm keeping the wick trimmed so the flame's tiny. No one will see its light even from the gate.

I've eaten all the biscuits and now I'm back on water. The beer gave me too much strength for my own good. I open the fridge to see what else I can eat and see someone's emptied out all my bits of food and filled it with packets and tubs and plates of cooked meat. There's even a pie. People have done this before, filled my fridge with food I couldn't stomach. I bet they filled my cake tins too. In the light from the open fridge, I'm finding tins in the cupboards and tearing their lids off. Just as I thought, bloody jam sponges and lemon curd tarts and apple turnovers. Flinging them across the kitchen helps, then trampling them into the floor. Why can't everyone leave me alone?

The fridge light is too bright.

Some interfering bugger will see.

I must shut the door, make it dark and safe again. Rushing to slam it, I see little jars of blood tucked in the door shelf.

Fatso and her cousins. I reach in, pull them out, cradle them against my chest. 'You're cold but it's all right. I'll warm you up.'

I go to my chair and curl up, my sheep in my hands. Fatso won't mind my callouses and split nails. She doesn't care about a thing except food. Maybe I'll fetch her some hay to nibble.

My boots are on fire.

I'm running so fast towards the broken red heap. There's black in there too, a tyre sticking up and it's turning, spinning, clicking. I've got to get there before it stops or I'll be lost.

'Save me,' someone calls from the heap.

Someone else is screaming. Me.

'I'm coming, I'm nearly there! Wait for me!'

I can see him now and he's climbing out, throwing crimson sheets of metal aside as though they were paper and grinning, smiling his welcome, the smile he gives me every morning when we wake, the one I get last thing at night before he gives in to sleep, the one I have with breakfast, dinner and tea, the one he flashes across the yard when I get home in the Land Rover from town, and the one he runs to give me when I come down from working in the wood.

'Julie, love, just in time,' he says clambering down the heap towards my open arms. He always says that, *just in time*, as though he hasn't been able to breathe without me.

He's down off the heap, and I'm so close. 'Ben,' I yell, flying towards him.

Scarlet and gold and orange surge between us and I can't see him for their blinding light.

I'm trying to swat it away, but it's too vast.

'Ben! Where are you?'

'I'm here, love,' he says behind.

I spin round and he says it again, this time to my left.

'I can't see you!'

'I'm here, love, right here,' say hundreds of voices at once. They're all round me, by my feet, round my head, diving under my outstretched arms and filling the air with swarming clouds.

'Ben,' I call, not loud enough.

He can't hear me for all the voices.

'Ben!'

Too faint. Yell, Julie, yell.

'*Ben*!'

It's only a whisper, and he can't hear me for the swarm.

'Save us,' the swarm cries in a myriad voices.

Ben's gone. All I have is this cloud of fireflies dipping and soaring and swooping round me.

'Save us.'

'I can't.' I slump to the ground, my cheek on the cool earth.

It's quiet and dark now. Even the fireflies have gone. I have nothing except the wet grass beneath me. But it's not grass, it's the chair cushion and it's soaked through.

'Ben.'

He's not here, Julie. He's dead, killed by a runaway tractor. He's never coming back and nor are your sheep. You are alone. You have nothing to care for and nothing to love.

'Stop it,' I moan.

No, I can't stop it. It's out of my hands.

It's dark and cold. I need a fire.

Hauling myself upright, I stumble out to the woodshed for an armful of logs. The grate's cold too, and stubborn, the paper damp and the sticks mutinous.

Light, you bastard, light, for God's sake! Can't you see I'm freezing?'

Calm down, then I'll ignite.

Forcing my hands to stop twitching, I coax the bloody fire into life, blowing into it when it hesitates, sitting back on my heels when it makes the smallest effort.

Now I can breathe again, watch the flames and sigh in the tiny warmth it's giving me. Then it rams into top gear and there's a wall of flame, just like the fire outside. There are fireflies too, tiny sparks in the soot on the fireback. Ben used to call them angels.

I need an angel. I want to bask in its holy light, feel its wings round me, listen to whatever rustling sounds it makes in my ears. But it's my arms that are round me and all I can hear are whispering moans. Rock me, hold me, make it go away.

CHAPTER NINETEEN

I don't know how long I've been rolling around in this squalor but I've heard the screeching brakes of the postman's van more than once, also a frequent cough from another vehicle that rings a bell in my brain but doesn't leave a message.

The world has gone on without me. The sun's kept on coming up, the rain's hissed down and the nights have kept me hidden, and this morning's sullen light has exposed the squalor I'm in. It's got to go. I've got to get things in order. I'll start with the kitchen, then tackle the mess in my mind.

Rubbing the pins and needles in my legs from huddling up to the fire for God knows how long, I see and smell my filthy jeans. How can I think properly with them round me?

But first – I need tea. Gallons of it.

Get the kettle on, find a mug, and the sugar. Toast, too – will sliced frozen bread toast? I want jam, as well. God, who left this mess on the floor? I almost skidded on what looks like the remains of fruit cake.

The kitchen looks better now. I've used most of my energy to sweep the floor but at least the cake crumbs have gone, the broken pastry, too. Now get the immersion heater on. Later I'll fill the magic machine and dump some powder in – my jeans and shirt will come out smelling sweeter, but I doubt a single wash will remove the ingrained grime.

It takes the rest of my strength to make tea and toast, but I manage to carry my feast to the fireside chair. Something digs into my thighs and I find the jars of blood. Sheep's blood. I put them on the table, on top of the piece of court paper, and resolve to dump the lot in the bin, but not until I've had my breakfast.

There's a bit of colour outside now.

Scarlet.

That means it'll rain later. Red sky in the morning, shepherd's warning, but I'm not a shepherd any more so it doesn't matter.

What does matter is the way my brain won't work properly. It's a mess. I can still add two and two together but can't think why I'd need to.

Better and better. I'm clean all over – skin, hair, clothes, the lot – and so is the house. I'm proud of my newly honed domestic skills. It all feels good. The washer's working overtime and the rubbish is about to leave the house forever. I've got a bin bag full to the brim ready to go outside but I'm not sure what's out there, or if I can face it.

There's only one way to find out.

Grab the door handle, don't stroke it, a big firm grasp like…like who? Like you.

It's easy when you remember how.

The light's too bright outside though it looks like rain, but a steady plod to the dustbin will have the job done in no time at all.

Noise. I turn too fast at the sound, and nearly fall over. Hanging on to the bin, I see the post van charging up the lane into a handbrake turn outside the gate. Bursting out, the postman dumps a wad of mail in the box. I stagger down to him.

'Morning,' he says, seeming eager for a chat, but I don't mind – I can practise using words on him.

He points at the barbed wire wrapped round the gate. 'Expecting an invasion?' He laughs merrily, pleased with his joke.

'I was,' I say carefully, 'but not any more.'

He's looking at the Land Rover now. 'All the air's gone to the top of your tyres.'

'You're new,' I say.

'Yup, been on this round a week – these lanes are fun.'

'I see you've learned to cope with turning in tight spaces.'

'It's the only way. Mind you, I've told my mates back in town not to buy second-hand post vans – they take some punishment on these rubbish road surfaces.' He grins and winks.

I try to smile back.

Talking to him helps words find their way out of me, and in the right order, and if he wants a smile, I'll try.

For him and only him. He's a stranger.

He's watching expectantly.

Maybe he wants tea and a chat at my kitchen table, the rural postman's perk, but I can't ask him. Not yet. Maybe tomorrow.

He gives a shrug and points at the box hanging on the fence near the gate. 'I've put tons of mail in there this week. You should collect it, or it might be pinched.'

I move towards it, and lift the lid. 'It'll be mostly junk.'

'Some look a bit important.'

I know what they'll be and they're not the least bit important.

'I'll look every day from now on,' I promise.

'Shall I hoot from the gate to remind you?'

'No, thanks – let's keep the countryside quiet.'

'Okey doke.' He breezes back to the van. 'See yer.'

Roaring down the lane, he leaves a month of screaming rubber on the tarmac at the crossroads. He also leaves me with the knowledge that I can talk, quite coherently. But though I'm back in gear, I know there's a hell of a lot more rubbish to clear out.

Where's the time gone to have such a backlog of post? Flipping through the pile, I home in on an OHMS from the Ministry. I knew it would be there. I also know what it will say. There are bills too, one postmarked June. Summer's arrived.

And hand delivered letters from my neighbours. Unable to phone, they've resurrected the ancient art of writing. I shrug and take the pile back to the house to put in the centre of the cleared table. I'll tackle it in a bit, after I've had a rest, after I've taken more dross out of my head. There was a germ of something in my head this morning, something shiny like a polished glass in a pile of dirty dishes, winking at me. I couldn't get to it for the rest, and I know I have to work through the pile before I can get hold of it properly, without dropping it. I don't want it chipped.

The washing finished, I drape it over the landing banister. Then I strip my bedding and bung that in the washer. I find clean sheets and make the bed. Too many pillows. Put some away. Tackle the bathroom, take those towels downstairs to join the queue for the washer, then rake out the grate. Don't need fires. I'm not cold any more now I've learned it's June.

And so to the letters.

Dear Julie, please get in touch. We're thinking of you every minute. Tons of hugs – Fiona and Jamie.

Dear Julie, says the next, *this is a picture I drew for you. Love from Ellie.*

She's drawn herself and Dan in their field with the geese and five goslings. Fiona's feeding the hens nearby, and Jamie's brandishing an axe in the doorway of one of the sheds. The shed where they kept the lambs is closed.

Dear Julie, says the next, *I don't know what to say except I'm thinking of you. Hope you feel strong enough to get in touch soon. We need to have a good chat. Love, Phil.*

No we don't, Phil.

Now for the Ministry.

Dear Mrs Sumner, I am pleased to inform you that the results of the tests carried out on your sheep returned negative. This means that your holding is no longer classified as an Infected Premises. Form D restrictions still apply. The disinfection of your buildings will take place as soon as a team is available. Yours sincerely, scrawl, scrawl, Regional Manager.

I knew it would say that.

Now I need air, lots of it, oxygen, neat if possible. I need it to fuel me, not steady me, and I'm going to tune my engine as fine as I can get it.

It's a week before I'm anywhere near fit, a week of patrolling my patch and filling my lungs with sweet summer air or rinsing the mire off in the rain. Walking through my fields strengthens me most. Long strides, skirting the bonfire of my living and the ashes of my dreams, backwards and forwards through leaping grass, or round and round, with my nose up and my mind working.

That bright germ in my head is more like a virus now, multiplying every day, leading me on. I'm nurturing it, feeding it with fresh air and sensible meals. I've even learned how to sleep.

The clean-up team have arrived and started devastating what's left of my farm, but I lock up the house and workshop before they arrive in the morning, and escape to my fields and the wood until they leave at five.

People hinder me. Noise does, too. And I know the world is poised to pour through the gate as soon as the farm's declared clean. When I'm stronger, I'll make the first advances, just so they know I'm back in command and something like the Julie they knew. That way, they'll breathe a sigh of relief and get on with their own lives instead of interfering in mine.

I'll have to be clever to do that, because I can't remember the old Julie. How could I? If I was a tree and someone cut me down, how could I be the same? Mind you, a felled tree looks much the same as it did growing, except it's on a different plane.

But I've got to try to fool them if I want to be left alone to work with my virus. I must give it an uncluttered environment to breed perfect offspring.

I love every minute in the wood, away from the din of diggers and the shouts and laughter of men. It's safe there, a church-like refuge where I can pause for thought under the dark green canopy of summer leaves or stand and wonder at the piebald light streaming down. I've always liked it. Ben teased me when I took it on as my own special project, told me that farmers' wives tended to prefer farm kitchens to overgrown woods.

The undergrowth is rampant. There's a tangle of searching brambles and hazel shoots have sprouted wherever I look, tall thin whips soaring towards the light. The wood's never been so bad but then I haven't had time. A lot's gone on since the turn of the year when Ben died in the ruins of the tractor.

The tractor. Something cold trickles through my veins when I think of the crimson monster that took my life when it took Ben's.

I wonder in which direction the virus will point me for retribution – the tractor dealer? Or the man on the assembly line, a Monday or Friday worker who didn't bother to tighten a nut or connect something properly before the tractor rolled out of the factory then murderously out of control down my back field?

So, virus, what's it to be?

Come on, tell me.

You've had plenty of time to work things out, and I don't want our quest for justice to last forever. I don't want to spend years tracking down the individuals responsible for destroying my life – true eye for eye justice must be swift as well as cold and hard.

Justice – a pretty word, a euphemism for revenge, and my revenge won't be a dish eaten cold. Mine will be frozen – air-dried and oxygen-hardened with razor-edged shards of ice lurking in its depths to clutch and tear out my enemies' throats better than any mediaeval instrument of torture.

Home now.

Enough thinking for today.

The men have gone, so I'll give the virus a bit of space to mull, and go home to eat and sleep.

Time to let the world back in.

'Fiona, it's me.'

I hear a gasp. 'Oh, *Julie*. Thank God. How are you?'

'Fine – the bruises are fading.'

'Bruises? God almighty, you've had more than a bruise.'

'So have you.'

Silence. She's thinking, but I'm ready.

'Can I come over, Julie – just me?'

'After the clean-up team goes at five. I'll put the kettle on.'

Masterly stroke that, to say things in the same way I always did. She must be fooled. And if I succeed with Fiona, the rest of my friends and neighbours will be a doddle. I don't want them interfering, and that's what friends do – meddle, think they know best, dole out advice, fill your cupboards with food, cloud your vision, or bung you up with their problems. If I'm going to make a good job of removing the squalid dregs of this world, I need to be unhindered by friends.

Another masterly stroke coming up. 'Better buy some milk on the way over,' I say, 'unless you want black tea.'

'Good as done.' She sounds animated now. 'Anything else?'

'Chocolate digestives would be nice.'

Smooth the way, Julie. Give her nothing to worry about.

She arrives just as the last man leaves.

A deep breath now, then I open the door and walk down to the gate. She leans on it, watching my every step.

'Hello there,' I say, trying a smile.

She's in like a shot, rushing to fling her arms round my waist and tuck her head under my chin. I smell her clean hair.

Now she stands back and looks into my eyes with that steady grey gaze that used to read my soul. Not today, though. I've got a barrier up, one she can't penetrate. She must not see the virus.

She's not frowning, so the barrier's doing it's job. Good.

'Julie…' She flounders. I don't recall her doing that before.

'Come on – a cuppa's the first thing.' I head for the house. 'Sit outside, shall we? Best to enjoy the sun while it's shining.'

I lead her to two rusty old folding chairs I've unearthed and positioned outside the kitchen door so we can look at the valley. I don't want to face her, nor do I want her to see my clean house.

After sitting her down, I fetch the tray, set it on a rickety table, and pour two mugs.

'How's Jamie?'

'The same.'

'That means fighting a cause, or engrossed in his wood?'

She laughs, and it's forced. 'Well, he's… okay.'

So his will to fight has gone. Not surprising really, but he lost only two sheep. I lost hundreds, and Ben.

'How are the children?'

She flashes me a look and sets her chin. 'All right, I think. Dan's obsessed with the goslings – they've helped take his mind off the lambs. But Ellie…' She frowns. 'Ellie's hard to fathom. There's something she won't share.'

Good for Ellie, I think. Girl after my own heart. 'Ellie's a bright child,' I say. 'She's seen a few too many horrors this year, and she's bright enough to work out what really happened.'

Fiona agrees. 'But I've never known her not want to talk things through with me or Jamie, and…and she withdraws from all adults now. Teachers, Sue in the shop, Jamie's customers – almost as though she mistrusts everyone.'

'Do you blame her?'

Such anguish fills Fiona's face that I'm in danger of dropping my barriers and inviting her into my thoughts. I must not. I need every scrap of energy to see my own cause through.

'Give her time,' I say, reaching for a platitude.

I turn away to watch the valley but I can feel her gaze, imagine her brow creasing. She's not stupid. She knows I've changed. Maybe she knows that, like Ellie, I don't trust a single solitary soul. But unlike Ellie, whose mistrust will fade with time, I will never trust again, especially any kind of authority. I'd believed in the police, and local and national government bodies who professed to be guarding my interests. I took it for granted they were on my side. Now they've shown they care nothing for me or my friends and neighbours. They rode through our lives with as much intelligence as a tractor and without the sensitivity of a hammer. They destroyed our trust, our security, and our respect, and I will bring them to justice.

Fiona interprets my silence as a signal that I've had enough company for one day. She gets up to go, and I don't stop her.

'Come and see us soon,' she says at the gate.

'Of course, 'I lie.

It's after she's driven away in her coughing Marina that I think of Jamie-style crusades and remember one of mine, the one before the mob came back to the valley.

Curious about it, I search the kitchen for my old battle book and find it fallen behind the dresser, probably swept there in one of my tidying sessions.

Reading through, I wonder who wrote it.

What a useless waste of time that was.

Not one of the people I attacked by mail answered. I didn't get a single comment or an excuse, not even a reassurance that my letter was receiving attention. No one took any interest in the ravings of a distraught female and not a single reporter took up my cause. It was a total waste of effort.

But though Jamie's probably trying to forget the lot of them, I won't forget and I have no one to consider – no husband or children, not even my sheep. Every scrap of time and energy I can muster can be used to fight this battle ruthlessly and totally.

And I will win.

I walk over to the waste basket and dump the book. I don't need contacts any more.

I've spent the last week working up in the wood. I'm in training, toning up my body with hard physical work and honing my mind to work as automatically and efficiently as my hands.

In just five days I cleared a wide path through the brambles. Now I'm working out from the path into the trees, dealing with all the timber I felled before Ben's death brought me to a halt. I'm sawing it all up into four-foot cords and stacking them in neat piles at the side of the path to dry off. All the small stuff and the brash left I'm building into huge piles for burning, but not now – the lush leaf growth of June is too vibrant to scorch and spoil with a blazing bonfire.

Bonfires.

Don't think about bonfires.

Think of nothing but what you're going to do.

Order your body to work and your mind to concentrate on the job in hand. Saw, lift, drag and stack and don't stop until this section's clear.

It's light enough to work every day from five in the morning until gone nine in the evening.

I take food and water up there with me to take at regular intervals, but I never rest for too long. I must work. Another week and I'll not only have the lot done, but I'll be at a peak of fitness in mind and body.

Working up here not only keeps me away from the men and their noise but also from my neighbours.

In the days after Fiona's visit, they trooped to the gate and I let them all in.

They brought their worried glances and their tentative observations that I'm looking a bit peaky, and did I want any more cooking done? I can't deal with it. I know they mean well but the social niceties of life sap my resolve and my strength. So does the way they shove the subject of dead animals and brutal officials under the carpet. If that's how they want to be then fine and I don't want to talk about it anyway. Action's what's needed, not hushed whispers about how suicidal Jack has become or how ill Carol is, or the endless ruminating on Mike and will he ever come home and maybe it's time he retired, poor old chap.

The wood calms me.

Working hard for long hours clears my mind of rubbish and brash, and by the time I'm through to the lane at the top my virus has sorted out one of the problems: how to track down all the individuals responsible for the killing of Ben and me and our community. Most of them are anonymous – from the idle tractor mechanic to the slaughtermen who laughed too much, from the police officers in their shiny urban shoes to all those bureaucrats straightening paper clips instead of returning my calls, and from the disinterested media and brain-dead digger drivers to the army personnel blindly following orders. I couldn't track them all down inside a year, because they're skulking behind a towering shield of anonymity.

And even if I knew or remembered their names, like the official who inspected Mike's farm, they're long gone, swallowed up by time and protected by their leaders who've moved them on.

Apart from John Reed.

He walked all over me. He destroyed me, and he subverted all trace of any decency and principle he had in order to destroy me. He will stand for them all.

So, I have one quarry. And I know how to find him.

CHAPTER TWENTY

First I have to clean up the Land Rover. It's the only vehicle I've got and it's going to town so it has to be clean to blend into an urban environment. Clean means anonymous. Maybe there'll come a time when I have to hire a car, an ordinary vehicle, a middle-range boring grey job that no one will notice, but for now the Land Rover will do.

First, the engine, a job I love. Filthy but rewarding when it ends up as finely tuned and oiled and greased as my plans. Next, I strip it down to its bones inside, turf out all the rubbish – the odd lengths of baler twine and empty feed sacks, the brochures and receipts and leaflets collected from various farm suppliers and thrown in the back, the rest of the grubby litter of sweet wrappers and empty water bottles, the dead insects and cobwebs, even the spare fuel can. It must not look like a farmer's vehicle.

So every day at dawn, it's down on my knees in the back with a bin bag for the rubbish then a hand-brush to root out the tiniest scrap. Finding hairs from Ben's old dog, I realise that the vehicle hasn't been cleaned out for years and part of me regrets removing all trace of our life. But no sentiment's allowed, just bucket after bucket of hot soapy water to scrub it all down inside and out, then a chammy leather on the windows, and even a buff up all over with a clean cloth.

It takes almost as long to clean it up as it took to clear the wood but I need constant activity to keep my mind in the right gear, and when I start the Land Rover up to take it for a spin, the way the engine starts and the gears change leave me grinning with pleasure. Ben would be proud of me.

Now it's my turn. Hair first. Shear off the mess of wiry spring growth down to a couple of inches. Good job I always hated hairdressers and taught myself to clip it evenly all over. It stands up a bit but water and a comb sort that out. Now my body. A good scrub and a levelling of split and broken nails works wonders. Clothes – clean jeans, an ironed shirt too, the newest I've got with all the buttons still anchored. Wearing boots most of the time except in bed, shoes are a problem until I unearth a sensible pair of slip-ons I used to wear at the practice.

God, I look different! Unrecognisable.

Now for town.

The library's cool on a scorching hot day. The reference section is as quiet as my wood apart from the whisper of turning pages and the occasional hum of the photocopier. I walk calmly down the aisles of books – don't clump, lift your feet, you're not in the fields now – to the medical section to scan the shelves for the Register of Veterinary Surgeons.

There's a free booth for me, a little island with a table and a pool of light ready for the tome. Flip through to R, God I've forgotten the alphabet. Think brain, think.

Got it. Got them. There are too many. John, find the Johns, or what if he's Michael John or Thomas John Gerald? I close my eyes and try to recall his identity card. Were there any other initials? I can't remember. Take a deep breath. Now start at the top of the Reeds, right from the Adrians and Alans and Andrews. Slow down, any name including a John will do so just make a list. I've left my pencil in the Land Rover, no, it's in your shirt pocket. For Christ's sake, Julie, calm down.

My eyes want to race down the page because my stupid brain thinks the John Reed with green eyes and no ethics will leap from the mess of words. It won't. Entries for bastards aren't highlighted.

Half an hour later, I have a long list of Reeds with John in their forenames. Why couldn't he have been baptised Archibald Winterspoon and solve most of my problems?

Now I have to work out how old they all are from the date they qualified, then think hard about how old my Reed was. My age? Younger? Trying to visualise him brings me so much pain and so many arrows from his green murderous eyes that I just make a guess – forty-odd.

I've ended up with five addresses and their phone numbers. Four of them are listed under their practice addresses. One address isn't a practice so I assume it's his home. It's in Wolverhampton so he's the nearest, but why isn't he part of a practice? My John Reed was too young to be retired and he had no trace of a tan so hadn't just returned from abroad. He's a Temporary Veterinary Inspector too so he'll be an ordinary vet, not working full-time for the State. So this Wolverhampton Reed must be in admin or research. But he's first to check. The others are too far away in Devon, Ayrshire, Derbyshire and Kent and I need action now.

I go back to the Land Rover and take a bite from the loaf I brought with me before heading for the bypass to head east for Wolverhampton.

I'm well prepared for a few nights away, with a bag of clean clothes in the back, a pile of blankets and a duvet to make a nest in at night, tons of bottled water and bread. I don't need more than that. I've got all the time in the world and no ties at home to keep me there. And I'll find him.

There's something about the open road, a sort of freedom, a lifting of one's head from the trough. I want to shout 'poop, poop,' Toad-style, or wave and smile at the drivers who overtake me on the M54. Most drivers overtake – the Land Rover's not used to their speed, though it did use its welly after that prat undercut me. I whipped past, pulled in sharply, terrified him. Put him in his place. No silly cake tin on wheels dares argue with the rigid steel chassis of a Land Rover.

Wolverhampton's awful, queues of cars at every roundabout. I pull off one, find a newsagent, and buy an A to Z. Fifteen minutes later, I park in Reed's leafy street, a few houses up from his; with a full view of the stretch between his gate and the front door.

I watch and wait.

An hour later, an elderly man raps on my window.

'You've been parked a long time. We have a Neighbourhood Watch round here, you know.'

'I beg your pardon,' I say with my best smile, 'but I'm resting after a long journey.' I look round. 'You have a lovely street.'

'And we want to keep it safe.'

'I'm sure you do. I'll go soon, don't worry.'

He purses his lips. 'You can't be too careful these days.'

'You don't need to worry about me,'I smile, 'and it's daylight. I'm just a woman, and I have no jemmy with me. Is that all right?'

He nods, relaxes, walks away. I watch him go into a house.

Another prat. How many more am I going to meet? But I know I've buggered my stake-out. In a quiet residential street, the Land Rover stands out like a blue plaster on a baker's floury hand. I'll have to park somewhere else and come back on foot.

I drive off, find a supermarket carpark half a mile away, then walk back to the corner where there's a bus shelter and a bench. Reed's gate is visible from here, so I skulk for an hour until schoolchildren alight and give me funny looks as though they know there isn't another bus today.

I had no idea how hard it was to fade into the background.

And why am I trying to? Why don't I march down the road, hammer on Reed's door and demand satisfaction? Wimp, Julie.

I walk away, turn right down a parallel street to Reed's, then right again through an alley festooned with back garden greenery, and end up bang opposite the windows of the Neighbourhood Watch king. A quick spin has me retracing my steps.

This is ridiculous. If I hang around any longer I'll be arrested again, and what the hell use is that?

Think, think hard. The phone. Call him, or his wife, and do a cold sell of some veterinary aid or car insurance, even a nice stretch of double glazing.

The phone box is clean, almost sterile.

'Yes?'

A man. Is it Reed?

'My name is Susan Green and I work for Gallup Poll. I wonder if you have time to complete a short survey? Your name will then go into a prize draw, and you may…'

'No, thank you.' The phone slams down.

Was it him? God knows.

And if it was, why is he at home and not out killing sheep?

Maybe TVIs have days off, now the main surge of the epidemic is over.

I've done my homework. I've listened to the radio this week. Only the remote regions of Wales and Scotland are being annihilated now and the government's pleased the daily outbreaks are decreasing. Any fool knows that if you remove half the nation's stock the incidence of disease is bound to lessen.

Why do the public accept such drivel and lies? And why does the media promote it? I don't understand the world.

I go back to the Land Rover to shut it out.

I have to move at eight when the supermarket closes, and still it isn't dusk. Bloody summer. It won't be properly dark until ten, so I daren't snoop until then. I set off back to the ring road and cruise round it. Round and round I go until nine-thirty, then I make my way back to Reed's area to park in a similar road, one with fewer houses so hopefully fewer security vigilantes. I'm not three yards from the Land Rover when someone stops me with a shout.

'You can't park there.' He's indistinct in the fading light, but his indignation shines across the road.

'Why not?'

'This is a narrow road and my car hasn't got a good lock. With an enormous vehicle like yours opposite my gate, I won't be able to swing into my drive.'

Beyond him in the drive is a average-sized family saloon.

'But you're already in,' I point out, holding on to my patience even though it's in danger of pinging out of my grasp. I could squash this fool and his car quite cheerfully.

'I might want to go out, and I'll need to make the same swing only in reverse, if you see what I mean. A monster like yours in the way won't let me.'

Breathe, Julie, and breathe again.

'Okay,' I say, traipsing back to a vehicle that assumes more enormous proportions by the minute. Anyone would think it was a forty-ton artic.

Ludicrous. All I've achieved is an interference in suburban rights of way and meetings with a few angry residents. There's nowhere to park and nowhere to camp without someone banging on the window to complain or report me to the police for loitering.

But where do I go? Home? No. Maybe I'll dump this Reed and head for the one in Devon, and when I've been hounded out of the south-west by an army of resident zealots, go on to the one in Kent. Would rural people do this? Would I hammer on the windows of a car parked where it shouldn't be? In my present mood I'd haul the driver out and beat his brains into the verge.

The M5 it is then.

The Land Rover likes trolling along at a steady sixty, sixty-five, mostly in the inside lane, and it allows my mind to work on plans for the next Reed address. This one's a veterinary practice at Totnes but I can't imagine why a Devon Reed would work temporarily in my area, so far off his patch. Did he need money? Was the practice in financial straits so he needed an extra job? But Devon got foot and mouth too, so why did he leave it, unless the Ministry insisted on complete anonymity by using vets from other areas? If they trawled the Continent and the Antipodes for extra vets to meet the crisis, why not Devon?

Soon after midnight, I'm already near Bristol.

If I go on like this, I'll reach Totnes before dawn, with nothing to do for hours except loiter and have my windows rapped on. I pull off into a motorway service area and note how full the carpark is. It must be the start of the annual rush for the south coast but I'm pleased they stopped here. I can hide in a crowd. Even the Land Rover doesn't loom too much with all these caravans and camper vans and immaculate 4x4 family wagons.

Food? Maybe, then back to the Land Rover for a bit of rest.

I lock it up, and march into the living hell of the cafeteria.

Inside five minutes, I can't bear the noise and the twanging tills. Doesn't the world ever shut up?

Sod food.

I lunge for the carpark and the peace of my own territory.

The Land Rover feels like home but the noise is too demanding, a continual drone interspersed with loud music and shouts and banging car doors. I reach for the ignition then roar round to the trucker's park where I become a tiny island in a sea of articulated giants with curtains pulled across their windscreens. I haven't got curtains but these drivers won't disturb me. Like me, they've got a job to do tomorrow and they need their rest. Settling down in the back, I pull my duvet round me. It smells of Ben. He and earthy sheep-tinged whiffs close round me to keep me safe.

It's him. He's in a green suit this time, not white, and it's the same colour as his eyes. He turns as I approach, and I get the full blast of his apple-green gaze.

'What the hell are you doing here?' His voice is harsh with authority. 'Clear off!'

'Mr Reed, I need you to come and look at my sick sheep. Please follow me.'

His eyes soften to aquamarine, and he obeys. I'm careful not to go too fast to keep him in the rear view mirror, and I lead him up, up, up into the hills, always careful not to lose him, not to go too fast or turn off too quickly. Then I lead him down a muddy lane, hoping his Audi has the weight to keep going. Funny how a lot of vets have Audis.

'I never had an Audi,' Phil says in my ear.

My head spins round to look at him. When did he get in?

'Any old estate car does for a vet,' he mumbles. 'Shame to spoil a posh car on these rubbish lanes.'

'What are you doing in my car?'

'Hitching,' he states. 'Got to get there by tomorrow – lots of sheep to kill.'

I stand on the brakes. 'Get out.'

'Julie, please!'

'Stop whining. Just get out.'

He's gone, but so is the Audi. Bloody hell, I've lost it. Damn you, Phil.

Someone bangs on the window. 'Hey, you!'

I ignore it and try to drive away, but the voice clings on. I try a sharp turn to shake it off but it won't let go. And I can't see where I'm going, can't see for that red light in my eyes. And what's that grinding of metal and hissing that's piercing my eardrums?

Bang, bang, bang on the window. 'Hey, you – don't you know this is a lorry park only?'

Struggling out of my dream and the duvet, I scramble into the front of the Land Rover to see a head framed in the side window.

I wind it down.

'Taking a risk, aren't you? You're too small to be in here,' he says, pointing at a long truck heading for the slip road. 'That artic only just missed you. If I hadn't stopped him reversing so fast, he would have driven right over you.'

'Pardon?'

'Wake up, love.' He has a sort of smile on his face now.

'You mean I can't park here, either?'

'Not a good idea.'

I don't believe this – he's leering.

'Fancy a cuppa? I've got all mod cons in my cab.'

'No, thanks, I've got a job to do. Got to get there – now.'

'What about a bite in the café?'

'I said no thanks.' I reach for the ignition, start up, and head for the slip road. But it's not until I'm back on the motorway that I see it's only four. It means I'll be at Totnes between six and seven, and that means I'll have another wait of two hours in broad daylight with the world and his driver constantly moving me on.

I pull off at the next services area instead, this time losing myself between a camper van and a Transit in the main carpark. I watch the world, and wait.

After reaching Totnes and locating the practice, I park by a row of small shops then walk back to note three marked-off spaces for vets in the practice carpark. They're empty. Good. I timed it right. Walking on to a bus stop, I lounge against the wall to watch the carpark and wait with the few people already there. A bus comes and two people get on. Another bus and the rest get on. More people arrive and leave but I'm invisible in their sleepy eyes.

At half past eight, a battered hatchback arrives to park in one of the vet bays and a woman gets out. She's likely the trainee, or a junior partner. At twenty to nine, a Volvo disgorges another woman. At five to nine, an Audi cruises in. The senior partner. Reed. The door opens and I see a foot touch the ground but then the driver's leaning back in for something and it seems like hours before he gets out.

He's too old.

Kent, here I come.

By the time I reach Exeter, the thought of the interminable stretches of motorway to Kent makes me feel ill. How reps cover all those miles, day in and day out, I don't know. They must be able to turn off their brains. I can't.

I turn off the bypass, planning to follow the coast road even if it will be slower. The Land Rover doesn't like high-speed cruises, and neither do I. We both work best in short intensive bursts, especially in a low and powerful gear.

It takes the rest of the day to get to Kent, hours and hours of queuing at roadworks and roundabouts and trawling round ring-roads and bypasses.

I have to stop.

I can't concentrate, nor can I understand why I'm in this unholy rush to get to Ashford – it's already eight in the evening so the practice will be long closed. A moment ago I even longed for home. Maybe I should go back.

What for?

But how did I get here?

Diesel, that's why. The tank's nearly empty. So is my mind. Unlock the cap, grab the pump handle and squeeze the grip. Go on, you can do it.

No, I can't, my head's swimming. I'm dog tired, desperate for sleep, dreamless sleep, but I know I'll either dive into a vivid nightmare or lie wide awake with my mind still in four-wheel drive. But I've got the sleeping tablets the doctor gave me when Ben died. One or even two of those should knock me out enough for my blasted body to gather some strength.

Get a grip.

The next minute I'm paying, handing over notes, trying not to look at the cashier. Her gaze is like headlights on full beam.

'Okay, love?'

I nod.

'Sure? You look a bit wobbly.'

'I'm fine.'

I grab the change and stumble towards the door.

'Don't drive if you don't feel good,' she calls to me. 'Pull your car over on that space beyond the air pump and take it easy a bit. You don't want to…'

Thank God, the door shuts on her voice.

I can see the Land Rover quivering in the distance and I must get there. It's the only safe place I've got. Climb in, start it up, clutch in, forward gear then off.

I can't do it. My arms and legs aren't listening. There's the air pump – head for that, go on, you can do it. No, yes, I can.

What's that infernal din?

'Are you okay?'

It's the cashier banging on the window.

'Shall I phone for a doctor?'

'No!' Is that me shouting? 'No,' I say, forcing my voice down, 'I just need to rest a bit.'

'I'll get you a cup of tea.'

'I don't need…'

'It's no trouble.' She's gone, but I can't run away from her. My legs don't work.

Now she's back, tapping on the window. Making a huge effort, I wind it down and reach for the mug she's holding up.

'I've seen it all before,' she says. 'You've been behind the wheel too long.' She points down the road. 'There's a pub down there with a motel thingy at the side – it's not expensive.' She looks hard at me again. 'Take my advice and book in for tonight or you'll end up being one of the accident statistics.'

The drink's warming me up, seeping into my brain and helping it work. 'This tea's good,' I say carefully.

'Tons of sugar in it,' she laughs. 'Best thing for the battle weary, and that's what driving is these days, a battle.'

'Thanks.'

'You're very welcome.' She leans against the Land Rover as though she's settling down for a good long chat. I gulp at the tea, needing its energy to help me escape from her. I can't cope with idle conversation – I've got a job to do.

What job?

Crawling away from the petrol station, I know I've got to take her advice. But why am I like this? A bit of driving and I'm a wreck, needing somewhere to hide from window-rapping fingers.

The motel thingy cruises up on my left and the Land Rover takes over. Before I can think properly, I'm staggering into reception and asking for a room.

The young receptionist doesn't look up. 'Have you booked?'

'No, sorry.'

She examines a register, runs her long blue pearl nail down a fuzz of print, looks up, eyes focusing beyond me. Turning, I see no one.

‘You’re lucky,’ she sighs. ‘This is the busy season, you know, and it’s always advisable to book ahead.’

She turns to pluck a key from a board. ‘Number Six.’

I stagger out into the carpark and somehow find a door with a six on it.

The key’s stiff but I’m in, leaning back on the door with my eyes closed and the world shut out, at last.

CHAPTER TWENTY-ONE

How long have I slept? Hours, days?

This ground is soft and warm and dry so I'm not sleeping outside, or am I? It's too dark to see but I can hear traffic.

Beams of light arch through a window, searching for me – please God, don't let anyone rap.

In the next set of lights I see a room. I'm on a bed, and there's a wardrobe and chest of drawers. Dead television screen, too.

Go back to sleep. Someone bangs again. Please go away.

They don't.

It's light, but no one is at the window.

'Hello,' a woman calls through the door. 'May I come in?'

Why does everyone insist on talking to me? I can't face them, but she'll never go away if I don't tell her to.

My legs are so heavy I have to push them off the bed and order them to walk to the door.

'Sorry to disturb you,' says a zealous face, 'but I need to clean the room.'

'Why?'

She frowns.

'It's gone eleven. You should be out by now.'

'I can't, I'm not…I need to stay.'

She's staring at me so hard I bet she can see right through me.

'You don't look too good.'

'Can't drive any more.'

She thinks a moment, head on one side. 'Look, love…'

Please don't call me love. Only Ben does that.

'…go along to reception and book another night. I'll give the room a quick tidy while you're gone.'

'But it's full up – the receptionist said…'

She leans forward.

'Take no notice of that jumped up little tart – they hardly have anyone staying since the travel stop was built on the Ashford ring road. You could have the run of the place if you wanted.'

‘Right, I’ll…’

‘Go on – she won’t bite!’

The daylight is blinding. I step outside, and my feet remember what they’re supposed to do.

It takes a lot of courage to enter the reception area – she’s bound to shout at me for not booking ahead.

Then it takes hours to pay for another night, and hundreds of words to convince the receptionist that I’m not ill, just exhausted.

At last I’m free. Halfway back to the room, I meet the cleaner.

‘Didn’t need doing, your room,’ she says with an approving smile. ‘Shame more people aren’t like you. You should see some of the tips I have to deal with – can’t understand how anyone wants to live in a mess. Still…’ She rambles on and on, and I’ll fall if she doesn’t let me back to bed.

‘See you tomorrow,’ she says at last, wheeling her bristling trolley away. I’ve only taken two steps before she shouts. ‘If there’s anything you want, just yell. Sandy’s the name.’

I turn to wave my thanks, then head for Number Six and bed.

I didn’t take a sleeper last night so dreams woke me, awful dreams in full technicolour, and I’m floundering when I wake, miserable to find the world’s still there. Maybe one day when I open my eyes, it won’t be. I’d like that, to be free, away with the fireflies who’ll help me find Ben behind some distant cloud and he’ll smile that smile and call me love.

It must be the small hours – not many headlights interrupt the dark. Tea, I need more tea. I can’t get enough. Must ask her, what was her name – Sandy – for more milk.

These piddling pots don’t cool the tea enough to gulp it down.

The sugar’s all gone, too.

Into bed, now. Make the hours pass.

She’s back, I can hear her trolley, but I’m ready for her this time. I’ve been up since first light watching television. I can’t remember what I’ve watched but it makes the hours go past.

I must get to the door before she raps on it.

‘You’re looking better,’ she says, head like a bird again.

‘Can you leave me more milk,’ I say, and the flow of words surprises me. ‘I’m drinking a lot of tea.’

'Course, my love.' She comes in and looks round the room. 'Holed up, are you?'

'Pardon?'

'I know what it's like, that need to hide. Can't do it myself – too many people depend on me, but I expect it's done you good. Mind you...'

She's off again, wandering through miles of words and I can't keep up even though the world's in some sort of order this morning. After about ten minutes, she pauses in her talking and spraying and wiping everything in sight. 'You could do with a little dog like my Merry,' she says. 'She listens to every word I say a darn sight better than my husband does, and dogs have a way of twining a lead round you and dragging you out of yourself. Merry does that – don't know what I'd do without her. Even comes with me to work and sits in the car waiting for me. People don't look after you like that.'

She's right. I remember how much Ben's old dog meant to him, and how I mourned it, like any other dog brought into the surgery too ill for treatment.

And isn't that why I chose veterinary nursing, to help every lame duck that waddled past? I should have a dog now, not for company or to love me for everything I've loved is dead, but to help me find Reed. A dog would get me into the practices without me having to spy on parking bays.

'I'd like to see her,' I say.

She beams with pleasure. 'Just let me finish your room then we'll go and take her round the garden behind the pub. 'She likes to take a break about this time.'

The dog, a small honey-coloured spaniel, wags at me, so I fondle its ear.

'She likes you,' Sandy says.

It mustn't like me too much, for its own safety.

She clips a lead on the dog's collar then we set off at a rate towards the garden. Every bush is examined, every plant, every tree with the serious intent of a pedigree born to seek.

'She's very pretty,' I say, and give her an elaborate account of some of the dogs I met in my work.

She's curious now. 'You worked for a dog rescue service?'

'Yes,' I lie.

'I can't bear to think about people chucking their pets out when they get tired of them,' she says, her face creased in anguish. 'I bet you wanted to take the poor little strays home.'

'Some of them were too big but I adopted one, an odd-shaped mongrel that no one else wanted.'

'A bit like my husband,' she says with a grim laugh. 'I wish someone would adopt him!'

She shouldn't joke about getting rid of husbands.

'What happened to your dog?'

She hasn't noticed the ice in my eyes. 'He died in January.'

'Oh.'

I can feel her eyes on me as we walk round the garden again.

She touches my arm and hands me the lead. 'Here, you take Merry for a bit. It'll help you feel better about your poor old dog.'

I take the lead and walk on briskly, skipping a bit to make the dog dance. Within five minutes, I've convinced Sandy that Merry loves me.

I've been here almost a week and I've taken Merry out for walks every morning while Sandy's been cleaning, but it's time to get back on the road and head east into Kent. I've got my brain back – thoughts germinate and grow and I can at least carry on a conversation with Sandy. She has a way of prising information out of me like a winkling thrush with a snail, and though I haven't told her any details, she knows my life has fallen apart. Maybe she thinks I'm on the run from a broken marriage or something, and that's fine. But I've shown her I'm an ardent dog lover.

I had a long scrub in the shower this morning then pulled on a clean set of clothes. I've even remembered to flatten down the spikes in my hair.

Tension's making hot wires of my muscles but at least I know I'm out of the gutter I've wallowed in since I fell off the road. Maybe my body needs these spells of sloth. Who knows, and who cares? I don't. I've got work to do.

I'm ready by eight, pristine, and hungry too. Pacing round the tiny room, I feel energy surging through me along with the need to get out and find Reed.

He's in the Ashford practice, I know it, and I've watched enough television news this last week to know that the Ministry is convinced the epidemic is almost over.

According to them, there's only the cleaning up to do. That means Reed is back at his normal work. I wonder how long it will take him to clean the blood off his hands.

I go to find Sandy scrubbing down someone's filthy bathroom and suggest I take Merry out in the Land Rover today to find somewhere better for a walk – a park maybe, or even a beach – and I promise to be back by eleven. When she smiles, I know she's pleased about me having more get up and go as well as confident about me abducting Merry for the morning.

Merry's fallen for me hook, line and rubber ball. She leaps on the end of her lead, desperate to be off, just like me. Land Rover, here we come.

It starts first time, obedient thing.

By nine, we've found Reed's practice and parked a good brisk walk away in a green residential street. Merry tugs me down the road for a few yards then starts exploring every blade of grass in the verge.

I find a phone box and squeeze us both in. 'I'd like a word with Mr Reed, please,' I say in a high-pitched and urgent voice. 'My cat's not well and can't be moved.'

'He's not in yet,' the nurse says. 'He's been delayed on an emergency but he shouldn't be too long. Would you like a home visit later?'

'Only if it's Mr Reed.'

'I can't guarantee that but...'

I put the phone down on her and head for the practice to lurk in the waiting room until he comes. He won't notice me in his rush to get on with the morning's clients.

'You're going to the doctor's,' I say to Merry as she bounces along, ears all over the place, 'so try and look a bit more under the weather, will you?'

The practice is modern, brick, and squat. As we cross the road, Merry lifts her nose and instantly loses her bounce, and I recall the fear that most dogs showed the minute they walked through the door of Phil's practice and caught the smell of suffering.

She looks up at me, nervous now, but it's a good thing. I don't want her showing rude health in the waiting room. Her tail is static by the time we've negotiated the doors, walked past all the anxious owners and their frightened pets to reach the desk.

'Yes?' The receptionist's tone and uniform take me back.

'I'm new to this area, and haven't registered.' I look worried. 'But my dog's ill. Could I see one of the vets, please?'

She peers over the counter at Merry, who's distinctly unhappy now. 'What's wrong with him?'

'She's a girl,' I say, suitably indignant, 'and she's off her food, very listless, has been for a few days.'

'We have two vets out today, but if you're prepared to wait one of the others will see you.'

She takes down my false details then I have to persuade Merry to one of the empty seats. She crawls underneath, as far away from her neighbours as possible.

By nine-thirty, I've glimpsed the vets on duty. They're those fast turnover young things whose aim every morning is to clear the waiting room by five minutes past nine. One started work at Phil's practice, but he didn't last long. Phil soon got rid of him, gave him a glowing reference when a better job came up and breathed a deep sigh when he'd gone.

Half an hour later, Reed still hasn't appeared. Anger's rattling through me. The woman in the next chair doesn't help, wittering on about how wonderful the vets are when poor old Mimsy doesn't feel one hundred per cent. Poor old Mimsy lies smugly obese in her cat cage, her eyes occasionally opening to amber slits, probably when she feels it's time for her next culinary treat.

I nod or shake my head at appropriate intervals, when really I'd like to tell the stupid woman that if she wants to overfeed a pet then perhaps she should keep a piranha instead of a cat.

Merry stirs by my feet. I reach down to touch her. Poor dog.

'Then, of course, everyone wants to see Mr Reed,' my neighbour's saying.

'He's so understanding,' says a man with an arthritic labrador.

Shall I tell them what he did to my sheep?

'Doesn't matter if it's a mouse or a moose,' the woman says with a serious shake of her grizzled head, 'he's just as gentle.'

A door opens and she goes to one of the young vets, and I smile when I think of how his fast turnover method won't work with her. She won't budge until Mimsy's last claw and plaque-coated tooth have been thoroughly examined.

'I'm new to this area,' I say to the man with the labrador, 'so tell me what's so special about Mr Reed?'

'Dunno, really. He's just got a way with animals. They aren't so nervous with him, like with the younger ones.'

They bloody well should be.

Have I got the right Reed? He showed something vaguely like sympathy for me towards the end of that evil day, so maybe he's gone back to his practice intent on removing the images of butchery that must plague him whenever he closes his eyes. But I must wait to see, twitching in anticipation of his arrival, forcing my hands to uncurl from their fists, trying not to rock in my seat.

The waiting area is tense enough without my nerves adding to the fray, and new clients turn up all the time. The phone doesn't help. No sooner has the nurse on the desk greeted a client or tapped something out on the computer than it's ringing again. And Mimsy's not out yet, so the queue's getting longer.

No one grumbles, but the owners flick surreptitious glances between their feet and the desk.

What the hell can I do? I can't wait much longer. Merry's due back with Sandy by eleven.

The phone rings again.

'Sorry it's been a long wait,' the receptionist says when she puts it down, 'but Mr Reed's on his way.'

I stretch for a leaflet about fleas from a rack, ready to bury my face in it when Reed walks through the door. But how am I going to see the green of his eyes without him recognising me? I haven't thought this through properly – that's why I'm twitching. The leaflet shakes; so does Merry. Her fear vibrates through my legs.

Mimsy's back. She looks spiteful in her cage, and her owner doesn't look much happier. The young vet does. Scanning the room, he spots me. 'Next?'

I follow him into the consulting room.

'What's the problem?'

He's terse from an overdose of Mimsy, and I know Merry

doesn't like him. She sits on my feet with her back to him.

'Very listless,' I say, 'and off her food.'

He reaches down and she growls. It's hard not to laugh. Attagirl, Merry, you show him who's boss.

He reaches for a muzzle.

'That's not necessary,' I say firmly. 'She won't bite.'

But she does, a vicious snap, and he's not quite quick enough – now he has a puncture mark and blood on the side of his hand.

Someone opens the door. 'Sorry to interrupt, Simon,' a man says, 'but I've just got in and need your help. Spare a moment?'

'Okay, John,' he mutters, dabbing his wound with an antiseptic wipe. He walks out without a word.

John. *John* Reed?

Merry in my arms, I slip to the door and peer through. On the far side of the desk, a slim man with mousy hair is disappearing through another door, and Simon follows him in. Reed comes back to close the door. Our eyes lock. His are blue.

Sod the Land Rover's liking for a sixty mile an hour cruise. I'm pushing it hard, storming up the M20 and onto the M25, bullying the sods who get in my way.

Even the trucks are giving me a wide berth. Behind me there's a black cloud of tyre smoke where yet more bunched-up vehicles have tried to avoid a pile up. I can't believe the amount of traffic – where are they all from and why the bloody rush? They haven't got to get to Derbyshire by tomorrow morning. They haven't got to track down a bastard of a vet, the fourth John Reed on my list, the one with green eyes and a soul worthy of a rat.

Hogging the outside lane, I blast the saloons and hatchbacks out of the way. Some are hard to shift until I drive up too closely to their tails. Something about my front grille filling their rear view mirrors does the trick and they sideslip to the centre lane with indignant flashes of their lights and their fists.

'Poop, bloody poop,' I yell at them as I fly past.

The hours are flying, too. It's mid-afternoon, and I've hardly got anywhere. I spent too long back at the motel trying to convince Sandy that the dog and I were okay. She looked surprised at my haste, and frowned when she saw her very unmerry dog, but I muttered that I'd had an urgent call from home so had to leave this minute. I should have told her straight that I'd done enough pottering round the country, enough skulking in corners.

Maybe she would have understood.

I don't believe it, the tank's on empty. How can I have used it all up before I'm halfway round London? I've no idea where the next services are, so I've got to get off the motorway and find a garage – as if I'm not delayed enough.

Calm down, Julie, or you'll never find one, and whose bloody fault is it for the delay?

Yours.

You're the one with the crackpot idea of befriending cleaners and taking off with their dogs just so you can sit in a waiting room hiding behind flea control leaflets for more than an hour.

And who's the one who wallowed in that trough of misery and uncertainty between Devon and Kent? You did. Now get down there and fucking find some diesel.

The pump handle's alive. It won't keep still. It doesn't know I've got to get to Derbyshire.

'What the hell do you think you're playing at?'

I look round to see a small man so angry his face is purple and his shirt's vibrating.

'I'm not playing, I'm filling my tank,' I say, trying to concentrate on keeping the nozzle where it should be, 'and what business is it of yours, anyway?'

'It is my business when you drive like a bloody maniac and risk not only my life but everyone else's on the motorway.'

He's going to pop if he doesn't calm down. Maybe a smile would help. I manage a small one.

'It's *not funny*,' he yells, nose coming up, his fists down.

I stop squeezing the fuel trigger and look at him, to see he's nervous despite his rage, and I bet his life is normally a straight road between one rule and the next. He's not usually brave. Something happened to him today. Maybe his wife left him.

'If you want a fight,' I say, 'then we should move our cars so we don't inconvenience all these people. Just hang on a second until I've filled my tank.'

He takes a step forward then one back, and I sense he's nearer tears than fisticuffs, hot tears of frustration because he's never hit a woman and he can't start now.

He goes, only to be back within seconds bashing the buttons on a mobile phone. 'I'm phoning the police,' he says. 'Drivers like you need hauling off the road.'

'I am the police,' I hiss, 'and if you blow my cover, I'll haul you off the road.'

Poor dear, he's gaping. He doesn't believe I'm a policewoman but he daren't challenge me. He's not the sort of man to follow through.

I go to pay.

Forcing my way back on the motorway, I push across to the outside lane and sit there.

I must not dither.

I've dithered far too much. All I've done for the last few weeks is take a vague stroll through the countryside in the hope that Reed would pop up in front of me, asking for forgiveness. Like some lost child in a supermarket, he'd take my hand and trudge beside me back to the Land Rover knowing I'd take care of his soul with a nice sweet dollop of retribution. He could then go cleansed to his maker.

Idiot, Julie.

This is war. Barge across the front line and snatch him.

CHAPTER TWENTY-TWO

I've got him. It was so easy. All I had to do was lurk outside his surgery until he came out to his car then follow him out of town, keeping my distance until we reached a quiet spot when I overtook him and forced him into the verge. Easy-peasy, as Danny would say. No more farting about with kidnapped dogs or pretending to be a client.

'What the hell are you doing here?' That's all he managed to say before I floored him. He should have known how strong I was. Farming has given me enormous fists and hefty shoulders.

He's out cold in the back of the Land Rover now, nicely doped on a sleeping pill. His car's gone, too. I drove it down an overgrown track into a mess of ancient woodland that looked as though no one had been in it for decades; and anyway, the car's now covered in a mat of brambles and dead branches so it won't be found. It can rot happily back into the soil along with all his veterinary potions and peculiar ethics.

The road home is through countryside devoid of stock. The Ministry's been bloodying its hands here too, for I pass farms with desolate fields and gates with tattered and redundant notices to Keep Out. The straw mats have drifted up against the hedges.

But I've got him. I've stopped one bastard from decimating any more people's lives and I've got him secure, curled up under the duvet, oblivious to the world and my plans for him. Sleep will do him good, though – he'll be the better for a few hours under his belt when the time comes to meet his judge and jury.

I must have been away a month but I'm going home, careering along the road, five miles, three, then the last bit with a sneaky bend to catch the unwary. Flying through the village, I see it hasn't changed a bit. In the light of what's happened over the last few months, I wonder why. No time to think. I reach the lane, then it's out with the headlights, let my eyes get used to the dark, and crawl in first gear up to the gate. It squeaks when I open it, but there are no lights on at Mike's so no one's there to hear me. The lights across the valley are watching, of course, but if I take the Land Rover right up to the lambing shed door, no one will see me hoist him out and install him in his new home.

Using only a torch for light, I drag his body across the pristine floor to the far corner, and make a duvet nest for him behind a stack of power-washed hurdles. It's a good move, using the lambing shed. When he wakes he'll recognise it, see where Fatso and her cronies hung out until they were thrown on the pyre like bags of rubbish. All my sheep are still here in spirit, despite the stink of disinfectant, so they'll not only keep him company, they'll remind him of what he's done.

He's just moaned.

'Don't worry,' I say, 'you're safe and warm now.'

His eyelids flicker, so I go back to the Land Rover and fetch my bottle of water. I can't have him dehydrated, and I do remember how dry those pills made me back in January when I was fool enough to think I needed sleep, fool enough to think I could forget what had happened to Ben merely by closing my eyes for a few hours.

Cradling his head, I dribble some into his mouth then lift his chin so the liquid goes down his throat. I've done that before to sickly ewes and lambs, poured glucose solution down their throats to give them energy. Men are easier to dose than sheep.

He's out cold again; out warm, I should say, for his nest is indeed cosy. But if I'm going to sleep well, I need fresh air first.

It must be gone midnight but summer nights aren't totally dark, and it's surprising how much I can see outside. I head for the workshop to plug in the torch to recharge it, then search for the roll of gaffer tape to bind his wrists and ankles together, just in case he tries to wriggle out of my plans for him. Last job – find the padlock from the front gate and click it on the shed door hasp.

The grass in my back fields is long, past my ankles, ungrazed since my ladies were killed. It smells lush, but there's another smell too. Ash from the pyre site. I stand for a moment to breathe it in, before moving on to the hedge where Ben left me. Pushing my bare hands into its leafy and thorny midst, I feel its scars, the heart permanently damaged, all twisted and bent. Next I climb to the wood, where I hear the ghosts of all my thaives trekking through to safety from their field of mud. I need to refresh my senses, inhale the spirits of all those I've lost, let them come back to help me during these final hours.

The bastard woke me just before dawn, that furtive grey hour before the sun gets into the right gear. From my pile of blankets next to him, I heard odd noises; not groans, more like whimpers. I fed him another sleeper with a few dribbles of water and waited until he was out cold before heading for the wood for my next job.

I've been burning rubbish for years but this is a new technique, and I must get it right if this bastard is to pay for what he and his kind have done. But I'm impatient. I want to light the paper under kindling as dry as I have become. I want to see flames accelerate through the scaffold of logs towards their prey, show him the full horror of what we've all been through, then purge every trace of him. Only when he has atoned for the ashes of our dreams can we rebuild our lives.

First the pit, a gaping scar some four feet by ten in the floor of the wood. It's taking hours of hard graft with a sharp spade and a mattock to dig down three feet but every back-breaking cube of earth and tangled root removed will make the up-draught stronger.

Next the timbers, stout thighs of fallen oak and ash hauled from the piles I built along the edge of the path. Some are as old and dry as I am, the sap long gone and fissures reaching as far as the heart. I lay them carefully across the pit for they are the foundation of the pyre on which I will build his bier.

Later, I'll build a sturdy scaffold of thinner branches for his final resting place, and a firm mattress of brash. Rotten twigs and shrivelled leaves will make a fitting bed for his withered soul and I will sacrifice all the holly saplings I can find for his shroud. He'll go to hell in a fury of crackling sparks and every one will be a memorial to the people and animals he has destroyed.

Enough for now, though. The sun's quite high, and I'm tired.

And I must go home to check he's okay, because I want him awake when the time comes.

I want to see his fear when he asks what he's done to deserve this. No doubt he'll moan that he was only doing his job and someone had to do it, but I've heard that too many times this year.

Maybe that's when I'll torch the diesel-soaked newspaper I'm going to stuff into every gap in the logs. A roar of flame should drown his whines.

Though his eyes are closed, he's awake, writhing feebly. Strange rasping noises are squeezing out of his mouth. When I squat beside him, his eyes flick open and he looks straight at me, into my eyes. I want him as conscious as this when I take him up to the pyre, so he'll see how it's built – almost identical to those whose construction he supervised; except that his were on a much grander scale. But mine will be more efficient.

He struggles to sit up.

'It's okay,' I whisper in his ear, 'it won't be long now.' I reach for the water bottle. 'You must be thirsty – try this.'

He splutters, but swallows some. I prise his jaw open, place half a sleeper on the back of his tongue and dribble more water in. I can feel his eyes on me the whole time and hear the words in his mind try to arrange themselves in some sort of order.

'Plenty of time for questions,' I murmur. 'Rest now. You'll need all your strength for later.'

I need to rest, too. This year must have sapped me more than I thought, and digging the pit has finished me for the moment. I used to be able to do hard physical work for hours. I was fit then, and happy. But my blanket bed is wonderful. It's too big for only me, but it's soft, as his will be once the flames have done their work and he is consigned to ashes.

What's that din?

An engine. A car, and it's coughing.

I must have slept. Did I lock the shed door? The padlock's not on the inside, so I didn't. Fool, Julie!

I get up too fast and have to waste precious seconds leaning on the wall until my head knows where it is.

The engine stops, and I hear the children's voices. Flying to the door and peering through a crack, I see them walking up the drive. There's no time to lock the door and hide.

'It's very quiet,' Jamie says outside.

'And the house door's shut,' Danny wails, 'so she's probably out. *No chocolate biscuits*.'

'Shut up,' Ellie says. 'All you think about is your stomach.'

'No, it isn't. I think about the goslings.' He's running, his steps light and swift. I hear him banging on the house door.

'Danny, stop it. She might be asleep.' Fiona's voice is sharp.

They head up to the house, thank God, so I can whip out, lock the shed door, then saunter out into their world.

I must do it, too. The Land Rover's here, so they know I'm home. I have to see them sometime, and didn't I half expect them today? Didn't I know they'd be snooping across the valley as soon as it was light? They've probably been doing just that, every day of the weeks I've been away.

I'm quick, so quick.

When I hear by their voices that they're at the house door, I pull off another strip of gaffer tape and carefully gag him, then I scoot outside, click the padlock shut, and stride back into my old world of friends and neighbours.

'Hello,' I call, rounding the corner of the shed, 'how long have you lot been here?'

Ellie and Dan race to me, and I just remember to act normally, lifting Dan up to swing round my head. Ellie is staring at me as though she can read my mind. She mustn't. None of them must ever again know what goes on in my head. They'd only yell, and try to dissuade me. I have to withdraw from them, but I must be careful not to arouse their suspicions or they won't leave me alone. They'll be at me constantly to talk everything out of my system, and then they'll cajole and tick me off and interfere. I have to pretend for a while that I'm the same person they knew.

Fiona comes straight into a hug, then – as always – stands back to look into my face. I grin at her, but she frowns.

'You look so tired,' she says, her gaze intense and probing.

'So do you.'

I turn to Jamie, see something has sucked the life out of him.

'Hi, Julie,' he says quietly. 'Glad to see you home again.'

'I took a holiday,' I say carefully. 'I didn't want to be around while the clean-up team was here, so I just got in the Land Rover and buggered off for a bit.'

'*Naughty word*,' Danny shrieks.

'So?' Ellie's voice is harsh. 'You'd say it, if people had done things to you like they've done to Julie.'

Danny crumples, takes a step backwards and stares up as though he's knifed me. 'I didn't mean to…'

I grab him again, and swing him round so he's shrieking with laughter. 'Come on, folks, let's go and see what we can find.'

We find a tidy house, stale biscuits, and green mould in the cake tins. I catch Fiona looking round my kitchen and I know she wonders why it's so organised.

'Didn't know what to do with myself a month ago,' I say with a good attempt at a chuckle, 'so I turned domestic. Sad, isn't it?'

'No,' she says. 'I've done that. Drudgery can fill the gaps.'

I fling the fridge door open and recoil at the smell of decay.

'Oops,' I say. 'Nothing to eat. No milk or biscuits, or crumbs big enough to feed a beetle.'

'What did you eat for breakfast?' Danny is serious. 'We knew you were home. We saw the Land Rover.'

'Oh,' I say airily, 'I had a bowl of fresh air with a good dollop of sunshine.'

He giggles. 'That's not enough.'

'Yes, but I came home too early, so the shop wasn't open.'

'We'd better go for you, then,' Ellie puts in. 'Mum, let's go now, otherwise Danny'll never shut up about chocolate biscuits.'

Fiona's undecided, and I suspect she wants to send Jamie and the children so she can get down to a serious discussion with me. I don't want one.

'Good idea,' I say quickly to Ellie.

Fiona gives in and goes, taking both the children, probably because she hopes Jamie will interrogate me.

'So, Jamie, how's things?' I say when they've gone.

'So so.'

'Found any good causes lately?'

'Don't have the energy, what with …' He flags, his eyes too bright. He moves to stare through the open doorway.

'I don't sleep,' he says, 'I can't sleep. Don't know about you, Julie, but this year's taken every ounce of stuffing out of me. It's hard enough to get the chores at home done, never mind satisfy my customers' demands. I keep getting new work, more than I ever dreamed of before…before all this, but…I can't do much.'

Irritation surges through me.

Jamie, a wimp?

I don't believe it.

Nor do I have time to worry about it.

I've got a bastard out there waiting for me, and Jamie's wallowing in self-pity; wasting my time, and wasting his life.

Pull yourself together, I want to say. Stop sucking your thumb, give yourself a kick up the bum, and get out there and get them.

Go for revenge, call it retribution if you want a nobler word, but don't wallow in my world.

He turns, defeat dripping from him.

I hear their car turning into the lane. I've got to be quick.

'Jamie, you're not helping the kids, and certainly not helping Fiona. Piece yourself together and find a new reason to go on. For God's sake, you used to inspire me, and now look at you! Go and find a cause, and I don't mean the sort you used to concern yourself with – all that fretting about the people who're starving on the other side of the world. Start on your own doorstep.'

He says nothing, so I move towards him.

I lean so close I can almost feel the stubble on his face.

'You're no friend of mine if you give in now.'

His eyes aren't shining any more, tears are running down his sallow face, glinting like Mike's did that awful night.

'But I haven't…'

I see Danny running from the car, weighed down with two heavy plastic bags, a determined grin on his face.

'Just look at your son.' I grab Jamie's shoulders. 'He wants a biscuit, so he makes sure he gets one. Be like him, Jamie.'

I push him aside, take the bags from Danny, and hoist them on the table. Fiona goes to lean against Jamie. Seeing them, Ellie looks exasperated.

'You're different, Julie.' She studies my face with her mother's eyes. 'Everyone's different, apart from Danny, of course. But I think you've got a *plan*.'

Found out.

I crouch to her level. 'Don't tell anyone.'

'Course not. Some things are secret, aren't they? I've got secrets. Will you tell me yours one day?'

'Probably not.'

'Okay.'

She understands. She knows what it's like to have her trust betrayed and her faith trampled into the mud, and she, poor soul, is more powerless than I am. I give her a consolatory grin.

The minutes are ticking past and I wish they'd go, wish they'd stop giving me the news of the month I've been away.

I don't want to hear about Carol having a stillborn baby and I certainly don't want to know that Jack's in hospital, doped to the eyeballs and asking for nothing but his shotgun, or that Mike's decided to stay at his son's and sell his own farm. Every word they say has me champing to be up in the wood again, building the latticework of logs and piling on the brash, and if they don't stop yabbing soon I'll just have to get up and walk out.

Ellie saves me.

'I'd like to go home now,' she says to her mother, looking at me with her steady perceptive gaze. 'I want to see the goslings.'

Fiona frowns, sighs, and gets up.

'Will you be over soon, Julie?'

'Soon enough,' I say.

'We'd like that, wouldn't we.'

Jamie blinks, looks at me with panic written in every groove of his face, then takes Ellie's hand. 'We would,' he murmurs.

Ellie scowls and pulls him. 'Julie's busy, but we can wait.'

I follow them out, and the bastard groans as we pass the shed.

Danny is instantly alert.

'What's that?'

They all stop and listen.

Oh please God, get them out of here.

'It's the ghost,' I say, without thinking.

Danny grips Fiona. Delight and fear dance over his face.

'I've heard it before,' I tell him. 'It's an old farmer from years and years ago. They didn't have chocolate biscuits in those days, so he comes back every time I open the tin.'

Danny imitates the moan, and tiptoes toward the shed.

'No, Danny,' I say sharply. 'He doesn't like being disturbed.'

He stops, uncertain.

Fiona's head whips round, and she studies me.

‘I didn’t hear anything – did you, Jamie?’

He shakes his head.

‘I should like to go home,’ Ellie states, ‘this minute. Please.’

They carry on to the car. A good job, too, or I’d be throwing them out. One last try at normality is required, however. They mustn’t go home and start trying to work things out.

‘It’s not really a ghost, Danny,’ I say. ‘Just the breeze. It does that sometimes when it blows through the gaps in the shed. In a gale, it’s more like an owl screeching.’

‘I want to hear it,’ he whispers.

‘Then you must come over, next time there’s a storm.’

They go, thank the Lord. I wave them off, then run for the shed the moment their car is out of sight.

CHAPTER TWENTY-THREE

He's really awake now, and I don't know what to do. I wanted to leave him down here until the pyre was finished but I can't if all the neighbours are going to start calling by. Nor can I feed him another sleeping pill – he must be fully awake when the time comes. There's only one thing for it, I've got to take him up to the wood with me, but how to do that without every nosy neighbour in the kingdom seeing what I'm up to? I wouldn't put it past Fiona to have binoculars trained on me the minute she gets home.

Peasy, Danny's favourite word, but just the right one. It'll be peasy, even in broad daylight, and I can't think why I needed to wait until dark. But first, force a quarter of a sleeping pill down him and take the tape off his mouth so he doesn't choke or suffocate. Can't have him dying too soon.

Reversing the quad bike and its small trailer through the wide door of the shed, I load him in. Floppy again, he fits nicely, his torso curved round and his legs drawn up. Curled up like that he looks very much like a baby. He doesn't have the innocence of a child though, nor does Ellie any more.

Don't think about her now, for Christ's sake! By all means afterwards, when she's been avenged, but not now – get the duvet over him. Next, the tow rope and a can of diesel tucked down the side, and don't forget matches and a stack of newspapers.

Conscious of the gaze of the valley on me, I also find a bundle of long-handled tools for effect. Sticking out the back of the trailer as I drive up the field, there won't be a single suspicion that I'm not carrying on as normal.

It's good to be back in the wood. I've parked him against a tree a few yards from the pit so he'll be able to watch me the minute he wakes again. Now I must fetch all the branches I need to construct the scaffold. First though, it's thinking time – making a pyre involves science. As each log burns, it will settle into the ash and the whole thing will drop, inch by inch. But it has to stay level otherwise he'll roll off.

After a lot of chin-scratching, I think I've got the technique. Using the thickest oak logs, I've built a roughly-buttressed wall round the edge of the pyre base. Three feet high should be enough. I'm filling it with thinner logs and stuffing brash and newspaper into the smallest gap so he'll burn evenly and efficiently, dropping down inside the wall as he goes. But it's all taking much longer than I expected. Maybe I didn't think it through properly. Come to think of it, the pyre that burned my sheep took almost a day to build, even with machines. But this one's tiny by comparison so am I making it too sound?

You're dithering, Julie. Just stop thinking about every little thing and get the bloody thing finished.

There's a weedy cry behind me.

I whip round to see he's awake and trying to keep his gaze on me despite his lolling head. He grapples with his balance then topples over. I go to prop him upright again so he'll have a good view of the last stages of my build.

'There we are,' I say. 'Does it pass your inspection?'

He stares at it, his eyes probably spinning in their sockets.

'Well?'

His tongue's got too big for his mouth. He can't seem to talk, apart from a few spluttered groans.

I pass him a bottle of water. 'Here, you do it this time – I'm fed up with bottle-feeding you.'

Struggling to hold the bottle between his taped hands, he drops it. 'Can't…Help me,' he splutters.

'Silly me,' I say, reaching down to whip the tape off, enjoying his flinch as the hairs on his arms come with it. 'So sorry, did that hurt? You poor dear.' I stand back to watch him struggle to unscrew the bottle cap. It takes long minutes but I'm not in a hurry any more. There's all the time in the world now the pyre's almost ready. I must have worried about it more than I needed, made it too complicated, thought too long about how the Ministry made theirs. What the hell does it matter as long as it burns fierce enough to expiate his sins?

He's having a lot of trouble drinking. Water's flowing off his chin, not trickling like Mike's tears. Jamie's did too this morning. Jamie. I wonder if he's got his finger out yet.

'Enough?' I take the bottle off him and go back to my work.

'Julie?'

White rage flares through me and I want to beat him to a pulp. I whip round and hiss, 'I only allow friends to use my first name.'

He stares, trying to assemble words. 'Why are you doing this?' he says at last, his voice a croak but fairly steady.

Good. That means his brain's unscrambling from all the gunk I've pushed down him.

'Why do you think?'

He shakes his head and frowns at his feet, at the tape presumably.

'I can't take that off yet,' I say. 'There's only me to see you don't escape. Unlike you, I haven't got police officers and the army to make sure this all goes according to plan.'

He looks confused. 'What plan?'

'The one to bring you to justice.'

'Justice?'

Does he think I'm a fool? 'Don't know much about justice, do you? Shame you didn't think more about it when you were wiping out people's hopes and dreams along with their stock. Did you think a fat compensation cheque from the Ministry would help us forget it all and carry on as though nothing had happened? Do you know what state you left us in, and do you care?'

He nods then shakes his head. 'I don't…'

'You don't care? Doesn't surprise me. All you had to do was wash your hands like Pilate and move to the next farm. Trouble is, water can't wash away what you did. Only fire cleanses properly.'

His eyes widen, and his gaze flicks between me and the pyre. 'But there's an emergency on.' His speech is steadying nicely. At this rate, his trial should be quite a reasoned affair.

'An emergency, is it? Maybe it hasn't occurred to you that this so-called emergency was spawned in negligence, years of it, decades of a laissez faire approach to agriculture that left our stock exposed to any old bug that happened to cross the Channel. Emergency, my arse. What sort of emergency demands you clear the nation of stock? Didn't you know there's strong evidence to show that most of the animals you killed didn't have foot and mouth, nor were likely to get it?'

He's shaking his head, but I'm not going to wait to let him put together his defence. I've had enough. The sooner I get rid of him, the sooner I can go back to the land and start again. And I will begin again. Ben would want me to.

'It's the betrayal of trust I can't forgive you for,' I say, holding on to the anger that's trying to spurt from me in white-water rivers, 'the way you ignored our needs and our feelings, the way you took away our belief in you as a good carers of our animals. For years you vets have been friendly faces at farmers' gates. For years, they've trusted you with their sickly lambs and calves and dogs and cats knowing that you'd do your best to put the poor things back on their feet. And how did you return that trust? You turned up at their gates armed with policemen and soldiers, and you lied and manipulated and bullied and bribed if not forced your way in.'

He lifts his hands, palms up, fixes me with his eyes. 'But Julie…'

'I told you *not to use my name!*'

'I need to use your name, if I'm to make you understand.'

There's a buzzing cloud round me and it's not made up of fireflies. More like thick smoke from a pyre, it's clogging my head and making my eyes sting. I have to get rid of it so I stride off up the wood to slash at holly saplings. But when I turn to haul them back, I see him crawling fast towards the entrance to the wood, using his hands in a paddling motion and dragging his taped legs behind him.

Running down the path, I grab his feet and drag him back to the tree. When he's upright again, his face marbles with terror.

'Please don't do this, Julie. You'll never get away with it.'

Get away with it? He's been watching too many cop soaps. 'Oh,' I sneer, 'so you're playing the frightened victim bit now, are you? You'd better shape up fast because I haven't finished yet. Where were we? Oh yes, your betrayal of trust.'

He swallows and opens his mouth but no words emerge so I push on. 'You betrayed yourself too and I can't understand that either. After all your training and your beliefs in doing something to reduce the suffering in the animal world, you toss it all aside along with every scrap of compassion you ever had just because the Ministry snapped its fingers and offered you a whacking great fee for doing its wicked work.'

'It wasn't the money,' he mutters.

'Oh, but it helped, didn't it, when you lost half your clients because they didn't have any animals left for you to tend? I bet your practice had money problems then.'

'It wasn't the money,' he says, stronger now, insistent.

'What then?'

He thinks a minute. I know he's choosing words carefully, but all he comes up with is, 'I wanted to help.'

'Help whom – the Ministry?'

'No – farmers.'

'Spell it out for me, will you? I can't make a connection between you destroying people, then saying it was to help them.'

He takes a deep breath.

'I knew what was going on – the God-awful hurry, the complete lack of any sort of system, and the…the bullying because an area had to be culled by yesterday if they were to cope with the hundreds of other farms that needed attention, but…'

I can't helping laughing.

'So you got sucked in? Don't give me that. Destruction on that scale can't be done on autopilot, not when you're a vet with ethics and principles. There isn't a carpet in the world big enough to sweep them under.' I turn away. 'Now, if you'll excuse me, I've got honest work to do.'

'Julie,' he says after I've stuffed the last gaps with brash and newspaper. Working with my back to him helps – not seeing his expression, that mixture of fear and bewilderment – but he keeps on calling me.

'Julie!'

'Stop it,' I yell, spinning round.

'I will not stop,' he says quietly, 'because it's the only way I'll get through to you.'

'How can you live with yourself after what you've done?'

He shakes his head.

'I can't. The images won't go away.'

'Well, you won't have to put up with them for much longer,' I shout, rage coursing from me now.

Grabbing the can of diesel, I wave it at him.

'Any minute now, your pictures will be on their way to hell, and you with them!' Throwing the can aside, I stride to his feet and tower over him. 'You think we farmers don't have pictures of our own, ones that will haunt us while we're living and after we're dead? Do you have any idea what's it's like to see your work and your life lying in a heap in your yard? It sits there, sometimes for days before growling machines come and scoop it up like rubbish to throw it onto the pyre, sheep by sheep, lamb by lamb. Do you think I'll ever forget the sight of them all, their heads bloodied and their feet in the air?'

He has the grace to lower his head but I can't stop.

'And do you think Ellie will ever forgive you for killing her lambs?'

'I didn't kill them.'

'You were one of the treacherous band. You might as well have killed my flock for all the help you gave when I needed you.'

That's got his head up. He looks straight at me, and I see him counting his sins.

'You walked away, Phil, when I *needed you most*,' I sob, my anger melting in a bucketful of tears. 'You *denied* me, *ignored* me. Instead, you chose to follow a set of insane rules, and let that arrogant bastard Reed trample all over me and my living.' My legs give way. I slump to my knees, but I won't take my eyes off him.

'I wanted Reed to pay for his crime, but I couldn't find him. I searched the country for him, and failed. That's why I chose you, and now I see I could have saved myself a lot of trouble and time because to betray our thirty-year friendship is the most heinous crime of all.'

His bottom lip quivers, and I don't know why.

Is it fear, or has he only just realised what he's done?

I don't care, nor do I want to hear his defence or his last confession. I must finish it now.

After going back to the pyre, I pick up the can of diesel and drench the whole thing until it's running out from the base.

Last job.

Fetch the holly.

Drag it down into a pile.

Then I go to pick him up. He's heavy, limp in my arms. He doesn't struggle at all, just lets me lay him on the pyre, his eyes fixed on mine the whole time. It's only after I've tied him down with rope that he speaks.

'It was necessary to kill,' he whispers.

I break off holly sprigs to frame him in dark green glossy leaves. 'And this too is a necessary killing,' I whisper. 'When it's done, I'll grow from the ashes and so will all the others.'

I tell him about Ellie's distrust of adults, a distrust that will stay with her for the rest of her childhood, if not her life.

I tell him about Mike giving up everything he's ever known before his time, before he could pass the farm to his son and his grandchildren.

I tell him about Carol's dead baby, and how that will affect her family forever.

And I tell him about the only hope Jack has left in his life – a longing for oblivion.

'So you see,' I finish, shrouding his face carefully with holly, 'someone has to pay for all this tragedy, otherwise how can we afford to go on?'

I stand back for a last look then reach into my pocket for the box of matches.

CHAPTER TWENTY-FOUR

The fireflies are back, my glittering crimson friends, flying low, darting round my feet, wings bright and voices clear. But why so many? Thousands more than my sheep. No, millions – they've brought the souls of every animal in the kingdom to swell my battle cry with their shrill song and the white noise of their flight.

I lift my arms and they soar to caress my skin, skim through my hair, surround me in a swooping cloud.

I sing their tune. 'Welcome.'

They don't like my voice. Why, when I'm their saviour? Don't they know they've only got me to avenge them? Now they bombard me. With their stings. Swatting hurts, and they regroup to whip my face with hard-knotted cords of scarlet and orange. And they grow into great daubs of colour, wind round me, suffocate me – save me, Ben!

He's coming!

There's the thump of his boots.

I bet he's got the hugest grin on his face.

He'll save me from this smothering shroud.

He'll find me.

'Julie! Oh God, just in time.'

He always says that – *just in time.*

He can't live without me, he needs me. His beefy hands hold me and he's pulling me free, but too hard. Don't tear my skin, Ben! Don't spoil my amazing muscles!

Flap, flap – the fireflies' wings are thrashing, black now, soaking up the orange and scarlet. Too much black, a mountain of it. Ben, quick, don't let it take you from me again! I want to see you. Let me see!

'No, Julie!'

Black, all black. 'Please, Ben, show me where you are.' Whispers. Murmuring footsteps. Mice? Insects, or have the fireflies burned their wings and turned into scurrying beetles?

No more black now – I see green, pale green. Cabbage-water eyes. Not Ben's. His are brown.

'You're in good hands.'

'Go away, I don't want your hands!' Fight, Julie, fight him. Kill the bastard!

More hands, more whispers. A needle.

'Don't kill Ellie's lambs!'

'Julie?'

'I'm not here.'

'Julie, open your eyes.'

'No, green eyes mustn't see me.'

Hands touch mine, small hands, not Ben's. 'Julie, it's me.'

'I don't know you. Get off my land! Can't you read the notice? The bastards put it there.'

'How are you today?'

'Go away. You have no right.'

'Hello, love.'

Don't call me love. Only Ben calls me love.

More hands. Strong. Leave my arms alone or there won't be enough of them left to hold Ben! They don't listen to me. They're pulling me up, up.

'No!' Someone screams. Maybe me.

'Come on, my lovely. Breakfast.'

'My turn for breakfast? You sod, Ben, skiving off to do the farm work, man's work. As if I couldn't do it just as well as you! Don't pull me!'

'Julie, love, you have to sit up.'

'Don't call me love!'

'Look – it's your favourite.'

I look. Green eyes, too close. My hands lift and curl into claws to scratch them out and stuff them down his throat.

'You little…'

'I'm not little! Can't you see I'm five feet ten in my socks?'

It's a woman, in a green uniform, and she's grinning.

'Welcome back, Julie!'

'Where the hell am I?'

'Safe, my love.'

'Please don't call me love, and get me out of this, this…' I've just seen my shroud. It's green. 'I will not have green!'

'Now, now, Julie.'

'I'm going home!' Pushing her aside, I leap away and tear the green stuff from me in one swipe. I am naked. No one sees me naked, only Ben.

'Where are my clothes?' I reach a door in one stride. 'Give them to me or I'll go like this.'

More bloody arms and hands. When will the world stop clutching at me?

Whispering shadows. I'm watching them through my eyelids, those shifting silhouettes flitting across in front of me, and when it all goes dark I know they're closing in on me. They must not find me. They can't see me if I refuse to open my eyes so I must be constant, not even allow myself a peep, then they'll give up and go away forever. I don't want them, or their arms.

It must be five minutes since I saw the last shadow. Carefully now, lids – open slowly, only a crack, not even a millimetre.

A window, and bars!

Listen for sounds. No whispers. No shadows. I am alone. Carefully, oh so carefully, I turn my head to see walls, and hanging pictures. They have bars too! But there are no arms lurking, no hands to grab me, no green eyes to burn holes through me.

I've opened my eyes wide and the bars have gone – they were my lashes! Idiot, Julie.

Looking round, I don't know where I am apart from in a room painted green, cabbage-water green. Come on now, what's its proper name? Think, brain. Eau de nil? Maybe nowadays it's called Mint Julep, or Cucumber Crush. Now you're being silly – it's Reed Green.

I see I'm lying in a bed, still wearing a shroud. Where are my jeans and boots – in that cupboard lurking in the corner? If I'm quiet, maybe I can get there without being dived on and clutched at again. I must try.

I watch one of my bare feet inch its way out from the sheets. Now my calf – what a strange name for part of a leg – and my toes, feeling the floor. It's soft. Good, I won't make a sound. I have to go home and I can't do that without clothes – someone would arrest me for indecent exposure. Arrest? But I'm arrested already, to stop me from…what?

The other leg's out now, and my arms. Look at those muscles! No don't, concentrate on getting across the floor without a sound or the armed whisperers will be back.

The door opens and I freeze halfway across the room. 'Julie – brilliant stuff,' says the woman in green. 'You're up!'

No use pretending I'm not here. I straighten up, glare, open my mouth and let words empty themselves over the floor in the hope they'll frighten her away. I'm sure I used to do that – batter people with words – and I'm sure they used to shrivel.

'Ooh,' she says when I've finished, 'you *are* feeling better.' Closing the door behind her, she walks across to tidy the bed. I study her rump, a sturdy beast, then turn to take one more step and open the cupboard. No jeans, no shirt, not even a pair of knickers. Just a blanket, a cellular thing, a green one.

'I'm sure you've been very kind,' I say, pronouncing each word carefully, 'but I'd like to go home now. Please find my clothes.'

She turns to face me with a silly grin, hands on hips, head cocked to one side in a parody of incredulity. It reminds me of someone – Becky, that's it, at the practice.

'Is your name Becky?'

'No,' she says, 'it's Anne.'

Thank God. 'Who are you?'

'An auxiliary nurse.'

'So I'm in hospital?'

She nods but doesn't move.

'Have I been ill?'

'Yes – very poorly.'

My head's too heavy for my shoulders. If I don't sit down I'll overbalance, but I must ask her something.

'How long have I been here?'

She takes a step.

My recoil's so swift and violent that I crash into the cupboard. Ordering my legs not to buckle, I lean against it, wondering why the room is in orbit. She's fast. Despite her weight, she's at my side in a flash, both her hands out to stop me falling.

'Don't touch me,' I growl. 'I won't be clutched at any more.'

Quick again, she fetches a chair from beside the window, to manoeuvre it under my sagging frame. 'There now, rest a bit while I find you some clothes.'

It's later when I learn I've been in hospital for weeks, crooned over by indulgent nurses, and judging by the consistency of my brain, doped to the eyeballs. But Anne fetched me a T-shirt, sweatshirt and track suit bottom so she's top of my list of favourite people, though she won't tell me the whereabouts of my own clothes. I miss my boots more than anything else. Those size 10 brutes that kicked everything out of the way.

Everything else is a mystery, especially the pasty young doctor. In his room, he parks me in a chair then sits opposite not saying a word, chin in hand, concentrating on a pad on his knee as though it's a Times crossword. In his other hand sits a biro, the end flattened and crimped. When he's not writing, he sucks and nibbles the biro, or rocks it between two fingers. Fiddle, suck, twiddle, suck, scribble. Better than biting his nails, I suppose.

He's a weedy little specimen, so etiolated that he can't go outside much; and he doesn't look as though he has the strength to peel the back off a strip of Elastoplast. His hands are fascinating, though – bone white, half the width of mine, and with the long fingers of a pianist. He'd have no problem manipulating and delivering a breech lamb. I tell him so on the first day.

The biro stops in mid-twiddle. 'Lambing needs small hands?'

I nod.

'Yours aren't.'

'No, but my ewes would prefer yours.' What am I saying?

I know he's trying to read my mind now. I won't let him. I'll start a war of silence and I'll win. For my prize, I'll go home.

'Tell me about your ewes,' he says, and I can tell he's forcing indifference into his voice. I meet his gaze until he blinks then I play his game and look down to study my knees.

It's a week later. Our confrontation is at stalemate. The end of his biro is in ruins. I smile within.

'Why are you fighting me, Julie? I'm not your enemy.'

Yes you are, I protest in silence, and you've taken me captive. Don't you know I'll fade to nothing in this prison, just like you have? White-hot fury comes from nowhere, and I get up and head for the door. He moves too fast for someone with spindles for legs – and his hand's on the door before mine.

'I'm your prisoner?'

'No.'

'Then why are you stopping me going back to my room?'

'I want you to tell me about your ewes.'

My hands are doing it again, lifting, ready, and if I had my boots on he'd be pulverised into the carpet quicker than a beetle.

'Don't you see?' He speaks quietly.

'What?'

'You have to cooperate.'

'Why?'

He lets go the handle. 'That's the only way you'll ever go home. I assume you want to?'

'Why bloody should I, when there's nothing left?'

'Sit down again, and tell me about it.' His hand stretches to take my arm, but I take a step back. I will not let him touch me. No one will ever touch me again.

'Don't worry,' he says calmly. 'I won't touch you. Trust me.'

'I trust nobody.'

'I know.'

I can't help it; words fly from my mouth like arrows. 'You don't know anything, not the first bloody thing about me!'

'So tell me. Start with your ewes.'

'They're dead.'

My room has shrunk. I'm sure I could cross it in three strides last week but now it's hardly more than two. I can't do a circular walk either with the bed taking up all that room and the cupboard in the opposite corner. I need a field to pace, a good fifteen-acre field of short sweet grass. But my grass will be so long now that it's not grazed, and by autumn it will be rank, no use to man or sheep. Will I have to hire a contractor to cut it, one of those wiry lads that look no older than sixteen yet control massively horse-powered monsters with the ease of someone hoovering a carpet, their music thumping from their cabs, their bodies fit from miles of bouncing merrily over the hills and through valleys?

Say it, Julie. Say the word.

'Tractor.'

There, it wasn't hard, was it?

Yes. As hard as telling Biro about me. And he's as sharp as a tin opener – give him the slightest lead, and he's prising the lid off my secrets without my permission.

Like yesterday.

'Tell me about your friends,' he said, after – in passing – I mentioned Jamie's work. Despite my resolve to speak in truncated sentences and only give vague details about my life, Jamie's coppicing techniques just fell out of my mouth. I can't even recall what prompted them.

'Which friends? I have a lot.' Used to. Real friends would have sprung me from this prison by now.

'Tell me why you're upset.'

'I'm not. Just angry…'

Oh idiot, Julie. Why did you tell him that?

'Who are you angry with?'

'You! Who else?'

'Yourself, perhaps.'

That was it! I couldn't take another word, and I was through the door and crashing back to my room before he could twiddle his biro again. But he followed, found me pacing my cage, then asked politely if he could sit down.

'Do what you bloody well like,' I shouted, 'but stop digging holes in me. I will not tell you any more, even if it means I have to stay in this dump for the rest of my life!'

He went out and I reduced the cupboard to splinters.

Why do I do it? Okay, there's never been much of a lid on my anger but I must control it now, to show that doctor I'm fit, to show the nurses I'm an ordinary soul at heart, one who's kind to animals, and people if they deserve it. I have a big heart, a soft one, one that only needs a hug to make it pump out gladness to all and sundry. Ben used to hug my heart. Used to. I don't have him any more, or my ewes, or my friends, so what's the bloody point of trying to behave so I can go home to an empty bed and deserted sheds and fields worked by someone else's tractor?

More days have crawled by. I have a new cupboard and every morning Anne teases me about it still being intact.

'Oh ho,' she says this morning, stroking its easy-clean surface, 'I'm impressed.'

'Bully for you,' I growl.

She sits down on the edge of the bed where I'm lying studying the ceiling and her tone changes faster than an April sky.

'For God's sake, Julie, isn't it time you gave yourself a kick up the rear?'

'Difficult to do that lying in bed.'

'Well, sod you,' she says, getting up. 'I'm not going to help anyone who can't be bothered to help themselves.' She slams out of the room.

The only friend I've got in the world is leaving me.

I leap out of bed, charge into the corridor, and chase after her.

She comes back, not speaking until she's closed the door.

We face other, me looming over her, she twice my width.

'You will not behave like a child any longer,' she says in a low tone, dead serious. 'You will *not* sulk, smash up furniture, treat Doctor Wilkinson like an idiot, or use me as a whipping boy. You will put the pieces of yourself back together and start returning a bit of the care the staff here give you. Understand?'

'Yes, boss.'

'And don't be cheeky.' Her face melts into a grin. 'Hark at me, acting like I run the place. Feel better for it though, and so will you.' She perches on the bed and pats the space next to her.

'That's better, now listen to me, Julie. I'm only a nursing assistant so maybe I shouldn't say this, but I've lived long enough to know what makes people tick. I've watched you change from a frightened rabbit into a vicious fox and it won't do you any good. All they'll do is shove drugs down you and keep you here until you're old and grey. You don't want that, do you?'

'I don't know.'

'Don't you want to go home?'

I suck my bottom lip to stop it trembling, then shake my head.

'Do you know what you want?'

I can't speak.

'You can tell me, Julie, and if you don't want anyone else to know, I shan't breathe a word. Trust me.'

'That's what everyone wants me to do, and I can't.'

'Then learn.'

Okay, here goes. See what it sounds like out in the open. 'I want to know what happened in the wood.'

She frowns. 'I don't know anything about a wood, so you'll have to ask someone who does. Start with Doctor Wilkinson.'

'Do I have to?'

She doesn't answer, just gives me a meaningful look.

Later, when I get to my session with Biro, I ask him straight out. He frowns, too. 'I don't know. Your friend didn't tell me.'

'Friend?'

'Fiona Casey – the one who saved you from the fire. She came in the ambulance with you, and she's been to see you every week.'

'Where is she now?'

'At home, I assume. Would you like to see her?'

Would I? Dare I?

At my next session, Fiona's there. She stands up when I enter and she looks straight into my soul.

'Hello you,' she says, her grey gaze as steady as a moonbeam.

Her hair is short as a boy's. Gone are the curtains that swung forward when she spoke. She looks about eighteen.

'I like your hair,' I manage.

'Short as yours, now,' she says with a smile, and lifts a hand to touch it. A scarred hand. Whorls and ridges of burned skin. My stomach turns a slow back somersault.

CHAPTER TWENTY-FIVE

Fiona's been every day for more than a week, but she still hasn't told me what happened in the wood and I daren't ask. If I do, she might not want to visit me again and then I'll never go home.

'We have to make a contract, Julie,' she says today.

'You have to trust her to act on your behalf,' Biro puts in. 'In effect, you have to give her a sort of power of attorney to act for you where your health is concerned. Will you do that?'

'Okay,' I say, not looking at him. Taking the biro out of his mouth has unstopped a dam of words and I want to plug it so I can ask Fiona when I can go home.

She must have read my mind. 'You can't go home yet, Julie, and certainly not until you promise to let me help look after you.'

I scowl at her.

'But I'm not ill.'

She leans forward to touch my arm.

'That's the problem – you won't accept the truth.'

'Okay, I admit it, I have been ill, but I'm not now. I feel all right and I *need* to go home.'

'Where you'll have no one to help you or keep you company.'

Anger stamps through me.

How dare she remind me about Ben not being there, or my sheep. I wrench my arm away from her and swivel round in my chair so I can't see her, only to remember something Biro has droned on about for weeks, something about running away from life. Turning back, I hang my head.

'Sorry, Fiona, I won't bolt again.'

She laughs softly. 'At least you stopped this time! The old Julie would be halfway to the horizon by now.'

'Would she?'

I don't need to ask, I know, and not because Biro has gone on about it for too long.

I know the old Julie either verbally thumped the people who stood in her way, or hid from them.

The old Julie couldn't suffer fools for a millisecond, the old Julie barged through life convinced she was taking it on the chin and giving back as good as she got, when really she was hiding behind strong words or pulling down the blinds so she could wallow in private. All running away.

Fiona looks hard at me.

'You have to learn to look after yourself.'

'Okay,' I recite, 'I thrashed my engine and didn't put a good enough grade fuel in it. I've also suffered more this year than most people do in a lifetime, and I'm too quick to retaliate and I don't recognise the warning signs and…'

She frowns. 'Stop it. You're parroting what you think people want you to say. Don't you see what you've got to do?'

She looks too serious. I want to talk about ordinary things. I want to hear her say they miss me, or that the chair by their Rayburn is waiting for me. Maybe Biro won't let her.

'Oh God,' I sigh with more than a touch of melodrama, 'all this talk about me and what I've got to do, or not – I hate it!'

She slumps back in her chair as though she's given up, but when Biro pulls the pen out of his mouth, she leaps in before he can speak.

'Julie, you must help me because I can't do it all by myself.'

Something about her expression tugs the inside of my chest. I try a smile, but she ignores it.

'Did you believe the doctor when he said you're ill?'

'I have been ill,' I admit, 'but not now.'

'Julie, what happened to you is serious and you have to learn how to mend – not only that, you have to let people help you.'

Biro butts in.

'We've talked about this, Julie. You're suffering from hypomania, a bipolar mood disorder, and it's a chronic condition. It won't go away. You have to accept that you've got it, and may always have it, but that both your manic and depressive tendencies can be controlled. Only when you believe that, will it stop controlling you.'

'And you also have to accept,' Fiona says, piling it on, 'that you can't carry on the way you were, before you were admitted to hospital.'

'What way's that? No one's told me yet.'

She does something I've never known her do – drops her gaze before she speaks. 'Jamie and I want you to come and live with us for a while,' she says to those tiny scarred hands in her lap.

Something in her manner tells me I have to behave, or I'll end up with the green whispering room as my permanent home and my mind the consistency of soup forever.

Fiona looks up, face stiff.

She means business.

I have to concede.

'I'm not good at being nannied,' I mutter.

She smiles. 'I don't *want* to nanny you, just help you learn. We all think the world of you, and you've been through so much this year, more than most people could imagine. Please accept that you need friendship and help, just until you know how to…how to find peace again. That's all we want.'

So I give in to them, and we start to work out this contract of cooperation, as Biro calls it.

I agree to take my medication regularly.

I also agree to stay with Fiona for a while so they can help me recognise the warning signs of abrupt changes of mood, those dives into misery or frenzied attempts to fly without wings that I assumed had something to do with Ben dying.

That I'm a chronic case is news to me.

When she's gone, I go back to my pale room rumbling with anger at being treated like an idiot, but I have to learn to do as I'm told if I'm ever going home again. Taking a deep breath, I stand by the window and practise a bit of self-discipline, half of me wanting to go back to Biro and tell him exactly what I think of him and his fussy manner, the other half wanting to run.

A bit of deep breathing works, dammit. In minutes, I'm having a hard job not to laugh at my mulishness. Okay, staying with Fiona might cramp my freedom but it won't be forever, and I'll be able to soothe ointment onto her hands as often as needed.

Don't just lie there, get out of bed! Lean on the windowsill. Feast on the morning. It's dazzling out there, a cockle-warming day, and even the serried concrete buildings have a glow about them. Not so the few trees I can see. They're forlorn, their leaves ochrous and needing a lick of varnish.

The door opens and a nurse peers in. 'Eight o'clock,' she says with question marks engraved all over her face.

'Pill time,' I say like the robot I've become.

'Good girl, Julie.'

There's a good girl, Julie, I mimic to myself, longing to slap her silly face for treating me like a ten year-old. But I have to learn – eight o'clock means medication.

At my session with Biro, his pen is tucked into the breast pocket of his shirt for a change and his mouth is too slack without its usual dummy. 'Two of your friends, Mr and Mrs White, want to visit you this afternoon,' he says.

Carol and Jim? So I do have friends.

All the doubt I've endured drips from me, all the private agonising and wondering whether or not my neighbours have forgiven me for interfering in their lot. If Fiona hasn't persuaded them to come, they must want to see me. Does it mean I'm nearly ready to go home?

Biro's speaking. 'Would you like to see them without me?'

Stupid question when he's done nothing but hover in the background for the last week. I can't talk to Fiona properly when he's there.

'You can choose to see them in here, or in your room.'

'My room, please,' I say as politely as possible, thinking it's the only home I've got at the moment.

He pulls the pen out of his pocket and opens the door for me and I scoot back to my room.

Anne comes in after lunch. 'I have to sit in with your visitors a while, but I'll go when I think you…'

'…won't smash the cupboard in a rage?'

'Don't even joke about it,' she says sternly, despite the grin slashing her face.

I won't smash the cupboard. I am learning not to let my anger rule me. Fiona's helped me most with that, and it's almost as though she's opened up the top of my head and poured a good dollop of her enviable tranquillity into me. And I feel I can wait until I go home to the valley before I ask about my wood. Fiona's comfy kitchen is the best place to talk about what happened. There I'll be able to deal with it.

'Hello, Julie.'

They haven't changed a bit. Carol's thinner, of course, and my insides shrink when I remember she lost her baby, but her eyes are as bright as ever. Though gaunt faced, Jim's fatter round the gut and his shy smile makes me want to hug them both. I resist the temptation. I must tread carefully.

Anne slips in with two chairs for them then perches in a corner by herself, hands folded in her lap. Though her mouth's set, I can tell she's pleased for me. But I'm struck dumb.

'...Weather's bearing up,' Jim says.

I nod my head vigorously.

Carol rummages in her bag and brings out a rolled sheet of paper. 'Amy painted this for you.'

The last one I saw was the maelstrom of red and orange and black. Please let this one be lollipop trees and rainbow flowers.

Please, Amy.

It's my farm. I recognise the house and sheds and fields, despite the painting's total lack of perspective and the addition of pink, purple and yellow flowers bordering the house.

And here – fields full of sheep and lambs.

Gulping furiously, I look up at Carol.

She reaches for my hand and squeezes it, and I don't mind the contact. 'Amy said it was a message for you. That your fields will be full again, just like ours.'

Two more gulps, and I'm in control. 'How are the children?'

'Madly enjoying the summer holidays. There's nothing like good weather and adventures outside to soup them up.'

'And your mother?'

Jim laughs. 'Positively blooming,' he says. 'She could bake for England.' He pats his stomach.

Clutching the painting like the lifeline it is, I ask them to tell me everything and they do, months of valley news, work they're doing on the farm, and their plans for new stock once they have clearance from the Ministry. After an hour, they've filled me and my room with sights and scents of summer and home, despite the pain they must be feeling about their lost child.

‘I’m so sorry about your baby,’ I say, forcing myself on, ‘and I’m sorry for interfering. If I hadn’t, maybe you wouldn’t...’

Carol sits bolt upright, eyes flashing.

‘Don’t you *dare* say that! We needed you that day – you gave us the strength to stand up for ourselves.’ Her tight expression softens. ‘And we need you now, Julie. *Please come home to us*, and liven us all up again, like you used to. You’re the warmest blast of fresh air the valley’s ever had!’

Jim gives a mock groan. ‘And I need you, so Carol’s mother has someone else to bake for.’

It’s then I notice Anne is still in her corner, relaxed now and listening to the conversation as though she’s known us all her life and has dropped in on her neighbours.

Feeling my gaze, she stands up, and starts for the door.

‘Please don’t go,’ I say, ‘unless you’ve work to do.’

I hold up Amy’s painting. ‘Look at my home,’ I say, hearing pride in my voice, and she comes to peer at it. She points to the clump of lollipop trees behind the farmhouse and asks if that’s the wood I’ve being going on about.

Something’s not right – I can feel tension stiffen Carol and Jim. I look up to find them exchanging glances.

‘Tell me,’ I say quietly, ‘I need to know. Did you see a fire in the wood?’

Carol bites her lower lip and nods.

‘What else did you see?’

She frowns. ‘Nothing. Only the ambulance in your yard.’

Is she protecting me from the truth? Why won’t anyone tell me? But I daren’t ask any more – nothing must spoil this neighbourly gathering for it’s strengthening me by the minute. I leave my barrage of questions unspoken.

Sarah comes next, two days later and after two nights of me thrashing through the mush of my brain, trying to remember.

I’m confused and wary.

Biro’s not telling me anything, nor is anyone else.

Why not?

Sarah’s just the same. She’s had her hair done for this occasion, bless her, and her curls shake as she prattles on about nothing. In best visitor mode, she’s making a determined effort not to mention Jack. In a brave moment, I decide to do it for her.

'He's coming on,' she says after a moment's thought, 'though how I'll cope when he comes home, heaven knows.' She goes on to tell me at great length that her son and his family have moved into the farmhouse and she's enjoying her daughter-in-law's company but finding it hard to accept the way they're bringing up their child. 'Still,' she finishes, 'times change, and we have to go along with that.'

'Tell me, Sarah,' I say after gathering some of my old bluntness. 'What did you see the day I came to hospital?'

Her frown is deeper this time. 'See?'

I nod, trying to hold her gaze but she won't let me. She studies her hands then twirls her wedding ring. 'I didn't see anything – I was visiting Jack in hospital that afternoon and came home to hear you'd been taken poorly too.'

It's useless.

No one wants to help me sort things out. All my neighbours are doing is what they've done for centuries – go on and on about the valley and its weather, its stock or lack of it, and what old Mrs So-and-So will do if her son/daughter/husband/third cousin twice removed doesn't do something about God knows what.

Anger starts to knot me inside, and I struggle to stop it rocking the equilibrium I've fought to build up. To divert the fire, I start to prattle too; about the nurses, and how I'd like Sarah's recipe for orange cake, and even how much I look forward to coming home.

Then, without warning, my voice begins to stumble through buckets full of doubt that I'll ever see the valley again.

Sarah cocks her head.

'I'm surprised at you, Julie. Of course you'll come home!' She leans forward looking as though she's going to wag a finger at me. 'It's quite enough that Jack went down the road of no hope, so don't you start!' Her curls shake. 'It's a shame we all drained so much from you this year.'

She leaves me later with a promise to fill my cupboards with her cakes on the day I go home, and a threat to visit more often than she'd be welcome. 'I need your company too,' she says over her shoulder as she trots down the corridor, 'especially with Jack the way he is! I need to have lots of good moans then go home the better for it. Don't let me down, neighbour!'

Is that what I am, a prop? Is that now my role in the valley, to burst through it in top gear or provide a broad shoulder for everyone else to offload their woes? Bugger that.

As soon as she's gone, I march down to the nurse's room and demand to see Biro, this minute, and no I can't wait, not unless they feel like ordering new furniture for the whole of the ward.

Biro isn't in, or Anne, so I spend the rest of the day prowling and pacing, and the whole of the night feeling bloody.

Why can't everyone just open their mouths and tell me what happened in the wood – and why do they look away when I mention it?

Hasn't anyone got the guts to look me in the face and reel out my crimes so that I can count my sins, grovel for mercy then start all over again with a clear horizon and an empty heart?

CHAPTER TWENTY-SIX

'You made a bit of a fuss yesterday,' Biro says the next morning. 'Tell me why.'

'No.'

'Fine.'

He scribbles, and I'll scream at the bastard if he so much as kisses his biro. Willing him to do so, I watch him twiddle then raise the end only to drop it when it's a whisker from his mouth.

He looks up grinning, damn and blast him. 'Choose your weapons,' he says in a voice I don't recognise, one full of suppressed laughter. 'Pens or words?'

A fight, at last.

'I thought duals were at dawn,' I say carefully, 'and it's already after ten o'clock.'

'Time isn't significant here, as you've probably noticed.'

Oh yes.

'Except when it's time to go home,' he adds.

'You or me?'

'You, Julie. We need your bed.'

He's chucking me out? I'm not angry now, just bloody scared, too scared to move.

He lobs his pen onto his desk as though he's throwing me over his own horizon. 'Mrs Casey is coming for you tomorrow but today, just to help you wind things up, you have another visitor – he's waiting in your room.'

'Who?'

'Someone who'll help you, according to Mrs Casey.' He studies my quaking form. 'Trust your friends, Julie. I do.'

It seems to take the rest of the day to haul my feet back to my room. Pushing the door open, I see his outline framed by the window and wonder what to do next.

He turns. 'Hi, Julie.'

I see a different Jamie to the one I recall. There's something about his face that has my thoughts leaping, but all I can do is stare. He grins and his eyes flash, just like they did in the old days.

'They didn't say it was you,' I whisper.

'Fiona thinks it's time I came.'

'Time?'

He nods and holds his hands out. What else can I do but give him mine? I let him hold them a long time. It feels safe.

'Come over here.'

He pulls me to the window. We lean on the sill in silence.

'Poor trees,' he says eventually, 'surrounded by buildings and concrete. No wonder they're so tired.'

I have to say something, anything. 'How's your wood?'

'Good. The understorey of oak and ash I planted last winter is doing well. They're all growing straight and true. Bit like me, really.' He turns to me. 'I did what you told me, Julie. I started again from my own back doorstep.'

'Did I say that?'

He nods. Is he going to tell me what happened in my wood?

'You kick-started me,' he goes on. 'Ellie said only the other day that I'm better than the Dad she used to know.'

Thinking of Ellie, I smile. I miss her more than almost anyone.

'She's a wise child,' I say.

'She takes after Fiona, not me, and she says she's going to help to mend you, because it'll help her mend, as well.'

Little Ellie. I can't wait to see her and Danny, but first I must know. 'Tell me what happened, Jamie.'

A gut-deep sigh emerges from him.

'Something came back to me that day,' he says, looking out the window. 'Something Mike said, all those months ago when I asked him how he knew that you were rescuing your thaives.'

He turns to perch on the sill. 'He said the only way to know what was going on in the valley was to open my eyes.'

'And what did you see?'

'I saw something in you that didn't sit right with me. Then when I got home, I watched you take the bike and trailer up to the wood.' He gives a forced laugh. 'Think you can fool a tree feller, Julie? No one works their woodland in high summer, so why would you need to take a trailer full of tools up there?'

‘You must have had binoculars on me.’

‘I did, and when you didn’t come down, I came looking.’

‘What did you find?’

‘Don’t you remember?’

My breathing is light. I daren’t take too much air into my lungs for fear of lifting off. ‘I need someone to tell me,’ I say carefully. ‘I’ve been waiting for someone to tell me.’

‘No one knows, apart from me and Fiona.’

Why didn’t they tell anyone else? Most people would have run from the horror of what I was doing, straight for a phone and the emergency services. Not Jamie though, and now I know it must have been him gripping my arms while Fiona fought with the flames and the knots in the rope that tied Phil down. I don’t remember much after that.

Swallowing is difficult, but I manage it. ‘Poor Fiona.’

‘Her hands will mend, Julie.’

‘And Phil?’

‘You had better ask him yourself. He’s waiting to see you.’

Phil is hiding his burns in a long-sleeved shirt, but he’s taller, I’m sure. His stoop’s gone. He comes over to the window to lean against it, just like Jamie did, and we stare out at the bright day – our thoughts separate, but looking for a bridge .

‘I’ve done it, at last,’ he says.

‘What?’

‘Put myself out to grass – retired. The veterinary world can now breathe a sigh of relief.’

I try to smile. ‘You should have done it years ago.’

He turns, and when his eyes bore holes through my already crumbling armour, my tears gather for a mass dive.

As they emerge, the sunshine splits them into a thousand glittering fireflies.

‘Come here,’ he says, his arms coming round me.

‘Forgive me,’ I say, as I tuck my face into his neck and he strokes my spiky hair smooth.